Praise for Jeff Abbott's previous Jordan Poteet mystery, DO UNTO OTHERS

"For ages I've been saying that fame and fortune awaited the man who could write charming and funny mysteries set in small-town America. When I read Jeff Abbott's *Do Unto Others*, I knew that the position had been filled."
—SHARYN McCRUMB

"A haunting story of a small Texas town overflowing with decade upon decade of dark secrets."
—R. D. ZIMMERMAN

"Abbott's debut has both light and dark tones, is thoroughly readable, and presents a well-drawn gallery of suspects."
—*Ellery Queen's Mystery Magazine*

Please turn the page for more rave reviews. . . .

"Jeff Abbott is a major new talent, Jordan Poteet a refreshing and delightful new series character, and *Do Unto Others* a powerhouse debut."
—Susan Rogers Cooper

"A promising debut and a fine new author I shall watch with interest."
—Margaret Maron

"Abbott's debut mystery is a bright, often funny portrayal of the social mechanics of a small town where, as the narrator/accused/detective quickly discovers, everyone has something to hide."
—*Publishers Weekly*

By Jeff Abbott
Published by Ballantine Books:

DO UNTO OTHERS
THE ONLY GOOD YANKEE

THE ONLY GOOD YANKEE

Jeff Abbott

BALLANTINE BOOKS • NEW YORK

This book is for my mother,
Elizabeth Norrid,
one of the truly great steel magnolias,

and for my father,
Roland Abbott,
for the love of books he gave me.

Copyright © 1995 by Jeff Abbott

All rights reserved under International and Pan-American
Copyright Conventions. Published in the United States by
Ballantine Books, a division of Random House, Inc., New
York, and simultaneously in Canada by Random House of
Canada Limited, Toronto.

Library of Congress Catalog Card Number: 94-96828

ISBN 0-345-39438-0

Manufactured in the United States of America

First Edition: May 1995

10 9 8 7 6 5 4 3 2 1

ACKNOWLEDGMENTS

For their contributions to this book, I'd like to thank: my agent, Nancy Yost, for her unending enthusiasm; my editor, Joe Blades, for his continuing encouragement and helpful suggestions; and the staff at Murder By The Book in Houston, Texas, for their support and friendship.

I'd particularly like to thank Robert Power, M.D.; Kelly Peavey; Megan Bladen-Blinkoff and Paul Messina; Karen Bell of the Smithville, Texas, Public Library; Sergeants Corky Marshall and Jim Nilson of the Austin Police Department Bomb Squad; and Smithville Chief of Police Lee Nusbaum for their expertise. Any errors are my fault, not theirs.

And as always, Austin's Black Shoes: Jan Grape, Susan Rogers Cooper, and Barbara Burnett Smith, for their willingness to visit Mirabeau repeatedly (despite its lack of a really good bar).

AUTHOR'S NOTE

Since Mirabeau is a fictional place, the stretch of the Colorado River it sits on is also fictional, and therefore is not under any environmental protection other than the laws of Mirabeau itself.

CHAPTER ONE

THERE WASN'T MUCH TO BEGIN WITH IN Mirabeau, so I was awful surprised when someone started blowing up parts of town. I mean, we did need a little excitement—but no one in his right mind thought explosives were required.

The first local landmark to go was Fred Boolfors's toolshed. Early one Monday morning it popped open like a jack-in-the-box on fire—spewing trash, back issues of *Playboy*, and Fred's unparalleled collection of borrowed lawn-care tools fifty feet in the air. No one was hurt, but I think his immediate neighbors were pissed that their trimmers were returned in small pieces.

The police were investigating the remains of Fred's shed when Pepper Tepper's doghouse got blown sky-high. I should explain that no one here calls Pepper by her full name except her owner, Clyda Tepper. Pepper's the most spoiled, orneriest French poodle you can imagine. No wonder the French are so rude with dogs like that around.

Pepper is Clyda's pride and joy—and that woman has spent unholy amounts of money to make that canine look as stupid as possible. It's fortunate Clyda never had children. God only knows how she would have sent them dressed to school. Probably adorned with giant bows on their heads and asses. Clyda also spared no expense on Pepper's doghouse. It was a miniature version of a French château, complete with wood trim, a slate roof, and a little tiny flagpole with French and Texan flags. Rumor had it that Clyda had installed a little stereo system to play "La Marseillaise" when Pepper entered.

Anyhow, about three days after Fred's toolshed kissed the sky, so did Pepper's château. Fortunately Pepper was off at Le Pooch Salon in Bavary getting her nails clipped. She was undoubtedly put out at having to sleep in a common dog bed. Clyda was sure Pepper was the target of some anticanine campaign and claimed to see poodle-hating Iraqis lurking around every corner.

At that point, with two pipe-bomb explosions in town, people began to get a mite nervous, myself among them. My name is Jordan Poteet and I run the library in Mirabeau. I found myself checking if anyone had borrowed books on explosives or if any returned tomes featured wires sticking out of them with attached timers. (The answer was no.) I wondered if someone bore long-buried hatred for Clyda (or Pepper) Tepper or Fred Boolfors. I didn't wonder long.

I'd spent the night at my girlfriend Candace's house and I wasn't quite over the guilt. I don't feel contrition about spending time with Candace; her company is pure pleasure. But I felt guilty about not pulling my weight at home by staying out all night. See, I came back to Mirabeau several months ago to help take care of my mother. She's dying a slow death from Alzheimer's. I'd given up a good career in textbook publishing in the faraway land of Boston to come home to this little river town halfway between Austin and Houston. My sister Arlene (who I just always call Sister) and I split duties on taking care of Mama. Fortunately, we'd had the recent help of an in-home nurse, so Sister had been able to go off the night shift at the truck stop she cooked at and enjoy a more normal life. But whenever I was away from the house, and not at work, I felt like a shirker. Even when I was lying in Candace's arms.

It was a beautiful Thursday morning, with early-summer light beginning to stream through the louvered shades in Candace's bedroom. The first rays fell across my eyes and woke me gently. I could pick out the details of the room: her white frilly lamp shade, the clump of friends' pictures on the wall (I was glad it wasn't Kodachromes of her parents staring down at us on the sweaty sheets), the delicately flowered blue-and-yellow wallpaper, the comforter that we'd crumpled in the night. Men won't admit it, but they love sleeping in a woman's room. There's an indefinable feeling of lying on a lady's sheets, resting on a lady's pillow, even breathing the air a lady breathes when she's in her private place. I rolled against Candace, buried my face in her sweet-smelling brown hair, and began to nibble at her ear.

She gave up playing possum. "I never should have let your long legs in this bed," she said, pushing me away playfully. Since she's barely five feet two and I'm a whole foot taller, she can't push me too far.

"It's not my long legs you should be worrying about," I said innocently.

"Hmmm. Is that so?" She kissed me and it turned into one of those five-minute, ignore-the-morning-breath affairs, full of heat and groans and raw-edged laughter deep in the throat. Our relationship was new enough, I told myself, that this fervor made sense. I kept waiting for the boredom to set in. Except for one other relationship, monotony had always entered the picture, but it hadn't yet with Candace. That worried me no end. This could be love. I thought of saying just that to Candace, but the words caught hard in my throat and instead I kissed her. I'm a show-er, not a tell-er.

I broke the kiss and smiled down at her. "I probably should get over to the house and check on Sister and—" I started, but didn't get to finish.

"I don't want to hear about your duties right this minute, Jordy. You have your own duty, right here." She was right—I was standing at attention, so to speak.

"I know, honey, but—"

"No buts. Look, y'all have that nurse now, so quit worrying so much. You and Arlene are getting a break. Now you can enjoy it, can't you?"

I shrugged, leaning back on the pillow. "I'm trying. But it's not easy, even with all this generosity coming from Bob Don."

Candace rolled over in disgust. "I've always counted patience as one of my few virtues, Jordy, but you have just about exhausted mine with Bob Don Goertz."

I'd learned a lot since I came home. I'd learned just how exhausting it was to be a caretaker. I'd learned being a librarian was a tough job that was underappreciated. And I'd learned my daddy wasn't my daddy. Two months ago I'd landed in the middle of a murder investigation where I found myself a suspect, along with Bob Don Goertz, Mirabeau's reigning car-and-truck czar. One of the unpleasant secrets that had come out during that investigation was my mother's long-ago (hell, not that long ago, I'm only thirty-two) affair with Bob Don when she and Lloyd Poteet were briefly separated. I was the product of that affair, and Lloyd (who I thought was my daddy) raised me with kindness and love and never let me know. Since Lloyd had died several years ago, Bob Don had been aching to be a father to me. Now Bob Don was trying to make up for three decades in two months. He'd nearly killed me with kindness. Part of his help was hiring the nurse to take care of Mama so Sister and I could pretend we had normal lives. Candace had been a pillar during that tough time, but I think she was sick and tired of hearing about Bob Don.

She spoke from beneath her pillow. "Now what has he done?"

"He insisted on giving me some land. Several acres down by the river." Mirabeau sits on a curve of the Colorado River, pretty and lush and verdant. The river winds through the gently rolling hills and the stately loblolly pines that encircle Mirabeau and never fail to surprise folks who think Texas is one big desert. The eastern half of central Texas is like a garden that God made just for us fortunate few that call places like Mirabeau and Smithville and La Grange home.

A blue eye peered at me from under the pillow. "And him giving you land is a problem?"

"I feel funny about it. I never owned land before. What do I do with it?"

"Well, I own plenty and it's no shame." Candace's folks are the biggest bankers in Bonaparte County. She works with me at the library on a part-time basis and fills the rest of her time with volunteer work. The small salaries that annoy librarians are of little worry to Candace. "What you do with land is simple. You keep it and let its value climb until someone wants to buy. Then you sell it and make a little money off of it." Having completed her introductory lecture in Candonomics, she threw the pillow at me as I sat up and I caught it. "Does your guilt about not being a Poteet know any bounds?"

"I haven't changed my name yet and I don't intend to," I answered with dignity. Jordan Poteet was hardly melodious, but Jordan Goertz? It sounded like a Danish laxative.

"Well, sugar, if you're not coming back to bed, go get the paper and scandalize the neighbors." Her smile was warm and inviting. Damn her for complicating my life more. She was smart, funny, and—with her blue eyes, thick brown hair, and pert nose—gorgeous. Well, if she was a complication, let my life stay forever difficult.

I leaned down and kissed her rosebud mouth. "How about I go get the paper, come back in here, open the shades, and then we scandalize the neighbors?"

"Mmmm. Maybe we'll make the society page."

I stumbled over to where I'd shed my clothes last night and kicked into a pair of jeans. Out of consideration to the blue-haired moral vigilantes of Candace's neighborhood, I pulled on a shirt. I brushed my blond hair out of my eyes and opened the door.

The morning sky was hazy with summer clouds and the promise of later heat and humidity. Birds sang in the trees, obviously early and already gorged with breakfast worms. A gentle breeze stirred against me as I walked barefoot across the dewy grass. I savored the early coolness—it wouldn't last long on a July day.

I saw the curtain in the house across the street dance back slightly, then settle. Miss Twyla Oudelle undoubtedly had me in her binoculars as I made an immoral spectacle of myself, appearing on Candace's lawn, fresh from a night of unblessed debauchery. Miss Twyla was basically harmless and sweet, but she'd been one of my science teachers in high school and I felt a little self-conscious with her watching me on my girlfriend's lawn. I bent to get the paper, wondering if I should turn and wiggle my butt at Miss Twyla. It was just then that the first mailbox exploded.

Across the street and two houses down, a half-oval white mailbox burst open like a flower of dynamite. I jumped up, stunned, staring at the wooden stump where the mailbox had been. The percussive noise rang in my ears.

I'll never admit to having catlike reflexes, and I was so surprised I didn't move. I just gaped at the chunks of hot metal that were now in the street. I hadn't had the requisite five seconds to find my voice when the neighboring mailbox, this one in Miss Twyla's yard and right across the street from me, detonated. Miss Twyla was fond of country decor and she'd mounted her olive-green mailbox on an antique metal milk tank. The cylindrical urn blew apart like a rocket running into the ground. I'd halfway turned when I felt a hot pain in my arm and I fell to the ground.

I heard but didn't see the next two explode. Pain shot through my arm and I felt Candace's hands on me, her voice screaming in my ear. She pulled me inside right before her own mailbox erupted and peppered her front door with shrapnel.

I'd suffered enough. Not from the pain in my shoulder or arm, although I'd been hit by flying pieces of Miss Twyla's milk urn. My suffering was Candace smothering me with the pillow of overworry.

I'd been rushed to the Mirabeau hospital, where I was pronounced damned lucky. The shrapnel that hit my arm tore no muscle and severed no artery. The wound was explored and cleaned. Candace had wrenched my arm pulling me into the house, so I was awfully sore from my wrist to my shoulder. When I woke up, my arm was bandaged and slinged and Candace was holding my hand. It didn't take long for the police and the reporters to show up. I had been the only person outside at the time and consequently was the only casualty and witness, making me the hub of inquiry. The attending physician made me stay an extra day to be sure I wasn't in shock.

When I got out of the hospital, I wanted to see the mess that was in Blossom Street. Candace walked with me, holding my hand as we surveyed the shattered stumps. Six mailboxes had exploded in their weird dance, one right after another. Candace's fingers trembled against mine.

"God, sweetheart, I think of what could have happened to you . . ." she said, and I squeezed her fingers. I didn't want to contemplate that myself. I felt luckier than the guy who falls into the outhouse and finds a gold mine. I poked a sneakered foot at the remains of Candace's mailbox.

"Hell, now I don't know where I'm going to have my dirty magazines sent." I pretended to pout.

She laughed, nervously, and caught herself in time from giving my arm a playful punch.

"Jordy, dear, I'm so relieved you're all right." Miss Twyla's booming alto nearly made me jump. Miss

Twyla herself had toddled up behind Candace. She was still a large woman at seventy, tall and full-figured, with her heavy plait of gray hair pulled back into a long ponytail. No other elderly lady in Mirabeau wore her hair like that and I always thought it looked great on Miss Twyla.

Miss Twyla hugged me hard and I embraced her back as best I could. Stepping back, she turned her chocolate-brown eyes on me and set her big hands on her broad hips. In her trademark khaki skirt and white button-down shirt she looked as formidable as she'd been when you screwed up your lab assignments. "Jordy, I cannot tell you how upset I am that my mailbox injured you. I just feel terrible."

"Good God, Miss Twyla, that's not your fault. We obviously have some lunatic running around town." I tend to gesture when I talk, and when I forgot, motioning with my hurt arm, I winced. Miss Twyla frowned in sympathy. Maybe I'd get some of her famous pecan-spice cookies out of this.

"First a toolshed, then a doghouse, now mailboxes." Candace shook her head. "I don't get this at all. What's the point?"

"Maybe we just have an unambitious terrorist in our midst," Miss Twyla conjectured.

"Or he's working up to something bigger." The implication of that comment hung in the air. Candace squirmed and Miss Twyla frowned again.

One of Mirabeau's police cruisers pulled up slowly in front of us, driven by Junebug Moncrief, our resident chief of police. Junebug and I grew up together in Mirabeau and had been close as children. We'd drifted apart as teenagers, and there had been an old competitive tension between us when I'd returned to town. After all the hoopla over that murder in the library a couple of months ago (where Junebug had thoughtfully not arrested me although I'd been the prime suspect), our friendship had started up again, albeit a little uneasily.

"Hey, Jordy." He nodded to me in his unhurried drawl. "How you feeling today?" He adjusted his eyeglasses to the light, looking every inch a small-town officer with his immaculately pressed uniform, his brown burr of hair, and his weathered Stetson. His face was a well-crafted one, strong with character, and one that people trusted.

"Fine, thank you. So what was it? Dynamite? Tomahawk missile? Nuclear detonator?"

Junebug cleared his throat, as unrushed as ever. "Well, the lady from the Austin Bomb Squad is gonna come back out and take a gander. Looks like blasting caps with an attached timer and battery. It left lots of fragments for the folks at the Austin Bomb Squad to analyze."

I swallowed. I'd heard that blasting caps—usually used to set off dynamite charges—had been found in the rubble from Fred's toolshed and the château de Tepper, along with the remains of an eight-inch pipe bomb. My spine felt a cold tickle, like a ghost's nip.

Although I'd already given Junebug a statement, he asked me to retrace my steps of that morning—where I was on the lawn, what I saw. I told him, omitting only that I'd seen Miss Twyla spying on me in the yard. No need to embarrass my favorite teacher. Junebug jotted down more notes after I'd finished, then asked me if I'd seen anyone near the mailboxes. I said no.

"Now, look here, Junebug," Candace intoned, "this has gone far enough. Jordy could have been killed. Just what are you going to do about this?"

Junebug began his monotonous answer, which was what I'd already read in our local paper, and I tuned out. I wanted a Tylenol and a cup of coffee. Then I'd go to the library. Surely that would make for a Safety First day. Wrong.

* * *

You don't want former lovers to come calling. It's as awkward and messy as trying to change your oil with two left thumbs. And you especially don't want an old lover showing up at work. Not when your current paramour is there to make the scene complete.

I was in my office, planning the attack to weed rarely used books off our stacks. We have to go through this agony at least once each year, determining from our records which volumes have gathered the most dust and sparked the least interest. We sell them to dealers, hoping to make a little money back so we can buy more books. Lord knows our regular book-buying budget isn't growing much.

I heard giggles out on the floor from my two newest staffers, Itasca Huebler and Florence Pettus. I didn't doubt that some interesting town gossip was being told; I believe Itasca has a satellite dish implanted in her beehive. Itasca's in her forties, a funny, big-boned lady with a kind, rosy face and a barbed tongue to rival my own. Florence is closer to my age, a mother of two, who somehow finds it hard to believe ill of anyone. She'd grown up poor and black in Mirabeau, odds that didn't favor success. She ended up married to Joe Pettus, owner of a big carpet store over in Bavary. Florence worked at the library because she liked the people, the children, the smell of the books; Itasca was a tad more practical, having already outlived and outspent two husbands. I was grateful to them both; there'd been no full-time staff when I took over as chief librarian and both women had learned quickly and worked hard.

I listened to the laughter crescendo then abruptly cut off. No doubt Itasca was flinging the latest mud and Florence, too embarrassed to tell her to stop, had just murmured her standard line about getting back to work. Florence appeared at my door, apparently barely able to keep the laughter in.

"Oh, Jordy, you have a visitor. Out at the checkout counter."

"Who?" I asked.

"She didn't say." Florence murmured.

Great. Another book salesperson, no doubt, ready to pitch the latest best-seller that no small rural library could do without. I put on a smile and sauntered out—and saw Lorna Wiercinski perched on the checkout counter. The shock value of seeing Lorna was roughly akin to seeing Jesus sitting there with a HI, I'M BACK button. I confess that my jaw moved up and down without any sound emerging. I'm sure Lorna appreciated that up-close view of my molars.

"I've got something that's overdue, Tex," Lorna rumbled in her thick Boston accent. And yes, rumbled is the right word. Lorna's a big girl, nearly six foot, with long alabaster legs, a broad Slavic face, deep-set gray eyes, an admirable bosom (if size matters to you), and a stunning mane of jet-black hair. Dressed in a miniskirted business suit with black pumps that made her as tall as me, she would have gathered a crowd, not merely stuck out in one. She leaned back on the counter and fluttered her eyelashes. "I do declare," she intoned in an awful pseudo-Southern accent. "That boy's got the vapors."

After a long, arduous search, I found my voice.

"Lorna? Oh, my God—" I was always one for witty banter.

She smiled, a rich, luxurious smile I'd seen many times before. It was her patented cat-who-ate-the-canary-and-the-fish grin, full of self-satisfaction at her own cleverness.

"It's good to see you, too, Jordan." She crossed her legs and leaned forward. "Still breathing, Tex? Keep those involuntary responses going, babe. And what the hell happened to your arm?" I told myself: Okay, she's here. Just deal with it.

I stepped up and hugged her awkwardly, keeping my slinged arm close by me. I don't believe in just shaking hands with someone you've slept with (albeit in the past) for three years. She hugged back, a little too warmly for my taste. When I pulled my head back, she planted a kiss right on my mouth. A friendly peck I could have dealt with; Lorna's hello kiss melted toenails. My eyes popped wide and I saw a grinning Itasca and a frowning Florence.

Which of course, following today's theme of "Keep Jordy in Trouble," was when Candace returned from reshelving the stacks. To her credit, she didn't scream or rage or faint. Oh, no. What she did was far worse. She was icy calm and polite.

I broke the embrace and tried to think of a well-mannered way to wipe the kiss off my mouth and not insult Lorna. I instead sucked my offending lips into my mouth, thinking that hiding them from view might lessen my culpability. I looked instead like an old man who'd had his dentures yanked right from his gums.

"Candace, hi!" I said brightly. She smiled her chilliest smile, the one reserved for people who made a snotty comment about someone she liked. I stumbled onward, feeling totally uncool: "This is an old friend from Boston, Lorna Wiercinski. Lorna, this is Candace Tully—um, my girlfriend." I gestured feebly toward Candace.

No one could have ever deduced my taste in women from looking at these two. Lorna was tall, where Candace was petite. Lorna was dressed like a businesswoman in heat, à la the heroine of some Jackie Collins miniseries. Candace looked like she'd tiptoed out of Laura Ashley University with a bachelor's in Prim. Lorna was smiling, Candace was not. If I'd had one ounce of sense I would have kept talking, but I was a little too rattled by Lorna's unexpected appearance.

"Candy. How nice to meet you." Lorna offered a hand.

Candace smiled and took Lorna's hand. She looked ready to keep it in a jar. "It's Candace, Ms. Weird-chintzy. And how nice to meet you."

Lorna ignored the mispronunciation jab. After all, Candace had *nearly* gotten her name right.

"You'll have to forgive me, I've taken Jordan quite by surprise. He certainly wasn't expecting to see me. I've just arrived from Boston."

"Since he's never mentioned you"—a glare went Jordyward—"I'm not surprised. How nice of you to visit. And what brings you here?" Candace asked. I was awful interested in that question myself. So were Itasca and Florence, who edged closer.

"I stopped by to donate some books," Lorna said innocently, handing me a plastic bag. I regarded it with suspicion. She'd always been one for yanking my chain. Peering inside, I saw that Lorna felt that the Mirabeau Public Library was missing some key volumes: *The Collected Stories of Eudora Welty* (one of my personal favorites), *The Tourist's Guide to New England*, and—oh, boy!—the *Kama Sutra*. Now, would that go under sports or biology?

"Two of those might be for you, Jordan. Can you guess which ones?" Lorna smiled.

Since I already owned a well-worn copy of the Welty, it wasn't a hard guess.

Itasca made a snatch at the bag. "Shall I catalog those for you?"

I yanked them back, somehow keeping my smile in place. "I'll do that later, thanks, Itasca." Candace crossed her arms and one eyebrow went up questioningly.

"I have a proposition for you, Jordan." Lorna beamed and the air temperature continued its downward slide. I'd never thought of Candace as possessive before, but I knew her well enough to sense the seething under her calm exterior. Like I said before, Candace is plenty smart. For an old girlfriend to show up, all the way from New England—I took a deep breath.

"Do you now?" Candace asked. I drew closer to Candace to show my allegiance. She leaned (unthink-

ingly, I'm sure) against my hurt arm. I winced, but let
her stay.

Lorna pulled herself down from the counter. "Yes,
Candy, a business proposition." She blinked as though
shocked at the thought that she could have any other
suggestions for me. "I'd like to discuss it this evening
with you, Jordan—say, over dinner. Nothing wrong with
mixing business with pleasure."

"Gosh, Lorna, you've kind of popped up from nowhere and taken me by surprise." I wanted to convince
Candace that I hadn't been expecting Lorna. "Can't you
tell me what this is about?"

Lorna smiled at Candace. "I'd prefer to discuss this
privately with you, and not during your working hours."
She glanced around the modest library. "Not exactly
like your old office, is it, Tex?"

I squirmed at the nickname; up north, it had seemed
clever and given me the vaguest sense of home; now it
seemed silly. "No, it's a real different office. It's better,
if you ask me." I hesitated. "Well, Lorna, why don't
you come to the house? We can talk there. Say at six?"
I jotted down the address and directions for her.

"Fine, Jordan. It's wonderful to see you again, by the
way. You never did say what happened to your arm."

"I had a little accident." I didn't feel like discussing
Mirabeau's mad bomber. "It's okay."

"How's your mother?" she asked unexpectedly.
Lorna had been none too pleased that I'd left Boston—
and her—to come home to take care of Mama.

"About the same."

"I'm sorry. Well, I'll see you at six. Nice meeting
you, Candy." With that, she turned, nodded at Florence
and Itasca, and sauntered out the door, like a hurricane
moving in from the coast. The only difference was that
hurricanes are indifferent to the destruction and chaos
they cause.

I turned to Candace. "Now listen to me—"

"Candy! How dare she call me that, after I told her

what my name was. I'm no confection." Her voice was low and cool and anything but sweet.

"I'm sorry you saw her kiss me. She took me by surprise—"

"How stupid do you think I am, Jordy? Of course she took you by surprise. That was all over your face and I could read it like a book. Or in this case, a comic strip."

Itasca walked up to me and, very thoughtfully, wiped lipstick off my mouth with a crumpled tissue. She is always one for attention to detail, even at the worst possible times.

"I liked your friend," she announced bluntly, shooting a glance at Candace. I'm fond of Itasca because she's smart and funny, but I don't like her resentment of Candace's money. Itasca hadn't been particularly supportive of my relationship with Candace. "She's gorgeous and she's got style."

"Is that what you call style, Itasca? Her throwing herself at a man who left her months ago?" Candace parried. I handed over the bag of books and she peered inside.

"How transparent," she finally said. "Your favorite writer, a guidebook to her stomping ground, and a sex manual. Honestly, Jordan, is this the kind of woman you dated up north?" Note she called me Jordan. Big trouble ahead.

"I'm sure she was just glad to see Jordy," the generous-hearted Florence piped up. Itasca rolled her mascara-encased eyes.

"Some people might be critical of a lady like her that takes what she wants." Itasca stuffed her tissue back in her purse and took the opportunity to reexamine her own makeup. "I'm not."

"Takes what she wants?" Candace sputtered. "What on earth makes you think she's going to get Jordy back?"

Itasca closed her compact with an authoritative air.

"Jordy didn't seem too broken up to see her, did you, honey?"

Three pairs of eyes trained on me and I felt as embarrassed as a preacher with a broken zipper. "Look, Itasca, you're as wrong as wrong can be. Candace, I'm as surprised as you are to see her here. Those books are just Lorna's idea of a joke. I can't imagine that she wants me back, and I don't know anything about her business proposal."

Florence attempted peace. "Well, now that she knows Jordy's involved with someone else, I'm sure she'll leave him alone."

"Excuse us, please," Candace said, taking my good arm and leading me back to my office. She shut the door.

She crossed her arms, uncrossed them, and crossed them again. "Just one thing. You had no idea she was coming?"

"None. And I don't know what this secret business proposition is about either. When I left Boston, Lorna worked for a consulting firm that specialized in real-estate development. I don't have any idea why she wants to see me."

"She's a good kisser, isn't she?" Candace demanded.

"Of course not!" I bleated. What did Candace want from me? An undying pledge of commitment? We hadn't discussed future plans—too much had happened in those tense couple of months when we'd come together and realized our feelings for each other. After the double punch of a murder investigation and learning about my parentage, long talks about the days ahead held little appeal. I was concentrating too much on past lies and present woes.

"Look, I'll see her, find out what this is all about. If it's just a ploy to get me back in her life, I'll swat her on the ass and send her on her merry way."

Her frown didn't waver. "C'mon, you trust me to handle her, don't you?" I asked. "Whatever this is, it isn't trouble. We've already had our share of that to-day."

She nodded, nearly imperceptibly, then hugged me, being careful of my arm and shoulder. After a moment she let me go and went off into the stacks. I sank down into the front desk chair. My body and mind felt stunned—except for my lips, which tingled from Lorna's kiss. No trouble, I told myself, is going to come of this.

Of course, I was dead wrong. It was trouble, and in the worst way.

CHAPTER TWO

"IT'S NOTHING BUT DAMNED CARPETBAG-gers!" Miss Twyla fumed in my office. For Miss Twyla to utter the word *damned* portended serious trouble. She'd rushed into the library late in the afternoon. I'd felt tired and lethargic and my arm was awful sore. I should have listened to the doctor, gone straight home, and pulled a pillow over my head. Right now all I wanted was some quiet, an icy-cold Celis bock, and another Tylenol. If I didn't watch it, I'd get chemically dependent and end up on *Donahue*, discussing my woes with nine million people. "Librarians Who Are Injured by Prank Bombs, Then Have Close Encounters With Ex-Girlfriends." I'd do wonders for the show's Niel-sens, no doubt. Only problem was I'd be the sole pan-elist.

I had been ready to call it a day when Miss Twyla arrived, looking bad, mad, and demanding some of my time.

"What was that about carpetbaggers, Miss Twyla?" I leaned back in my office chair that dated from when vi-nyl was first invented and tried to find a comfortable position.

"Car-pet-baggers!" Miss Twyla repeated. I'm sure the term has more emotional weight with her than it does with me, since I don't recall using the word except in a history paper.

"Would you care to explain?"

18

"Have you had the pleasure of meeting Miss Lorna Wiercinski and Mr. Greg Callahan?" Miss Twyla asked.

I'd had all sorts of pleasures with Lorna but didn't care to discuss them with Miss Twyla. "Yes, ma'am, I know Ms. Wiercinski. We knew each other in Boston. I haven't met Greg Callahan—who's he?" I paused. "I'm supposed to meet with Lorna this evening about a business proposal."

"Well, hide the silver," Miss Twyla advised. "Those two are nothing but thieves. They want our land, Jordy."

I had this sudden image of Lorna bartering with Chief Manhasset, tossing a few extra beads on the pile. "What land?"

"The land you and I and some others own, that fronts down on the river. They want to buy it up and build condos."

"Condos? In Mirabeau?" Mirabeauans are house dwellers, except for the hardy few who call the trailer park home and those who live in the town's one, rather shabby apartment complex. So this was the reason Lorna was in town. Good—it had nothing to do with our former relationship. Then I remembered the kiss and Lorna's dictum that there wasn't a damn thing wrong with mixing business with pleasure.

"I know. It's stupid. Who'd want to buy a condo in Mirabeau? But that's what they want. And we've got to stop them. Condos would ruin that lovely view of the river, not to mention cause all sorts of nasty runoff into the Colorado. And possibly bring an undesirable element—weekenders." Miss Twyla shuddered.

"Maybe that wouldn't be so bad, Miss Twyla. It could pull some money into town." Mirabeau wasn't exactly lacking in funds, but aside from cotton and peanut farming, cattle, pig raising, a couple of bed-and-breakfasts, a few odd service industries, and some antique stores, there wasn't much to hold folks. Which made me, in reflection, even more curious as to why Lorna or anyone else would want to build condos.

"It's time for action!" Miss Twyla announced, and if she'd had a walking cane, I'm sure she would have stamped it to emphasize her point. "I'm calling a meeting of all concerned citizens tonight. Those developers might think they can ignore me 'cause I'm old, but they're dead wrong!"

"It seems to me that the easiest way to stop them is just not to sell them the land." The fire in her eyes scared me a little; Miss Twyla was one of those old ladies who, once they've gotten their dander up, aren't likely to put it back down until they've had their way. Plus most of the Oudelles, while respectable, had turned out crazy in their later years. Miss Twyla had taught chemistry at the high school and it always made us a tad nervous that she had so many poisons at hand.

"Of course, Jordy, but we must present a united front. I've gone to the county courthouse and found out who all owns the land these Yankees are after. It's you, me, Bob Don Goertz—" (Here she harrumphed—had the gossip about my relationship with Bob Don reached her? We had made no formal announcements, but Junebug, Candace, and a few others in town knew.) After clearing her throat, she continued: "Dee Loudermilk, and your uncle Bidwell."

I groaned at the thought of meeting with that group. First of all, let me clarify that Bidwell Poteet is no longer my uncle, although I may call him that just for purposes of torture. Uncle Bid redefines the term *small-town shyster.* He is possibly the least ethical lawyer produced by the Texas education system, which has never been shortchanged when it comes to producing lousy lawyers. But I liked Dee Loudermilk—she was the mayor's wife, and although her husband was deadly dull, I enjoyed Dee's wry sense of humor. I dreaded the thought of Bob Don and Bid together. Bid enjoyed bad-

mouthing Bob Don (in his ever so subtle fashion—as
subtle as a skeeter bite on the end of your nose).

"Is this really necessary, Miss Twyla? Maybe Lorna
and this Greg Callahan will change their minds about
buying the land if they see the town's not behind them."

"Hardly." Miss Twyla huffed. "They've already offered me an obscene sum for my acres."

An obscene sum? I could use that and I'm not
ashamed to admit it. I'd given up a lot, career-wise, to
return to Mirabeau, and librarians don't get paid diddly.
Sister wasn't exactly opening up a numbered Swiss
bank account with her earnings at the End of the Road
truck stop either. I felt uncomfortable enough with letting Bob Don hire a part-time nurse to take care of
Mama. Condos on the river didn't sound so bad.

"I have taken further action." Miss Twyla stood and
opened the door to my office. "Nina, please, join us."
She widened the door slightly to admit a young woman.

My first thought was: Oh, God, she's one of those
hippie herbalists. Mirabeau's had their share. These
folks (generally women) come out to small towns like
Mirabeau and set up shop selling herbs to the few tour-
ists that wander off Highway 71 and stop in Mirabeau.
God knows the locals won't buy their botanicals; those
folks who don't believe in herbal medicine won't touch
them and those who *do* know where to find them in the
surrounding countryside.

The woman looked a bit older than me, perhaps in
her midthirties. She was plain and her attire didn't help
much in my opinion. Her garb—a long, shapeless beige
dress—gave her the look of a modern-day shepherdess.
A series of sand dollars, shells, and beads ensconced
her thin, dark throat; she could have decorated a beach
all by herself. Her coal-black hair was cut short and not
stylishly. The dark hue of her complexion suggested
Hispanic ancestry, and her black eyes gleamed with intelligence behind wire-rim frames. She greeted me with
an earthy smile.

"Jordy, this is Nina Hernandez. She's an environmental activist from Austin. Nina, this is our town librarian, Jordy Poteet. Jordy also owns some of the land that those Yankees want."

I felt Nina Hernandez's eyes coolly assessing me, as though measuring me for some internal scale of worth. She gave my hand a two-handed shake. "I hope that you will stand firm, Mr. Poteet. Folks like Intraglobal Development will stop at nothing to get what they want."

"Intraglobal?"

"I take it that Miss Twyla has told you about Wiercinski and Callahan being in town."

"You make them sound like foreign agents," I said.

Nina sank into a chair next to Miss Twyla. "Don't underestimate these people. I've dealt with Callahan before. He's cool, ruthless, and determined to win." I wondered if she could be described the same way. The intense gleam in her eyes screamed Type-A personality, even if she was a tree hugger. "We already suspect that they've been in touch with your uncle and with the mayor's wife."

"Already? How long have these folks been in town?" I asked. Lorna stalking Mirabeau, possibly exchanging gossip with my friends and family—horrible thought. I hope she spoke kindly of me.

"Wiercinski just arrived this morning. Callahan's been here two days, staying at the Mirabeau B. Lamar Bed-and-Breakfast." Nina jerked her head toward Miss Twyla like an officer commending a private. "We can thank Miss Twyla here for ferreting out that information." Miss Twyla looked inordinately pleased with herself. I had to admit that Nina chose her allies well.

"Now, Mr. Poteet, we'll have to mobilize to fight Intraglobal. Callahan will certainly be rallying the forces of irresponsible development to combat us." The beads around her neck jangled gently, in odd counterpoint to her strident tone.

Miss Twyla told Nina that I was to meet with Lorna this evening. Nina eyed me like someone prodding Daniel into the lion's den.

"I don't know much about Wiercinski," Nina said, half to herself, "but she's got to be tough if Callahan hired her. He chews broken glass for dinner. Now, what you've got to do, Mr. Poteet, is—"

I don't usually interrupt folks, but for her I made an exception. I smiled. "Look, Ms. Hernandez. I'm sure your concern for Mirabeau is genuine. But I've known Lorna Wiercinski for a long time. I will listen to her business proposition and then make my own decision."

She stared at me like I'd leaned over and spat in her face. "I suppose you want to give them the benefit of the doubt, but let me assure you—"

"Ms. Hernandez, I don't take kindly to outsiders coming into Mirabeau—whether to buy land from us or talk us out of selling it—and then thinking we're a bunch of hicks who can't think independently and need to be told what to do." I stood and nodded at Miss Twyla, who was looking a mite uncomfortable. "I'll be glad to talk to you, hear y'all's side, after I've talked to Lorna."

"Lorna? Already on a first-name basis with the enemy, are you, Mr. Poteet?" Nina's smile faded.

"Yes, ma'am, I am." I wasn't about to admit to having slept with the enemy. "But that doesn't mean that I'm not going to evaluate both sides. Now, if you ladies will excuse me, I have work to do."

Miss Twyla gathered her purse close to her. "Jordy, the meeting's at eight tonight. At my house. I certainly hope you will be there."

"I'll consider it, Miss Twyla." I watched as the two women left, marching arm in arm to defeat the forces of development. That was all Miss Twyla needed: another cause.

I sat back down at my desk, but between thoughts of Candace and Lorna, I didn't get much work done.

* * *

Much to my surprise when I got home, Sister was getting ready to work a rare late shift. She had promised to cover for a friend. At the truck stop, Sister cooks the kind of comfort foods that truckers run speed traps for: chicken-fried steaks, catfish, thick jalapeño cornbread, butter beans with chunks of ham. It's amazing that her twelve-year-old boy Mark and I aren't fatter than hogs. I found her in the kitchen, sticking a pan of chicken enchiladas in the stove.

I leaned down and kissed the top of her head. She straightened and forced a smile. "Hey. Your arm feeling better?" She'd been terrorizing the hospital staff into taking excellent care of me. And now that her shock over my close call had subsided, she'd turned to her usual pastime: teasing me.

"If you were sleeping in your own bed, you wouldn't have gotten hurt." She yanked her white cook's uniform straight and ran a hand through her thick blonde hair. She's still one of the prettiest women in Mirabeau, with her high cheekbones and determined mouth, but she doesn't seem interested in getting hooked up again. After the rotten way her husband abandoned her, I wasn't surprised. "Good thing your hooter didn't get blown off. 'Course, small targets tend to survive."

"Very funny." I enjoyed having Sister tease me again. She'd suffered a shock, weeks ago, when I'd had to tell her about Mama and Bob Don. I suppose that technically we were only half sister and half brother now, but when you've been raised together you don't feel much different about each other. Plus, I wasn't about to start calling her Half Sister. Just doesn't sound right, you know.

I quickly filled her in on what had happened with Lorna and Nina Hernandez. Sister's lovely green eyes widened. She'd heard enough about Lorna when I lived up in Boston.

"That's what you get for dating a Yankee, Jordy," she admonished me.

"I beg your pardon?"

Sister looked at me like I was the town idiot. "For God's sakes, you were the one that complained Yankees were kind of brusque and rude and made fun of your accent. That just shows how unpleasant they can be. Well, this Lorna YMCA-or-whatever-her-name-is gets hold of a nice Southern boy who's been raised right and is more than presentable. I'm sure you treated her nicer than any of those Yankee fellers ever did. Why wouldn't she track you down and tree you like a coon?"

"Lorna's not the tracking kind, Sister."

"She's here, ain't she?" With that, Sister sailed out of the room in triumph. "You and Clo can eat those chicken enchiladas for supper. Mark's staying at his friend Randy's tonight. I'll be back at eleven." The porch door slammed behind her.

I pulled a cold bottle of Celis from the fridge and shook two Tylenol out of a bottle. Gulping them down, I sipped the beer.

"You sure are stupid, taking those with alcohol," a voice rumbled behind me. I put on my best smile and turned to face my own house's gentle ogre.

Clo Butterfield watched me, her beefy dark arms folded across her ample chest. Her black face was set in half stern disapproval, half amusement. Her salt-and-pepper hair was set in an improbable perm. I shook the little bottle of capsules at her.

"It doesn't say anything about that on the bottle," I said defensively.

Clo snorted, deep and low like a bull scrutinizing an amateur matador. "Ever-body knows you don't take drugs with alcohol. Didn't they teach you nothin' at college?"

I pointed with the bottom of my beer bottle at the oven. "Sister left some enchiladas cooking in there for our dinner."

"Thanks, but I got a nose. I can smell 'em." She frowned at my arm and my sling. "Can't believe the foolishness in this town, some idiot blowing up mailboxes. Come on upstairs. Let me look at your bandage, see if it needs changing." I followed our angel of mercy up the stairs, her white uniform tight across her heavy body.

"How's Mama?" I asked.

"Fine. Same as when you left here." If Clo disapproved of my nocturnal wanderings to Candace's bed, she wasn't going to say so outright. I followed her down to Mama's room, and we both stood in the doorway, looking in on my mother, trapped inside her private, shrinking world.

She sat in her bed, a colorful quilt made by her own mother tossed lightly across her legs. She didn't seem to feel the July heat. Clo had just washed and combed Mama's hair, and she looked like a small child, fresh from an afternoon swim in the creek. She stared, like a blind person would, at the small color television on her dresser. She couldn't stand the volume turned up loud, so the Channel 36 news anchor whispered his late-breaking stories to her uncaring ears. Her hand moved repetitively across the quilt, caught in a loop of echoes she could not break. My throat doesn't tighten anymore when I see Mama like this. I've learned to play the waiting game of Alzheimer's, reluctantly acknowledging that she will never recover and waiting for the day when she breathes her last. I sometimes hope for it so I can have more memories of her as she was, rather than have them supplanted by memories of the shell she is now.

In the past Mama would have been on her feet in a moment, demanding to know why my arm was in a sling, comforting me far beyond my need for it, doctoring me herself, making me laugh at her worry, smothering her little boy with a nearly irritating level of attention. Now she stared at me, through me, no more seeing the sling on my arm and her nurse standing next to me than she did air itself.

Clo spoke to her in a far gentler tone than she'd ever used with me or Sister. "Anne, Jordy's come home for supper."

Mama didn't even nod. She glanced at me as though I were a bothersome stranger and turned her attention to the television. My throat tensed. Mama's not even talking as much as she used to, when her babblings were annoying and I'd have to hold my patience to keep from pulling my ears off. Now the silence she offered was worse, like the quiet of a grave. I went over to her and gently squeezed her hand. She kept watching the screen.

Clo was undeterred. "I'll feed you your supper in a minute, Anne. I'm gonna take a look at Jordy. He hurt his arm out fighting organized crime." I smiled, but Mama did not. Today she was uninterested in my adventures.

With Clo following, I went to my own room. Her ministrations did not take long. She examined my stitches critically, made a noise in her throat, cleaned the wound with an antiseptic wipe from her nurse's bag, and put on a fresh bandage. "This damn world. Some say folks like your mama are crazy, but someone who blows up mailboxes, they the loony ones." She pressed the bandage onto my skin. "Weren't you scared?"

"I was too surprised. Now, today, that was scary." I told Clo about Lorna's reappearance in my life, Candace's disapproval, and my rocky meeting with Miss Twyla and Nina Hernandez.

"Dating Yankees. Don't you know better than that?" she finally opined.

"You don't think I was celibate all that time up there, do you?" I eased my arm into a fresh shirt.

"I think what you need, boy, is a little celibacy. Do you some good. Then you don't have womenfolk arguing over you. Celibacy never killed a man."

"Well, I have a feeling that if Candace has her way, I'll be home alone for weeks to come."

"Builds character," Clo rumbled. She patted my good shoulder and moved toward the door. "I'll go get Anne's dinner."

"Speaking of Yankees," I ventured, "my old girlfriend's coming over tonight. Apparently she has a business proposition for me."

"I'll just bet she does." Clo nodded. "Monkey business, most likely."

"I think I'll invite her to dinner. Sister made enough enchiladas for us all."

Clo didn't argue. "Let me know if your shoulder bothers you any. You staying here tonight?"

I pondered the possibilities. "Yeah, I am." I didn't imagine Candace was particularly aching to have me climb into her bed. Plus I needed some time to think.

The doorbell rang. I hate it when your past catches up with you.

CHAPTER THREE

LORNA STOOD BEHIND A BIG BOUQUET OF brightly colored flowers—a gift for Mama. The introductions were quick and to the point. Clo sized up Lorna and the flowers, made polite noises, and excused herself to go feed dinner to Mama up in her room. Lorna still wore her business suit (and looked as uncomfortable as anyone in a suit in the dead of Texas summer would be). She stood in the middle of the living room, shifting from foot to foot, casting her eyes over the white wicker furniture, the mural of family photos that covered one wall, and the antique coffee table that seemed to hold a patina of dust as part of its finish. I offered her a beer and she accepted.

"Thanks for the flowers," I said, my voice sounding awkward. "It was real thoughtful of you." I headed into the kitchen.

"You're welcome. The old homestead isn't exactly what I thought it would be," she called to me as I knelt before the fridge, getting a couple of brews.

"What did you expect?" I called back.

"A ranch, maybe, like in *Giant*. Not all these trees and greenery and rivers. God knows it's hot and humid enough. Where's the tumbleweeds and the dust devils?"

"You're too far east, Lorna. Texas is big, remember? Not all of it looks like the backlot of a John Wayne movie." I returned to the living room and caught her giggling over an old school picture of me; I was smiling with my two front teeth noticeably absent.

29

"Toothless wonder with a cowlick. You look like Dennis the Menace," she said, her clipped Boston accent flattening the vowels and cutting words abruptly. I hadn't heard anyone talk like her in quite a while, and memories started crouching, ready to spring. I pushed them back.

I handed her a cold bottle of Celis beer and she raised it in toast. "To seeing you again," she said softly. I quickly clinked my bottle against hers, unsure if I should return the toast. We settled on the couch.

She sipped cautiously and made a face. "What's this?"

"Belgian-style beer. Brewed in Austin," I said.

She sipped again, held the beer in her mouth, shrugged, and swallowed. It was an action so typical of her that I felt we'd been apart mere minutes rather than months. I forced my eyes away from her and stared at Mama's empty chair until she spoke.

"Beljun-staaaahl beeeyur," she repeated, laughing. "My God, I don't mean to razz you, sweetie, but your accent's gotten wicked thick. You sound like an extra from *The Dukes of Hazzard.*"

"Did you pahk the cah out by the yahd?" I parried, imitating her Boston tones. "I didn't realize that was the King's English dripping from your tongue."

She laughed good-naturedly, a booming, hearty sound. Lorna never did do anything halfway. "You're ragging back. The old Jordan. I guess your little Scarlett O'Hara didn't castrate you after all."

I shrugged, enjoying the banter despite myself. "She doesn't want to lose a good thing."

"She's cute—I'll give her that. I thought she might stamp her foot and say 'fiddle-dee-dee,' but she must be made of sterner stuff than I gave her credit for." She sipped at her beer. "If I'd only had a camera to capture your expression when you saw me. Sorry if I shocked you, but you know I always like to make an entrance."

"You always prided yourself on surprising me, Lorna. And thanks for the book donation."

She laughed again. "You know I'm devoted to fine literature. And *you* still surprise me, Jordan. Staying here." She glanced around the room. "Don't get me wrong. Your mother's home is quaint. Are you really happy living here?"

My face felt hot. I'm allowed to pick on Mirabeau, but I don't like it when other folks do. "I love it here. This is where I grew up."

"Don't get me wrong. I admire you for wanting to help your family. You always were a bit too noble for your own good. It's just—it seems a step backward."

"Excuse me?"

Lorna rose and began striding around the room. She paused at the coffee table. "First of all, darling, don't tell me you're reading"—she paused to peer down at the newspaper and magazines on the coffee table—"*The Star*'s Royal Family special edition and *Southern Living*?"

"Those are my sister's," I protested. I wasn't about to admit I flipped through tabloids for stories on my favorite royal, Fergie. I like big-boned redheads in bikinis. "Anyhow, *Southern Living* has some good articles on refinishing furniture."

"That you are even thinking of refinishing furniture shows how much you've slid, Jordan," Lorna opined. "I recall you were always one for cultural events, darling. What's on the bill this season at the Mirabeau Lyric Opera, the Mirabeau Symphony, and the Mirabeau Avant-Garde Playhouse? Rossini? Beethoven? Ionesco?"

"There's no need to be nasty," I snapped. She sat down next to me, that enigmatic smile still on her face.

"No nastiness intended. I'm sorry if I offended. I think Mirabeau is delightful. But my God, Jordan, your presence here just seems impossible."

"Why? This is where I came from, Lorna. I'd already spent most of my life here when you and I met."

"But it didn't seem like you were small-town. Oh, yes, you had that charming drawl to your voice, but you were so at-home in Boston. You seemed so at-home . . . with me."

I didn't have an answer for her.

She shrugged. "God, I guess I'm lucky that I didn't find you in overalls, out picking cotton, and singing 'The Yellow Rose of Texas.'" She smiled at me, her warm rich smile, and patted my hand. "Oh, well, you can take the boy out of the country but not the country out of the boy. Being at home obviously agrees with you, Tex. You just look wonderful."

"I am the exact same person I was up in Boston. And I wish you wouldn't call me Tex. It really, really makes you sound like a Yankee."

Having scored a point against me, she grinned again. "Oh, okay. I certainly *don't* want to sound like a Yankee. But you do look great." Her gray eyes took on a wicked amusement. Leaning back against the couch, she examined my backside. "Still have a butt you could bounce a quarter off of. I suppose you're running your ridiculous five miles per day." She giggled. "Are you still limber? I hope you haven't already read those books I brought you. I threw out my back on page thirty-six."

I rolled my eyes. Standard Lorna, shifting a discussion of what had been between us to merciless teasing to patting my fanny. She'd been the most aggressive, intimidating, rousing, lusty woman I'd ever known.

I wasn't about to let her work her spell on me. "Why don't I get some guacamole and chips to go with the beer?" I offered, escaping into the kitchen.

"Can I help?" Lorna asked.

"Just make yourself comfortable." I could hear her humming to herself as she examined more of the family photos. As I mashed avocados I found my mind drifting back to our first meeting. In many ways, Lorna was the type of girl you might meet in a bar—but of course we hadn't. I wasn't into guzzling Chardonnay while surrounded by ferns.

We'd met at an art exhibit at a posh gallery in Boston's Back Bay neighborhood, on Newbury Street. Brooks-Jellicoe, the textbook publisher I worked for, was publishing a volume on modern American art, and one of the artists featured was Fauve. Yes, that was his name: Fauve. One name, like Madonna or Cher or Liberace. Anyhow, Fauve was quite the respected creator of slabs of rock covered with paint. I think they were supposed to represent anger or angst or Angola—I forget which. The art-books editor, Robert Goldstein, was a good friend and asked if I wanted to accompany him to this exhibit. I've always liked music more than art, but Robert said there'd be cute women and free food. Editors love free food (and some of us like cute women, too).

The exhibit was crowded, people divided into chattering clumps animatedly debating art and music and who Fauve was sleeping with. I noticed how many folks were keeping their backs to the paintings. After I'd seen a couple, I didn't find that such a bad idea. They were ugly and didn't have a lick of artistic merit. Plus I didn't want anything interfering with my digestion of all that free food I'd consumed.

I saw Lorna before she saw me. She stood nearby, staring perplexedly at an expanse of craggy granite mounted on the wall. The rises in the stone were painted pink and the valleys were a mix of blues and purples.

I'll never forget what she was wearing: charcoal-colored suit pants, a tight white blouse with French cuffs, and an orange-colored blazer with a huge silver pin on it. Her look was cool, reserved, and a little provocative at the same time. Her thick dark hair was corded into a braid, thankfully with no bow on it. She stared at the picture and I stared at her, ignoring my friend Robert's lamentations about the New England Patriots and their losing ways.

I didn't see the heavyset lug until he was practically on top of Lorna, nearly knocking her over in a bear hug. She wrenched free, whirling. "God, Bertil, you scared the crap out of me!"

The man she called Bertil was big, around six foot four, with a thick burr of blond hair and a vacant look in his watery blue eyes. He placatingly placed his mitts on Lorna's shoulders.

"Sorry, Lorna. Didn't mean to startle you." He was either Swedish or drunk. Or both.

"I see you're using Absolut as this evening's cologne," Lorna observed. "Now goodbye."

"Wait, wait, Lorna, don't go—" Bertil lurched, obviously having partaken too much of the grape. He seized Lorna's arm and spun her back.

"Do you want to lose one of your meatballs?" she snapped. I had started to move forward to help her when another hulking type, this one a dark, thick-necked fellow, intervened, pulling Lorna and the Swede apart.

"Let her go, Bertil," the dark man rumbled.

"Oh, great, a male model to the rescue. I'm safe as long as you don't get hit in the face," Lorna said. She stepped back from both men. "Why don't you both just leave me alone? Go spend the evening learning how to spell."

He ignored her, determined to be a paladin. "This guy bothering you, Lorna?" He puffed up his chest, pushing it within an inch of the infuriated Swede. "Maybe I should make sure he behaves like a gentleman."

"You be a gentleman yourself, Trevor," Lorna demanded. "I don't need a bodyguard."

"Yeah, Trevor, she doesn't need you." Bertil gave Trevor's chest a little jab with his finger.

"Listen here, butthead, I don't—"

"Gentlemen, gentlemen, please! Control yourself!" The star of the exhibit, Fauve himself, intervened. He was a tall, thin willow of a man, wearing a ridiculous-looking copy of the small-lapeled gray suit the Beatles favored back in the Sixties. A curve of hair hung artistically in his face, showing his great sensitivity and a gentle nature. Fauve put a protective arm around Lorna, his hand perilously close to her right buttock, and flexed his fingers, as though ready to squeeze.

"Gentlemen, really, no need to fight. Ms. Wiercinski is my special guest this evening, so I do hope that you won't resort to fisticuffs over her."

"Go sculpt, Fauve," Lorna blurted, pushing his hand away. I didn't see it at the time, but I can imagine the glint that appeared in her eye. "They weren't fighting over me. They were discussing which of them hates your rock piles more."

"What!" Bertil exclaimed, his jaw dropping. (I later learned Bertil was a corporate art buyer whose boss was a close friend and admirer of Fauve's.)

"Lorna!" Trevor's face turned pale. (I later found out that Trevor was an aspiring painter who was panting to get under Fauve's wing.)

She whirled, leaving her would-be protectors squabbling. In her haste to flee them, she barreled right into me.

Her eyes locked with mine, but she lowered her gaze and pushed past me. "Excuse me." I followed her, the din of Trevor and Bertil's protestations fading with Fauve's outraged cries over their deplorable lack of taste.

I caught up with her as she left the gallery, venturing into the cold March air of Boston. "So much for culture!" she yelled at the night sky.

"Ma'am?" I called to her. "Are you okay?"

She paused and regarded me with her gray eyes. "Look, buddy, I don't need any more guardians tonight."

"I don't believe you do." I smiled. "You handled the Three Artistic Stooges in rare style."

She took a step toward me. "I take it you're not from Boston. *Style* usually has just one syllable."

Being teased about my accent always rankled me, but from her it didn't seem too bad. "No, not originally. I'm from Texas."

"So why didn't you leap to my defense? Aren't cowboys supposed to be chivalrous?"

"Only to womenfolk that need our help. You obviously didn't, ma'am." I turned *ma'am* into two syllables—and she laughed.

I tried not to waver on my feet, a sure sign of nervousness. This girl made me feel timid, but I rallied my courage for those unforgettable gray eyes. "I'm fed up with spray-painted rocks. Wanna get some coffee or maybe a drink?"

She considered me for a moment, measuring me on the internal ruler that women must in these dangerous times. "I don't usually go out with men I don't know."

I offered my hand. "Jordan Poteet." I never *ever* went by Jordy up north—I thought it sounded too hick.

She didn't laugh but she looked amused. "What a perfectly fantastic name. Definitely American. Unlike Bertil, Trevor, or Fauve." She took my hand and shook it, holding it a moment longer than necessary, as if taking my pulse. "I'm Lorna Wiercinski. Mispronounce it twice and die. It's not as American as your name, but hey, this is Boston, the great unmelted pot." She pointed down the block. "There's a pub on the corner. I know the owner, so if you give me trouble, he'll kick the shit out of you. We could have an Irish coffee."

Odd invitation, but I didn't mind. I offered her my arm. Judging by her expression, it might have been leprous.

"God help me. Just how much of a Southern gentleman are you?" She laughed, finally placing her hand on my forearm.

"Not nearly enough for my own good," I answered.

It was the strangest date of my life. We each drank three Irish coffees, sinfully rich with cream and whiskey, then after two hours of laughing and talking she asked me back to her apartment. It was an upscale condo not far from the gallery. I'd wondered if we'd end up in bed, but she wanted to play poker. With me and her neighbor, Mrs. Perkins. She'd suggested it. I'd agreed—a little too stunned to argue. And she'd gone down the hall to fetch Mrs. Perkins.

"She'll be right over," Lorna said, pouring us each a whiskey. "As soon as she gets her money and puts in her teeth."

"I hope she doesn't get them confused. Hate to have her ante up her molars."

She laughed. "I'll see your bicuspids and raise you an incisor."

As it turned out, the poker game was fun, and although I kept wondering what Lorna's bed felt like, I didn't get to sample it. Mrs. Perkins claimed she was on a fixed income (considering the neighborhood, her fixed income was most likely a trust fund), so I had to let her win her money back and we played into the wee hours. When the amiable Mrs. Perkins won the stunning total of twenty dollars, she toddled off and Lorna called me a cab.

"Would you have dinner with me tomorrow night?" I prayed this funny, smart girl would say yes.

"Yes, I would," she answered, almost shyly. "You see, you passed tests number one and two. First, you didn't presume you'd sleep here, and second, Mrs. Perkins liked you. She let you win at first so the game'd go on longer. Yes, I think dinner is a real possibility." Our good-night kiss was brief but sweet, one of those you hold in your memory like a treasure. And so it began— three years' worth of wonderful remembrances.

We discussed marriage once or twice, but Lorna was gun-shy, her own mother having been divorced three times. Said mother was somewhere in Toronto with a much younger man who didn't believe in matrimony. I wasn't sure I wanted to stay in Boston and Lorna seemed firmly planted in her native soil. So the topic was dropped and we just enjoyed each other. My return to Texas to care for my mother was a bucket of ice water in Lorna's face. I asked her to accompany me. She said no—she couldn't do that. And I left. So much for us. It hurt, but I hadn't looked back.

Lost in my memory, I hardly noticed her hand close over mine as I finished stirring the avocado and spices. Lorna's voice was low: "You haven't called—or written—in months."

I bit my upper lip. "I don't think you're here because I haven't stayed in touch. Which I'm sorry for. I guess I just thought it would be better if we broke cleanly." I took the dip and a big bowl of tostadas into the living room. Lorna followed me.

"So you're not coming back to Boston? Ever? Babe, what happens when your mother dies? Do you plan to stay here forever?"

Leave it to Lorna to ask all the tough questions in the first five minutes. "I don't know. I'll worry about that when it happens."

"Spare me, Jordan. That's never been how your mind works." Her voice was serious now, and her tongue kept darting out to moisten her lips. Nervous. "I didn't want to ask you such a difficult question, but I think I deserve to know."

"It's more complicated than just Mama's illness, Lorna. A lot has happened since I came back."

She sat down and scooped up guacamole on the corner of a chip. "So talk. Tell me."

So I recounted it all, starting with Beta Harcher's murder and my discovery that my daddy wasn't my daddy after all—and trying to have a relationship with my actual father. I'll give Lorna credit. She stayed quiet throughout the story. When I was done, she took my hand.

"My God, baby, I can't believe it. I'm so, so sorry. Are you okay?"

I nodded. "I'm surviving. But I don't plan on leaving town right when . . . Mama dies. That may not be for a long time anyhow, Lorna. And I have Bob Don to consider—and Candace, too."

"As soon as I laid eyes on her, I could see you marrying that Scarlett clone and playing the gentleman planter on her money."

"So you know about Candace's money?" A chip halted halfway to my mouth. "Is this part of your land-acquisition deal with Intraglobal, finding out who's got what where?"

She looked startled, then shook her head, dark curls jiggling around her face. "I'm not surprised you know about the land deal. I suppose word gets around in such a small town." She opened her briefcase and began to shuffle papers. "Perhaps it's best we simply put our former relationship on hold for the moment. It really doesn't matter. I'm not here to lure you back to New England. The truth is I'm here to offer you a reasonable purchase price for your land."

Her shift in gears was so abrupt I was taken aback. Not like Lorna. She'd already observed how I'd changed; perhaps *she* had changed as well. Fine, we'd talk business. Surely *that* would be less stressful than the earlier topic: us. "I know. Intraglobal Development wants to build condominiums, right?"

"An entire resort condominium community, Jordan," Lorna amended for me. "Designed for residents who desire a higher standard of living—"

"That should narrow down the candidates," I interjected, but she pressed on.

"—and those from Austin and Houston who seek a comfortable weekend getaway on the shores of the Colorado." She began to spread out maps; architectural drawings that included a golf course, pool, tennis courts, and clubhouse; construction schedules; and environmental-impact statements. She told me in more detail than I cared to hear exactly what the development plans were.

It still seemed ludicrous and impossible: Lorna Wiercinski, who had shared my bed and my heart and my sense of humor for three years, was *here*. I listened to her overrehearsed presentation, nodding over her figures, blinking at her studies for the potential market (the target demographic audience in the cities was *excellent*, in her estimation), smiling at her own excitement about the project, and wondering what kind of money they'd offer. I hadn't yet decided on a course of action. In any case, I'd hear both sides before parting with the title to my riverside acres. I'd promised that much to Miss Twyla.

"So that's basically it—a condominium resort community that will both provide a solid growth pattern for Bonaparte County and not interfere with the river's ecosystem."

"Lorna, I'm amazed. You actually parroted your company spiel instead of slapping your offer for my land on the table and telling me I had five seconds to make up my mind. Does your boss have you on morphine?"

She smiled a smile several wattages below normal and shrugged. "I know; it's so much more restrained than the real me. I've got to do it that way. Greg says I'm too blunt otherwise. Scare people off."

"This would be Greg Callahan?"

"Yes. I take it you've heard about him."

I opted not to share Nina Hernandez's less-than-charitable characterization of Lorna's colleague. "Yeah, his name's getting around town."

Lorna huffed. "I warned him to stay away from the local women."

"Excuse me?"

"Greg's a bit of a ladies' man. He doesn't have your studly height, but he has a hell of a lot more charm." Her voice lowered slightly to a tone I was ever so familiar with and I wondered just how much charm this Greg had.

"Charm's a passing commodity, unlike height," I said with a smile.

She examined me with mock gravity. "It seems to have passed you right by, if I may say so."

"You stopped long enough to look."

"Looking's free," she replied, scooping up more guacamole. "You can't find something worth having without doing a little window-shopping."

"So how much is my land worth to you?" We'd slipped into the gentle flirting we'd done so well and so often back in Boston. We used to stay up late, munching popcorn and watching videotapes of the *Thin Man* movies—and exchanging verbal salvos as if we were Nick and Nora.

I could hear Clo rumbling around upstairs, obviously preparing to join us. And the chicken enchiladas smelled nearly ready.

"I can't make the offer. That has to come from Greg. Maybe he can meet with you tonight."

"Let's eat first, then discuss this further." I called upstairs to Clo, then went into the kitchen. "You'll stay for dinner, of course," I said. I went into the kitchen and opened the oven door. Lorna leaned over my shoulder, sniffing at the casserole dish.

"Maybe I will stay." Lorna peered at the bubbling mix of cheese, jalapeños, and tortillas that smelled like a corner of heaven. "It just depends on what the hell's on the menu."

Watching Lorna eat her first bona fide Mexican meal while juggling conversation with Clo was a great entertainment value.

"Mrs. Butterfield, Jordan tells me you do a wonderful job with his mother."

"Try to."

"So, are you a lifetime resident of Mirabeau?" Lorna asked as she filled her plate with two thick, cheesy chicken enchiladas.

"Yes." Clo had obviously taken her monosyllabic pill while upstairs. She watched Lorna guardedly and began to eat.

Lorna gave me her don't-we-have-a-live-wire-here look and I smiled. It bothered me, though, that I could still interpret Lorna's glances so easily. Under the circumstances, it made me damn uncomfortable to have such easy nonverbal communication flashing about. How readily could she read my face? I suddenly felt as naked as a newborn.

"So tell me, Mrs. Butterfield . . ." Lorna attempted again. "You must get a tremendous amount of satisfaction out of nursing."

"I see why you like him." Clo jerked her head toward me. "You talk just as much as he does." With that, she popped half an enchilada into her mouth and began to chew with great dignity.

That silenced Lorna long enough for her to try Sister's culinary treat. She surveyed the spicy quagmire on her plate, scooped some on a fork, and popped it into her mouth. *Popped* is the correct verb, as her eyes then proceeded to pop in surprise and she rapidly popped the top on a new bottle of beer and began to gulp down the icy brew.

Clo and I smiled over the peppers on our forks and proceeded to eat them with great relish, little sweat, and no beer. When Lorna's vocal cords quit smoldering she stared at me with one eyebrow raised. "It's that war thing, isn't it? You lost, so when one of us comes down here you try to rupture our internal organs with this Tex-Mex concoction."

Clo made a choked chuckle and I was saved from replying literally by the bell. I scooped up the phone receiver, swallowed my mouthful of enchilada, and said a hello.

"Jordy, you must honor my request!" It was Miss Twyla and she was apparently reliving her previous life as a Byzantine empress. She clearly expected me to fetch every time she barked.

"Calm down, Miss Twyla. What's the matter—"

"The crowd will be such at tonight's meeting that my little living room can't hold them all. May we use the library instead?"

"I suppose so." I checked my watch. It was a little past seven. "Still starting at eight?"

"Yes, dear. Nina, Tiny, and I will call everyone and let them know of the change in plans."

"Excuse me. Did you say Tiny is there?"

"Yes, Jordy, and what a wonderful help he's been. I'm sure the meeting will be an orderly one with Tiny's help. I'll leave a note on my front door for those we can't reach by phone. Perhaps you can meet us at the library a little before eight."

"Certainly. See you then." I hung up. Oh, great. Now Miss Twyla had gotten Tiny Parmalee involved. My evening was complete. I would spend my evening with my ex-teacher with a cause, an environmentalist windbag who bossed folks around, and the fellow who'd bullied me and every other kid at Mirabeau Elementary. I'd have to make sure I'd hidden my lunch money before I headed over to the library.

Clo had finished eating and was rinsing her plate in the sink. Lorna's plate was also clean, except for the pile of sliced jalapeños she'd pushed to the rim.

Clo excused herself to check on Mama. I told her I'd be gone for a while, but should be home by ten. She agreed to stay with Mama until I returned, then went upstairs.

"Delightful woman," Lorna observed. "A graduate of the Nurse Ratched School, I take it?"

"Clo doesn't like Yankees."

"I don't get this Yankee garbage. Why do Southerners continue to mope about the war? I'm a little tired of being referred to as a Yankee and having it sound like I've got a venereal disease. People down here don't try to get to know you before they make judgments—"

"Sorry, but no sympathy. Now you know what I went through in Boston. Like the times folks made fun of my accent by repeating back everything I said, all the times I was asked how many oil wells I owned, all the times people wondered aloud if I was a member of the KKK." I cleared our plates and began to wash them. It wasn't easy using my one good hand, but I managed.

She was very close behind me before I realized it. "Then how about our own little Appomattox? I suggest an immediate peace treaty." Her palms, generous as the rest of her, slid up and down along my sides in a gentle rhythm. My body began to respond before my mind did. By that time her hands were in full exploratory mode and I dropped the plate I'd been trying to wash into the soapy lake of the sink.

"Lorna—" I whispered as I turned to her.

Her mouth covered mine and goddamn it, I let it. I've no excuse. It felt like we were back in her apartment in Boston, the ever-present noise of traffic outside her kitchen window. But as hard as she was kissing me, I was kissing back and cussing myself for doing so. After several seconds I broke the kiss and turned my head.

"My arm hurts when we get that close."

"I didn't even touch your arm."

"I'm—involved with Candace, Lorna. I care about her. I think I'm in love with her."

"You *think*? Love isn't something you think. It's something you know." She pulled back from me. "Look, Jordan, I'm not good at this confession stuff. I don't lay out my heart very easily. But I was wrong, dead wrong, to let you come back here without a fight. What was I supposed to do—say no, don't go take care of your mom? What kind of selfish monster would I be if I said that? I never loved you more than when you said you had to come back here to help your family. Everything you were willing to give up for the people you loved, it just amazed me. You're the most kindhearted man I've ever known." She broke eye contact with me and stared at the floor. "I can't compete with a sick woman who desperately needs you. I haven't known what to do for months now. I was paralyzed. Then I end up going to work for Intraglobal and I nearly died when Greg told me we were coming to Mirabeau to do this deal. I couldn't believe it. The coincidence just seemed too great. Then I realized: some things are just meant to be. God's dropping you back in my lap, Jordan. Your land and the condo deal—they don't matter except that they've allowed us to be together again."

I could still taste her on my lips. Turning away from her, I wiped my wet hands on a dishrag. For once in my life, I was speechless. In three years Lorna had told me she loved me maybe once or twice. She was not a woman given to emotional pronouncements. I was even less likely to voice the L-word, and I couldn't believe I'd confessed a depth of affection for Candace to someone else. I couldn't still love Lorna; I couldn't. I didn't need the complication. So why did I suddenly feel so weak-kneed?

Miss Twyla had provided me a coward's perfect escape route and I took it. "I have to go to a meeting at the library. Some folks aren't much in favor of this condo development and want to hash it out. I'm not taking their side yet, but I owe it to them to hear what they have to say."

"Don't." She reached out and turned my head back to her. God help me, I wanted to kiss her again. "Listen, babe, I know this has to be a shock to you. Seeing me again like this. But don't turn away, please, not again. Not when you can be so much more."

"I don't know what you mean."

"It's incredible that you're taking care of your mom,

CHAPTER FOUR

I'VE NEVER BEEN A FAN OF MEETINGS, BUT FOR Miss Twyla's sake, I put on my best public-librarian smile. I'd heard Lorna's side of the development issue—and fairness demanded I listen to Nina.

I'd arrived in time to unlock for the three of them. Tiny Parmalee stood close by Nina Hernandez and it wasn't hard to see why he'd evinced sudden interest in riverfront development. She was just the plain kind of woman that he always fell for.

Every time I see Tiny, I recall our first instance of quality time. He'd always been bigger than all the other kids, even since first grade (hence his nickname). He'd also been dumber. That's not a crime in itself, but coupled with his stupidity was a particular brand of meanness. Tiny was damned unpleasant and he took comfort in that.

Our first and only fight had been in third grade. Naturally it was at recess, the only time in the scholastic day that Tiny ruled as king. The boys played softball or touch football and the girls played tetherball or tag, chasing each other with screeches of delight. It was the autumn of 1971 and Mirabeau schools had finally settled into integration. It had been a surprisingly easy process; most people in Mirabeau who objected (and let's be blunt, most people did) had decided that it was inevitable and they might as well go along. Kids being kids, necessity won out over prejudice; to have two teams for softball during third-grade recess, every able-bodied boy was needed. So the whites graciously agreed to play with the blacks, and the blacks graciously agreed to play with the whites.

Tiny was not exactly on the cutting edge of societal change, then or now. If memory serves, he objected to his team losing because of a run batted in by a boy named Michael Addy. Michael was a fair fielder but a great batter, and his skin was as dark as an eggplant's.

Even in third grade Tiny towered over the other boys, and when he'd decided to beat up Michael for hitting in that run, no one seemed inclined to interfere. Michael was the biggest of the black boys but still no match for a genetic oddity of size like Tiny. He had Michael, his nose bleeding and mashed, in a headlock. The black boys stood in a group of their own, none daring to take on the giant. The girls, both white and black, huddled together, watching the dusty display of male violence with distaste and horror. I clearly remember one of the black girls screaming at the boys to do something. A few of the white boys stood in open approval of the spectacle, while others stayed silent, toeing the dirt of the field. And no one, including myself, dared to fetch the teacher, knowing what Tiny's ire would bring on us later.

I don't know what made me do it. I was not tall in those days; my growth spurt didn't hit until I was in high school. I didn't care too much if the white kids and the black kids got along. Michael Addy wasn't a friend of mine. I only remember thinking that if my daddy found out I stood by while another child was beaten, how disappointed and mad he'd be. I knew that from experience.

"Say it," Tiny huffed to the prisoner of his arms. "Say it slow, like I told you to."

To this day, I can hear the crack of Michael Addy's voice, his throat trapped in Tiny's heavy arms, a voice that begged for release: "I'm—I'm a dumb nigger."

"Good. Now say it loud so ever-body knows what you are."

I put my hand on Tiny's shoulder. "Stop it."

The shock in the crowd was not nearly as great as the shock on Tiny's pug face. He wore his hair in a crew cut then, and his hair was so white he nearly looked bald. He glanced at my hand on his stout shoulder. "What the hell you doing, Bo Peep?"

Tiny had altered my surname to *Bo Peep* and got no end of amusement from this ingenious pun.

"You made him do what you wanted. Leave him alone." I tried reason. "You better let him go before the teacher gets out here."

Tiny looked at me as though I'd just announced that he himself was a dumb nigger. He dropped Michael Addy, who promptly and wisely took the opportunity to put some distance between himself and Tiny, scrabbling across the softball field grass to relative safety.

"You takin' up for that nigger, Bo Peep?" Tiny squared his shoulders and looked down at me. I suddenly felt very fragile, but all of a sudden I was madder'n hell. Tiny had never bullied me physically, but I'd grown tired of that nickname and the way he pushed people around like checkers on a board.

"Just leave him alone. He didn't do nothing to you."

"I don't like losin' to an uppity nigger."

"You don't like losin', period. Well, ever-body has to lose sometimes. You can't always win." I wanted to turn and walk away, my speech complete, but I knew that I could not turn my back on Tiny Parmalee.

He wiped a bit of spit off his lip, his hand forming into a fist as he dragged it across his mouth. "You just love them niggers, don't you, Bo Peep."

"I just don't like you pushing people—" and that was as far as I got before he belted me. I fell to the ground, my lip cut and bleeding instantly. I'd never been walloped in the mouth before, and damn if it doesn't hurt like the dickens.

Instead of sitting there and crying about the agony in my lip like any sensible boy would have done, I instead meted out more punishment for myself by tackling Tiny, low near the ankles. He didn't have good balance because of his size and he fell, fortunately not landing on me. There was an *ooh* from the crowd and several boys, from the safety of distance, began yelling encouragement to me.

Tiny only knew power, not strategy, and I didn't know much about either. I had been in only one other fight in my life—and I'd lost. And my struggle with Tiny quickly degenerated into rolling around in the gritty dirt of the batting area, surrounded by screaming and cheering schoolmates who surged back and forth in rhythm with the fight like a fickle tide.

I was losing, though. We'd tussled past the fence that marked the boundaries of the old baseball lot, rolling onto unmowed grass. Tiny huffed and puffed like a dragon trying to rouse up a steamy breath of fire. I could tell his anger was boiling over; he should have dispatched me easily, but I was quicker and stronger than he had figured. If he didn't win soon, his standing would fall in the playground, and that he could not tolerate. Cussing, he pinioned me on my back and his hands closed around my throat.

"I'm a-gonna squeeze real hard, Bo Peep, unless you tell everyone what a nigger-lovin' faggot you are." His eyes softened, not in any mercy but in that he sensed victory. A drop of his sweat fell into my eyes, like Chinese water torture. His raggedy fingernails pressed crescents into my throat. I thought about all of Tiny Parmalee's weight crushing on my windpipe and tried not to be scared.

"No," I gasped. "No."

Tiny leaned down harder on my throat and dark circles began to form over his face. The screaming of my classmates was far closer, but seemed to be growing distant. I felt his fingers digging into my neck, seeking out the air in it like it was an intruder. And, shockingly, I saw the glint of murder in Tiny Parmalee's eyes. His rage was so intense that, had we been alone, I'm certain he would have killed me. He was the sort of boy who would set a worm on fire and laugh at its wriggly dance of death. I stared back into his eyes and he saw that I saw what he was, the gaze between us as intimate as lovers. His grip tightened.

My hands lashed out and my right one caught metal. I had a vague memory of a stake thrust in the ground, tied with a yellow ribbon at the top, marking a corner of the softball field. Only an adrenal surge gave me the strength to pull the stake out and bring it down in Tiny Parmalee's back.

Honestly, I didn't do much damage. My aim was horrendous and I didn't hit his back so much as pierce his side. It didn't even crack a rib, though it cut through some flesh and bled profusely. I've no doubt that it hurt like hell.

What undid Tiny was his scream. He howled as that stake scored him, and his scream was like a girl's—high-pitched and full of powerlessness and fear. Breaking his throttlehold on me, he reeled away, holding his side and screeching at the blood that spilled from him. He was the only one screaming on the playground now; the other children were stunned into silence.

I didn't do a victory jig. I opted to roll over, gasp repeatedly, and finally throw up in the mashed grass of the field. I lay there, unmoving, until a teacher cradled my head in her lap and told me I was okay.

In the simple mathematics of recess and playground and combat, that scream defeated Tiny Parmalee. He'd been the bully and the aggressor, but he'd been the one to capitulate—and worse: to scream like a girl. I'd done the unimaginable in taking him on. A few thought I'd cheated in using the stake, but the bluish bruises on my throat spoke for themselves about the equality of the struggle. We both were suspended for a week, much to my father's delight (in that I had done the right thing in taking up for Michael Addy), to my mother's horror (in that I'd stooped to fighting), and to my sister's embarrassment (in that she had a crush on Tiny Parmalee's cousin and I'd set back her campaign to win the boy).

Our first day back, the principal met us in the office and forced us to shake hands. I coughed and did so, averting my eyes from the bruises on Tiny's face. Had I really given him those? Or had his parents reacted differently to the fight than mine did? Tiny shook my hand and stared blankly into my eyes.

"I don't want to hear anything about you boys fighting," the principal chirped. "I don't want to hear about it happening here or away from school. And rest assured, if it happens, I will hear about it."

It didn't. Tiny and I avoided each other like the plague. If we passed in the halls, we didn't speak or even acknowledge one another. Our friends tried to goad us into fighting again, but we ignored them. Michael Addy slipped a note to me in my math book one day that simply said THANK YOU. I ate the slip of paper before my teacher could see it. Michael and I ended up going through the rest of school together without mentioning the fight again. Michael went to Texas Tech on a baseball scholarship and now coaches for a high-school team in Richardson, a big suburb of Dallas. Tiny barely finished high school, did a stint in the army, and now worked with his daddy, a long-haul trucker.

So that's why I don't care much for Tiny Parmalee. We'd had no further run-ins and I'd only seen him once since I returned to Mirabeau. We'd passed each other on Mayne Street as I went into a store and he was coming out. He'd given me the briefest of stares, which I ignored.

Now he was favoring Nina Hernandez with long, goofy looks. She didn't look too delighted with his attentions; in fact she seemed downright apprehensive.

"Tiny. Ms. Hernandez." I nodded as I unlocked the

library doors. Nina smiled thinly and moved inside. Tiny lumbered near me and regarded my arm, still in its sling.

"Heard you nearly got blowed up," he said, sneering. There wasn't direct malice in his tone, just a sort of general bullying that lay underneath like filth under a rug. "What a damn shame that'd be."

"Thanks for your concern," I answered, not wanting to waste much air on a response to him. Miss Twyla prevented any further pleasantries by coming up to us both, thanking me again for the use of the library.

The last folks to occupy the community room on the library's top floor was a Lamaze class, so there were no chairs set up. Apelike, Tiny just popped the metal chairs open and set them wherever he happened to be. I used my good arm to help Nina drag the chairs into the proper positions.

"I think your new assistant likes you," I murmured to Nina.

She stiffened as if I'd stepped on her toe. "Mr. Poteet, I'm sorry we got off on the wrong foot this afternoon. It's just that I feel strongly about stopping Intraglobal. And you should be as concerned about saving the river as Mr. Parmalee is."

"Oh, I am. I'm just not so certain that our Tiny friend is motivated by ecological desires." I could be friends with her if she could take a little teasing.

"Tiny's a fine man," she muttered, watching her new charge as he scratched his forehead while blankly surveying a map of the world that hung on the wall.

"Yes, he is. And don't worry about all his eccentricities. He's a victim of society." I meant it nicely, but Nina misinterpreted. She snorted at me, pushed her glasses back up on her forehead, and went to confer with Miss Twyla. So much for teasing.

By eight everyone had arrived. Aside from Miss Twyla, Nina, Tiny, and myself, there was a scattering of forty or so people who didn't own land by the river but had gotten riled up by Miss Twyla. Also present was our esteemed M?yor (and my boss), Parker Loudermilk and his wife, Dee. I remembered that Dee owned some of the land that Lorna and Greg Callahan wanted to buy. Parker, I've no doubt, was looking for whatever favorable impressions he could get out of the situation. Parker's not bad as bosses go—as long as you watch your back.

I saw with some amusement that my old friend Eula Mae Quiff had embraced this latest cause. If there's action anywhere in Mirabeau, Eula Mae's usually hovering nearby drinking it all in. She's a best-selling romance novelist and my favorite of the town eccentrics. (And it's a wide and varied choice.) Tonight she wiggled beringed fingers at me while she chattered with Miss Twyla and Nina. I figured the outlandish dashiki she sported was to show her concern for the environment, other cultures, and general world harmony.

I took Eula Mae aside when some other folks began talking to Nina and Miss Twyla. "What are you doing here? You don't even own land on the river."

"Well, pardon me, Squire Poteet," she sniffed, running a hand through her graying curls. "I didn't know you had to have a title to the sacred acres to care about saving the Colorado."

"I'm not convinced the river's in danger, Eula Mae."

"Well, our way of life is. I don't want a bunch of snotty Houstonians down here on weekends, jamming up our streets and spoiling my view of the river." She patted my good arm. "Do you need the money you might get from the land sale, sugar? You just let me know. I'll be glad to loan you some cash. Is your hospital bill making you fret?"

"That's not the point, Eula Mae. We don't know much about what tactics this Nina Hernandez is going to use to stop this development. I think she gets ornery if she doesn't get her way. I just want for there to be reasoned discussion, not a bunch of mudslinging and hysteria."

"Honey pie, you're talking about money and people and land. Reasoned discussion isn't part of that equation. Look at all the problems they've had over in Austin with greedy developers from out of state."

"Look, I know one of those so-called greedy developers—"

"That big-boned Yankee gal with the Polish name?" Nothing got by Eula Mae, and I didn't miss the amused glint in her eye. Teasing me is probably Eula Mae's favorite pastime, aside from ogling men and deciphering her royalty statements.

"Yes, that would be her, Eula Mae." I glanced around to see if Candace had arrived yet—but then, I didn't know if she even knew about the meeting. "Listen, I know Lorna, and I don't think she'd be involved with anything unsavory—"

"Jordy, that girl drips unsavory like week-old barbecue," Eula Mae said. "Itasca told me about her little entrance at the library. And I can only imagine the two of you together. Actually, it's nearly romantic. Poor lonely Southern lad, cast adrift in the big, heartless city. I'll guess you met her during one of those dreadful winters and needed a bedwarmer. I bet that chest of hers could heat all of Massachusetts." Yes, Eula Mae actually talks like her books. It can be real amusing as long as she's not talking about you. "And how does Candace like your little visitor?"

"Fine, just fine." I definitely didn't want to be discussing my love life with Eula Mae. If I wasn't careful, I'd read it again in the fat pages of one of her potboilers.

She patted my arm again. "I gotta go say hi to the Terwilliger sisters, sugar doll. I'll catch you later." She toddled off in the direction of some of the elderly ladies that hovered near Miss Twyla, undoubtedly members of our local widows' and spinsters' Mafia. If they were on Miss Twyla's side, I nearly felt sorry for Intraglobal.

My former uncle Bidwell Poteet (blessedly former since I found out that Bob Don's my dad meant that Bid isn't my biological uncle) also appeared, scowled at the audience, and broke into an unexpected grin when he saw me. To my horror, he made a beeline for me. It was sort of like being hounded by a small, smelly Chihuahua. Uncle Bid is hairless (as far as we can tell, and I'm not about to investigate past his pate) and he always reeks of stale cigarillos.

"Well, boy, I see you nearly got yours." He poked at my slinged arm.

"Try to hide your disappointment," I answered dryly.

"Seriously, Jordy, you are okay, aren't you?" His husky voice lowered and I thought: It can't be—not genuine concern for me. I regarded him suspiciously. Maybe I'd misjudged the old toot.

"Yes, I'm fine, Uncle Bid, thank you for asking."

His scrawny shoulders heaved in relief. "Good. If you died, I don't know who you've got those riverfront acres willed to—and having it tied up in probate right now could sour the deal for the rest of us."

"Your consideration for my well-being is touching. Like bad heartburn." I glared down at him. "Why do I have the feeling you'd sell Intraglobal your land even if they were building a nuclear reactor next to the town?"

"Hell, boy, money's money. If you had one scrap of sense in that brain my brother wasted all that money eddicatin', you'd know that." He jabbed a finger into my chest (about as high up as he could reach). "Get some sense in you, Jordy, for once, please. Sell to these folks and don't listen to that shell-wearin' Austin hippie up there."

"I'll consider that as strongly as I do all other advice you give me," I promised.

The insult went over his head, since it didn't have far to jump. "All right, then. You got any questions on how to unload that land, you see me." His chocolaty dark eyes squinted at me. "I might just buy your land first, you know, then sell it to Intraglobal. I'll give you a fair price. Think it over, nephew." He sashayed off, greeting people who forced smiles to their faces, and sat in the back row. He must've thought the seating chart was by IQ.

I wasn't terribly impressed by this show of Poteet family love. If Eula Mae was right and this development had anything unsavory about it, Uncle Bid'd no doubt be nearby, adding his own unique stench to the pot.

Miss Twyla called the crowd to order. I took a seat near the back. As Miss Twyla was explaining the purpose of the meeting, Candace slipped in and sat beside me. She took my hand and squeezed it. "And how was your little dinner?"

I'm not one for public affection, but I kissed her— and then wondered if she could tell my lips had been kissed.

"Fine. She just mostly wanted to talk business."

"I bet she did." She gave me an enigmatic look and turned her attention to Miss Twyla.

I glanced around the room again. Bob Don, to my surprise, was not present. I thought for sure he'd want to hear about a land deal that affected him personally. And I felt momentarily stung; he'd given me this land, and now the situation was getting complicated, and he wasn't here to be with me. Maybe I didn't matter to him as much as I thought. Wrong; he'd been at the hospital when I'd gotten hurt.

I hoped our mad bomber didn't know about the meeting; he could take out quite a few people with this gathering.

Miss Twyla ran the meeting like one of her high-school classes. Quickly calling it to order, she summarized Intraglobal's intentions—and voiced her own (and others') opposition to the development. After this brief statement, she called Nina Hernandez to the front to tell everyone what "the battle plan" would be. I grimaced at the idea of getting myself into any mess that required a battle plan.

"Ladies and gentlemen of Mirabeau," Nina intoned with grandiose dignity, "I warn you now; Gregory Callahan is not a man who will take no for an answer. Intraglobal has the resources and the money to get what they want, regardless of whether or not you want this development in your backyard. They will build without regard for the sensitive ecosystem that surrounds Mirabeau"—here I distinctly heard Uncle Bid snort— "and they will despoil the river, the river that has nurtured the town of Mirabeau for over a hundred and fifty years. I've dealt with Intraglobal before, with their attempts to develop in other small towns, in both the South and in New England." She paused, letting us realize that once again the battle was joined.

She produced charts, bar graphs, and tables of data on an easel to show just how much the river would suffer under Intraglobal's stewardship. She spoke with conviction and assurance—and I found myself liking her more. "They ruin towns, then move on. They don't have to win again. You can stop them," she concluded.

"Excuse me, Mother Earth," a voice called from the back of the room, "but why the hell should we want to?" Uncle Bid being his usual charming self. He'd risen from his customary predatory crouch to his feet.

"And you are, sir?" Nina asked, obviously irritated at the interruption. One could only hope she'd sic Tiny on Uncle Bid.

"Bidwell J. Poteet, Esquire, Attorney-at-Law," Bid purred in response. "And as one of the concerned landowners, I don't see a single reason why we shouldn't sell. Intraglobal is offering good money for this land and the resort community could bring a lot of money into Mirabeau." There was a buzz of general assent from one corner of the crowd. Apparently some folks supported that view, and I couldn't blame them.

Nina wasn't fazed. "The reason, Mr. Poteet, is the

way that Intraglobal does business. They probably won't hire local contractors to build this development; they'll bring in big-city folks. They target towns like yours that haven't needed to have serious environmental controls yet and they get their plans approved before the voters can put any sort of ecological leash on them. They'll build with no regard for what pollutants they spill into the Colorado." She slammed her hand down on the podium we'd pulled out of storage. "We can stop them. You don't have to have this kind of development."

"We need development, missy!" Bid brayed back at her. The Miss Twyla corps of supporters glared at him as one.

"Not this way!" Miss Twyla opted to enter the fray. "I don't necessarily think that development is wrong, Bidwell, but we want to control how it happens, not just sell our land to folks we don't know diddly about and let them ruin it and the river."

I raised my good arm. "Excuse me, Ms. Hernandez. I had dinner with one of the Intraglobal representatives this evening. She showed me environmental impact statements that indicate the effect on the river would be minimal."

Nina smiled nicely at me. "Those statements are prepared by Intraglobal, Jordan. They emphasize whatever Intraglobal wants them to emphasize. I'm sorry you were deceived."

Well, that shut me up. I kept my mouth open for a moment in case inspiration hit, but shut it when a sad-eyed Eula Mae shook her head at my naïveté.

The Lord Mayor of Mirabeau (not his official title but that's how he fancies himself), Parker Loudermilk, rose to his feet and cleared his throat. He had plenty of Cherokee in him and his complexion was dark, his eyes brooding except when he had on his mayoral smile. His daddy had been mayor for fourteen years, and when he died, no one else ran against Parker. It just seemed natural to have a Loudermilk as mayor. Parker was not a tall man, but he had the most erect posture I'd ever seen, like someone had shoved a metal beam along his spine. And I knew from city staff meetings that special cough of his meant all us peons better grovel in the mud. "I think, Ms. Hernandez, that the fine citizens of Mirabeau can rely on their elected officials to protect their environment."

"Your wife owns some of the land," Tiny called out, then looked embarrassed. His first venture at public speaking. If I'd liked him I'd have been proud of him.

Nina favored Tiny with a gracious smile and turned back toward the mayor like he was cheese on a cracker and she was starving. "That's right, Mr. Mayor. Mrs. Loudermilk does own some of the involved land. Do you think that you can maintain your objectivity when Greg Callahan starts throwing money at y'all?"

Mayor Loudermilk huffed. His thin, politically weaselly face pinched tight. He didn't like folks challenging him and I sometimes wondered if he didn't have a pronounced violent streak under that suave exterior. I'd seen him break pencils with a smile in staff meetings when he thought someone was challenging his authority, and I heard he ran his construction company like a military unit. Junebug and I joked about it after the meetings, but I really didn't care much for the man. It was a shame; his daddy had been a real fine fellow.

"I don't really need to worry about the money he might throw at me, Ms. Hernandez, but I thank you for your concern for my moral fiber."

I saw Dee Loudermilk put a restraining hand on her husband as she rose to her feet. She was prettier than Parker Loudermilk deserved, a slight, wispy blonde beauty with eyes of fierce hazel intelligence. Dee used to be like Candace, doing mostly volunteer work. She'd discovered art, though, a while back and had become a potter. I had one of her own pots in my backyard, an object of strength and sturdiness if not of beauty. Dee's metaphysical stretches of the boundaries of ceramics escaped any meaningful interpretation from me. I liked her a sight better than I did her husband.

"It's my land, not Parker's. I had that land before we married, so it's not his concern," Dee said. Parker didn't look like he agreed with this economic assessment but he wisely kept his mouth shut. Dee's voice rang out clear as a bell; I guess it was used to out-yelling her husband.

"Regardless, I'm sure that Loudermilk Construction would be interested in bidding on the development work," Eula Mae put in. She's self-employed and got more money than God, so she doesn't have to be cordial to our elected officials.

Parker bristled. Dee smiled at Eula Mae; she was a better politician than her husband. "I won't sell until we know more about what these Intraglobal people plan, and that's a promise."

"I'll be glad to answer that for you, Mrs. Loudermilk," a man's voice, nasal in its Northernness, called out from the back of the room. The voice belonged to a man in a tailored summer gray Italian suit, certainly the finest duds Mirabeau had seen in some time. The floral pattern on his tie would have gotten him thrown out of all the beer joints I knew of. His hair was starting to thin, with strands of blond still clinging to his freckled pate. His face was intelligent, with a rough sensuality to it that suggested he was a man who took a coarse and easy pleasure in life. Lorna stood to one side of him, looking cool but perhaps a touch uncomfortable. I saw her eyes seek me out and she stared hard at me for all of ten seconds. I glanced away and saw that if I wasn't willing to return Lorna's stare, plenty of other fellows were. I hoped Uncle Bid, seated right in front of her, wouldn't drool.

The man on the other side of Lorna was someone I knew: Freddy Jacksill, a local real-estate agent. He was sticking to Lorna and the balding man like sap on bark. I saw another form move behind the three from the stairs and find a seat. A stunning young brunette I recognized as Jenny Loudermilk, the mayor and Dee's daughter. She looked like she'd gotten her hand caught in the cookie jar—*hiding* cash. I didn't miss the glances that Parker and Dee exchanged—or Miss Twyla and Eula Mae exchanged—at this latest development.

"This is a private meeting, Callahan," Nina barked. The look she gave the man was one of pure loathing. "I'd appreciate it if you'd leave."

"This is a public building," Greg Callahan (I'd already guessed who it was) answered smoothly.

"Um, he's right, Nina," I spoke up. "Meetings held in the library, unless previously approved, are open to the public." There, no one could ever say I hadn't memorized the library's bylaws.

"These good people aren't interested in your lies," Nina retorted. Tiny bolted to his feet, presumably to play bouncer. Nina jerked a hand at him and he stayed put.

"She's got him trained like a dog," Candace whispered to me.

"Lies, Ms. Hernandez? I'm not here to lie," Greg Callahan said smoothly. "My associate, Ms. Wiercinski, along with our new friend, Mr. Jacksill, thought that we ought to set the record straight." He pointed an elegant, pale finger at Nina Hernandez. "This woman is nothing but a radical and an environmental extremist!"

A murmur ran through the sparse crowd. "Wrong," Nina snapped back. "I have no political agenda. My only desire is to protect the river—and to expose Intraglobal for the wasteful, pernicious business that it is. I wouldn't quarrel with sensitive, responsible development. But you, Mr. Callahan, have no regard for people or the land they live on."

"Ridiculous!" Greg Callahan sneered back. I envied him his glare; it was a right effective one. "You'd throw yourself over a blade of grass to keep someone from building a patio, Ms. Hernandez. And folks, let me tell you: it wouldn't make much sense for me to invest in riverfront property then trash the river, would it, now? Who'd buy a single condo? No one, that's who." He cast his penetrating blue eyes across the gathering. "Investment, ladies and gentlemen. That's what this resort would be. I'm going to spend so much on the riverfront that I'd ruin my own business if I polluted it." He jerked his head toward Lorna and Freddy Jacksill. "We'll be holding a meeting of our own, to really tell the truth about Intraglobal. Tomorrow night at the Sit-a-Spell Café. Y'all are all invited." I thought he should've left that last part off; Texans do not take kindly to having their accents or regionalisms adopted by others.

Miss Twyla stood. "I won't be there. I've already heard enough from Nina to know I'll never sell my land to you."

Eula Mae was not about to be upstaged. "And I'm going to put my considerable resources behind Miss Twyla's campaign to save the river."

Callahan smiled thinly. There was the vaguest hint of malice lurking there. "Perhaps you'll change your mind, Ms. Oudelle, Ms. Quiff." He'd done his homework, you had to give him that. He nodded confidently at the crowd. "I urge everyone not to pay too much heed to Ms. Hernandez. She's a bit upset right now because this is her third attempt to interfere with Intraglobal's business, and every time she's failed. She's a loser. Until tomorrow night, ladies and gentlemen." He turned on his imported heel and strode out, with the confidence of a rooster leaving a sated henhouse.

Freddy Jacksill stayed right in Callahan's personal space, probably busily calculating the amount of money he could make as the local agent for helping Intraglobal. Lorna hung back for a moment, then left, favoring me with another glance.

I patted Candace's hand and whispered, "I want to talk to him."

I followed them out, hearing Uncle Bid cackle, "See! Jordy's chasing that fellow to sell him his land. Y'all

ain't going to win." I decided I'd worry later about setting Uncle Bid straight—as straight as someone as
crooked as he could get.

I hurried out the back entrance from the stairs. (The
upstairs meeting room is accessible by a side door, so
folks can have meetings after hours without going
through the rest of the library.) Lorna, Greg Callahan,
and Freddy Jacksill were standing by Freddy's Taurus,
its RIVERTOWN REAL ESTATE sign big on the driver's-side
door.

Greg Callahan watched me as I ran up to them.
Crickets chirped around us, a deafening chorus of them
in the live oaks that towered near the library. The sun
was setting and his eyes looked hard in the fading light.
I said, "Lorna, aren't you going to introduce me to your
friend?"

Lorna shuffled slightly. I don't think she was happy
with the upshot of our last conversation. "Sure. Jordan,
this is Greg Callahan. Greg, this is Jordan Poteet, my
old friend I told you about."

"Jordan, fabulous to meet you." Greg shook my hand
with what I considered an abundance of fake warmth.
"Fantastic town you've got here. Really homey and cozy."

"Thanks. We'd like to keep it that way."

Greg fixed me with a smile. "Now, Jordan, I hope a
smart gentleman like yourself isn't going to jump on
this environmental hysteria bandwagon. I assure you all
the information that Lorna presented you is absolutely
valid. We're not going to shoot ourselves in the feet by
ruining the river."

"Jordan," Freddy Jacksill interrupted, "why don't you
give me a call tomorrow and I'll set up a meeting at my
office, where we can discuss Intraglobal's offer on your
land."

I made myself smile at Freddy. I couldn't say I actually disliked him; but he was one of those people who
so nakedly curries favor that they annoy the living hell
out of you. He was in his mid-forties, portly, and not

dressed in the height of fashion. I always saw him on weekends, squiring potential buyers, usually young yuppie couples from Austin who fantasized about country living.

"Well, Freddy, that might just have to wait a spell. I'm not sure I want to sell my land. I'd prefer to give it some thought before I make any decisions."

Greg smiled heartily and squeezed my good shoulder. He didn't ask what had happened to my arm. "Of course you would, Jordan, and I know that a reasonable guy like you is going to make the right decision. You're a clear-thinker."

I resented someone who didn't know me making such gross generalizations; I could be as muddy-thinking as they came, if I put my mind to it. My distaste for Greg bolted in my chest; why was Lorna working for him? I smiled politely. "Well, I'll be glad to attend your meeting and hear you out." I glanced at Lorna. "You're very lucky to have Lorna working for you. She's a remarkable woman."

That elicited a smile from both Lorna and Greg. "Isn't she, though?" he said. "I'd be lost without Lorna. She's my details lady." He grinned at her with a nearly proprietary air.

"Great. Well, then, I'll see y'all both tomorrow." I shook hands and turned to leave.

"And we'll see y'all tomorrow, too," Greg chirped. I tried not to break stride. Yankees. They never seem to get that y'all is plural, not singular. Someone needed to have a talk with Greg on how not to alienate the locals. I decided that if I chose to sell my land, I'd coach Greg on the intricacies of Mirabeau etiquette.

I returned to an assembly that was frothy with outrage at anyone who might even glance askew at our beloved Colorado River. Uncle Bid and his supporters had departed. Candace leaned over and whispered to me, "So did you cut a deal?"

"Not hardly. That fellow is slicker than a watermelon seed."

"Well, Eula Mae announced she's donating fifty thousand dollars to the antidevelopment cause."

"Good Lord!" I whispered back. "I didn't know she had that kind of cash to burn." I glanced over at Eula Mae; she was absently twirling her hair with a finger. I hoped she had the money to back up her promise. The Loudermilks were silent. Nina's voice droned on, outlining how they would use Eula Mae's seed money to raise a massive war chest to inform the public about the perils of Intraglobal's invasion.

The meeting didn't last much longer. I didn't pay much heed; I kept watching the obvious glares between the Loudermilks and their daughter, who had kept her seat in the back of the room. Something was amiss in Mirabeau's first family. Jenny Loudermilk tossed her rather luxurious locks in prime Barbie style and ignored her parents. Miss Twyla gave a final inspired speech on how we should ban together to fight this godless (not quite sure where theology crept into the equation, but Miss Twyla was on a roll) development.

"We will stop this!" Miss Twyla vowed. "Whatever it takes, we will stop this!" God, was her timing lousy.

I'd escorted Candace home. We hadn't talked much. I told her Lorna had been mostly businesslike at dinner, calmly outlining Intraglobal's strategy. She didn't ask for an explanation of what constituted *mostly*. Her goodbye kiss was quick and dry.

When I got home, I discovered Clo in the living room. She was watching her favorite program, *Star Trek*.

"You never miss that one, do you, Clo?" I asked as Captain Kirk dueled a barbarian with a bad overbite.

"That Lieutenant Uhura, she looks just like my girl."

"Really?" I said. Clo had been tight-lipped about her private life. She'd mentioned a granddaughter once.

"She's dead now. Dead for ten years." Her voice was

softer than usual, slack without its stridency. She stared at the screen, watching the battle. "You see, Jordy, I know what family pain is, too. Your mama's asleep now. If you don't mind, I'll sit here and watch the end of this. It's nearly over."

"Sure, Clo." I hadn't expected such a remark from her. She folded her hands in her lap, as though keeping something in them for an angel, and kept her eyes on the television. I went upstairs, washed my face, and came back down to the kitchen for a glass of milk. I sat there awhile, feeling that if I went into my own living room I'd be intruding on her grief. After a few moments I heard her click off the television. I stood and went back to join her. I walked Clo out to her little Ford Tempo and watched her drive away, only a good-night passing between us.

I locked up, left the porch light on for Sister when she came in from her irregular shift, checked on Mama's gentle rasp, took some more Tylenol for my sore left arm, and went to bed.

At some point, deep in the night's belly, a phone awakened me. I finally answered it.

"Yes?" my voice creaked.

"Jordy? This is Chet Blanton." The name finally registered with me—Chet was the manager of the Mirabeau B. Lamar Bed-and-Breakfast, and a library patron with a pronounced penchant for Agatha Christie. "I'm sorry to call you so late, but it's an emergency."

"What—what's wrong?" I managed to mutter, my brain smogged with sleep.

"I don't want to go into this over the phone, but your friend—she's in trouble. Please, could you just come over?" Chet's normally hearty voice sounded pinched.

I sat up in bed, wide-awake. I told Chet I'd be there in a minute and hung up. I stumbled into clothes, eased my left arm into its sling, peeked in to make sure Sister was back from her shift (her snoring was a dead giveaway), and as though on autopilot, drove to the Mirabeau B.

Lamar Bed-and-Breakfast. A police car stood in the driveway, its lights flashing. My wristwatch indicated two in the morning, but I pounded on the door anyway.

Chet met me at the door, dressed in a rumpled robe, his heavy face white.

"What's happened? Is Lorna okay?" I asked, pushing past him.

"She's okay, I think. Follow me."

Chet turned and we ran up the stairs of the elegant, antebellum home he'd converted. The second story held the eight guest rooms.

In one of the rooms, I saw Lorna crouched on a bed, one of Junebug's deputies talking to her. Her face was in her hands and she didn't see me. I noticed blood on her right hand, oozing from a badly torn fingernail. I moved forward for her; Chet's arm stopped me.

"You better see this," he whispered, steering me down one more room.

"Which one is Greg Callahan's?" I asked. He pointed two doors down the hall, back toward the stairs. "Number four."

The room he showed me was comfortable looking, decorated in classy antiques, and with a faint smell of fruit and potpourri, and the gassy odor of death. I stepped in and looked where Chet pointed.

Greg Callahan lay sprawled on the Persian rug, his pale head bent at an unnatural angle, his eyes staring up at the slowly turning ceiling fan. He's drunk, was my first irrational thought; but there was no air of liquor. I didn't start to gag until I stepped closer and saw the length of barbed wire cruelly and deeply twisted into his neck.

CHAPTER FIVE

EVEN AFTER A MORNING OF GETTING OUT OF
the hospital, an afternoon of Miss Twyla and Nina be-
rating me, and an evening of concern about Lorna, I
couldn't rightly say I'd had the worse day in Mirabeau.
That distinction rested with poor Greg Callahan.

I sat sipping a Dr Pepper in the small waiting area of
the Mirabeau police station. Lorna sat next to me, holding my hand. Her own hand felt clammy. One of the officers came in, the door pinging as he opened it, and I
could smell the faint grittiness of rubber and gravel
from the parking lot. The summer-night air was warm,
but I still had goose pimples from what I'd seen.

While the police began their investigation of the murder scene and the ambulance arrived to trundle off
Greg's body, I got Lorna down to Chet's kitchen. She
had been silent as I seated her at the kitchen table and
I wondered whether to get her whiskey or coffee. Suddenly she had screamed, burying her face in her hands.

"My God, he's dead, he's really dead!" She sobbed
uncontrollably then, and I just held her, whispering into
her dark hair that she was okay. Finally she believed me
and stopped crying. I held her and thought about what
I'd seen in the few moments I'd had in Greg's room.

I had carefully knelt by Greg. I saw the ends of the
wire had been fashioned into loops, probably for a better grip for the killer. I swallowed; death by barbed-wire
garrote was a sickening thought. I forced myself to look
at Greg's savaged throat. The wire had cut into his neck

deeply, and the barbs had left little tears in his flesh. God, like simultaneously being strangled and having your throat cut. I could only hope it had happened quickly.

One of his hands lay open, and I could see small wounds on his palm, like stigmata. I shuddered. It must have been agony for him, having that torturous noose tightening on his gullet and, when he tried to pull the choking cord off, getting metal thorns in his hands.

He was still in his suit and the dribble of blood from his neck stained his starched collar. His blue eyes bulged, the lids half-closed. I gingerly touched his wrist and felt the silence.

I stood, wanting to get back to Lorna. I glanced around the room. A half-empty bottle of whiskey stood between two used glasses. On the desk was a scattering of loose change, a receipt from the Sit-a-Spell Café, a closed laptop computer with some small disks stacked like playing cards next to it, a sheet with the Mirabeau B. Lamar stationery near the phone. Writing scrawled across it, with doodles surrounding the text: NINA HERNANDEZ=EARTH BITCH. Below that, a telephone number: 555-3489. That was a Mirabeau number, I thought. But whose? I didn't recognize it, but then I'd hardly memorized the phone book in my copious spare time.

"Goddamn it! Get the hell out of there!"

I nearly jumped out of my skin. I turned to face a very, very irritated Junebug.

"Junebug—"

He rumbled forward, grabbed my sore arm (mind you, my *sore* arm), and hustled me out into the hallway. Chet looked shamefaced and sick. I pulled my sling free from Junebug's grip with what little dignity I could muster.

"What do you think you're doing, Jordy, tainting a crime scene?"

"Tainting? I was just looking—"

"What you were doing, clueless, was leaving hair and fibers and probably fingerprints that are now going to have to be weeded out in my scene-of-crime work." Junebug shook his head.

I opened my mouth to retort, then shut it. He was right. I'd had no business in there. My own curiosity and shock at seeing Greg dead, who I'd only talked with a few hours before, got the better of me. I took a deep breath and fought down a spasm of nausea.

"You're right. I apologize. I didn't think." I glanced down the hall. "Can I go see Lorna?"

"In a minute." Junebug whirled his sirens on Chet. "You stand guard here till Franklin tapes off this room. No one gets in, Chet. Do you understand?"

"Yes, Junebug," Chet said miserably. Fortunately Franklin Bedloe, one of Junebug's deputies, galloped up the steps that moment and took over. Chet looked vastly relieved. I stood in the hall waiting while listening to Junebug chew out the officer sitting with Lorna for not securing the crime scene. The rookie tried to tell his chief that he'd just been concerned about Ms. Wirechinski (he nearly had the name down), but Junebug wasn't having any of that. I heard him speak in low, kinder tones to Lorna and she sniffled an answer.

We three civilians were relegated to the kitchen while the authorities took over. Lorna refused Chet's offer of whiskey, but coughed out that she would like a glass of brandy. One of the policemen sat stonily in our midst—I guess making sure none of us headed for the border. He gave Lorna first aid for her injured finger while I watched.

After thirty minutes Junebug came back in and said, "Jesus Christ. Jesus H. Christ." Chet, ever the professional host, offered Junebug a drink. He refused and watched Lorna carefully.

"Ms. Wiercinski," he finally said, "I'd like you to come down to the station with us and answer a few questions. If you feel up to that."

"Of course, Mr. Moncrief." She rose unsteadily, then as if suddenly remembering that I was there, took my hand. "Can Jordan come, too?"

"Of course," Junebug answered. "I'm not quite sure why he's here."

"I'm an old friend of Lorna's. We knew each other in Boston." I didn't want to go into more detail while Chet was there. He's a rotten gossip.

"He's a good old friend to have." Junebug nodded, and so we had ended up here. Junebug had asked us to wait in the lobby for a few minutes and had disappeared into his office. I was dying to know what had happened but thought it wouldn't look too cool to be grilling Lorna when Junebug came back. Her fingers laced with mine and I didn't pull back. My arm felt stiff and sore and I tried to keep the sling still and close to my body.

"Y'all come on back," Junebug returned, and escorted us into the station's one interrogation room. I felt distinctly unwell; I presumed we'd get questioned in the less accusatory surroundings of Junebug's office. Lorna and I sat on one side of the table, Junebug across from us. He scratched his crew cut and blinked at our entwined hands. He didn't comment, but he was doubtless wondering what my relationship was with Lorna.

"Now, Jordy, maybe you can tell me what you're doing in the middle of this," Junebug said.

Lorna glanced at me. "Jordy? I've never heard you called that before."

"Please, Lorna, not now." I took a deep breath and recounted Chet's phone call.

Junebug listened without comment. "Now, Ms. Wiercinski, maybe you can tell me what happened."

Lorna ran a thin fingernail across her bottom lip. She briefly explained her and Greg's presence in Mirabeau. "Okay. About eight-fifteen we went to the library because Greg was upset—"

"Wait a second, ma'am. Who's *we*?"

"Me, Greg, and a local real-estate agent, Freddy

Jacksill. I had dinner with Jordan"—one Junebug eyebrow went up, then settled back where it belonged—"and then I'd come back to the bed-and-breakfast. Greg had already heard about the meeting and he was upset. He abhors Nina Hernandez; says she's an extremist who always gets in his way."

"Wait another second!" Junebug exploded. "What's this all about?"

Lorna told him about the ongoing animosity between Nina Hernandez and Greg's company. Junebug made notes. "Okay," he said, "so he wanted to bust up this meeting."

"Not exactly. He just wanted to let people know that Nina is dead wrong about Intraglobal and clarify what we want to do here. He wanted to announce his own meeting—which would have been tonight."

"How had he heard about the library meeting?"

"I don't know, Mr. Moncrief. I guess Freddy Jacksill told him." She went on to describe Greg's arrival during Nina's speech and the ensuing charges and countercharges. I helpfully filled in what had happened before Greg and Lorna's arrival.

"And after you left the library?" Junebug prodded.

"Greg was very confident that he'd win, but I could see that he was seething. He really hates Nina Hernandez. I mean, he really hated—" Her voice broke off as she corrected her tense. Junebug offered a tissue and she waved it away. "I'm okay.

"Anyhow, after we left, Greg, Freddy, and I came back to the Mirabeau B. I was tired and a little upset"—a glance at me spoke volumes—"and I wanted to go to bed. This is my first deal working with Intraglobal and I'm not accustomed to all this confrontational crap. Greg had calmed and seemed ready to celebrate. He said that Nina would mess up her campaign to stop us and we'd be able to get the land for the river resort. He wanted to have drinks with Freddy and me, but I begged off. So he and Freddy went into

Greg's room. Around nine-thirty I went to bed—" She broke off, sounding uncertain.

"Is that all, ma'am?" Junebug seemed to sense she was holding something back and his tone was pressing.

"I dozed off, but then I woke up. I heard Greg's voice yelling at someone. Whoever it was wasn't yelling back."

"Did he sound afraid?" I asked, ignoring Junebug's scowl at my intervention.

"No, more mad than afraid."

"You didn't hear Mr. Jacksill talking with him?" Junebug asked.

"No, not that I remember."

"What happened then?"

"I went back to sleep. I woke up later, maybe around midnight—I heard a door slam down the hall. But I rolled over and went back to sleep. Then—a little before two—I woke up again. I'm not sure what woke me up, I just snapped awake."

A slamming door, I thought. Chet had told me while we waited for the police to finish their preliminary examination of Greg's room that Lorna and Greg were his only guests at the moment. So it must've been Greg's door that she heard.

Junebug listened to her carefully, as though a clue might drop from her unsuspecting lips. "Think again, miss. Did you hear a noise? Someone crying out? Another door slam?"

Lorna pursed her lips. I could see the effort of her recollection as she dredged through her shock. "I'm sorry. I don't remember anything. I think I woke because I was thirsty."

"Okay," Junebug said. "You were thirsty."

"I decided to go down to the kitchen for some apple juice. I opened my door and started for the stairs. I passed Greg's room and I could see that the door was ajar. I . . ." She stared at her clenched fingers.

Junebug didn't prompt her; neither did I. We both

sensed that she had to tell this at her pace. After a long intake of breath she continued: "I knocked at the door, very softly. I thought maybe Greg fell asleep with it open, but that would have been very unlike him. He was a maniac about his privacy. So I pushed at the door. It was ink black inside, what with the curtains down. But my eyes were used to the dark now, and I could see his bed hadn't been slept in. So I stepped inside the room—I remember my hand went out for the light switch. The lights came on—I was looking at Greg's bed. I couldn't see his body from there. I didn't know he was there. And then these gloves closed around my mouth and my throat. . . ." She took a long, shuddering breath.

Junebug leaned forward. "Okay, Ms. Wiercinski. Please describe what happened very carefully. Take as much time as you need."

Lorna, her closed eyes tight lines, nodded. "Okay. One glove went over my mouth because I started to scream. The other went behind my neck"—she pantomimed for us—"holding me at the base of the throat. I just stopped dead, because as they closed around me this voice whispered to me, 'Make a sound, bitch, and you're dead.' "

"A man's voice or a woman's?" I asked. Junebug didn't seem to object.

Lorna shook her head. "I couldn't tell—the voice was a ratchety, harsh whisper. A man's, I think. Maybe."

"What about the gloves? What kind were they?"

"Thick, coarse. Not like driving or dress gloves, but like heavy work gloves."

"Of course," I said. "Whoever used that garrote on Greg would have to protect his own hands from the barbs. Pulling it taut could be painful."

"From the way the person was holding you, Ms. Wiercinski, could you tell if they were bigger or smaller than you, or around your own size?" Junebug asked, ignoring my valuable insight. He'd probably already thought of it, anyway.

Lorna shook her head. "I couldn't tell—the way he was holding me, it was at something of a distance from him; I wasn't pressed up against him. I—I thought of fighting, but I was too scared. I mean, everything I'd heard of what you're supposed to do—fight, kick, scream—my mind wouldn't do it. I just froze."

"What happened next?"

Lorna swallowed. "He—or she—pushed me face-down on the bed. I remember saying, 'Please don't hurt me.' He didn't say anything. He blindfolded me with what I later found was one of Greg's ties. Then he tied my arms together with the bedsheets. He shoved another tie in my mouth as a gag and put a pillowcase over my head. Then he shoved me into Greg's closet and said in that hoarse whisper, 'You just stay right there.' I could hear the closet door shut and the key turn in the lock." She sniffed. "I guess that's when you know you're staying in a real old house—when you have keys for the closets. I thought he was gone, but I couldn't be sure. I heard movements at different times, so I just lay there for a while and I started to get panicky. I was pretty sure he'd left, so I worked my way out of the sheets, got the gag out of my mouth, and took off the blindfold and the pillowcase. I peered out of the keyhole, but I couldn't see anything. I started screaming and kicking on the door; finally I kicked it loose. I saw Greg's body and screamed. Chet rushed in and got me out, and he called the police. I—I asked him to call Jordan."

Junebug said nothing, but tapped his pencil against his pad in an annoying staccato. "How long have you been in Mirabeau, ma'am?"

"Only a day or so. Greg's been here a few days longer." She frowned.

"And you can't even say whether or not the person who grabbed you was a man or a woman, how tall they were, or nothing?" Junebug demanded.

"Not with certainty." Lorna's jaw set. "If I could tell you, I would."

"Maybe you wouldn't," Junebug said. "We don't know you here."

I'd had enough. "Look, Junebug, I've known Lorna for years, and she is not a liar."

"I'm not about to take this from someone named after an insect!" Lorna stormed, but Junebug, placid as ever, raised a calming hand.

"Let's not dwell on this at the moment," Junebug drawled. "Perhaps you can tell me who might have had it in for Mr. Callahan."

Lorna propped her elbows on the table and leaned into her open palms. "Sorry, Mr. Moncrief, about the insect remark. I didn't mean it. I'm extremely upset."

He nodded.

"Jesus. I can't believe anyone would kill Greg." She looked over her polished fingernails at Junebug. "My first guess would be Nina Hernandez. I mean, there was certainly bad blood between them. And I did hear him arguing with someone, but I didn't hear another voice. Maybe he was arguing with her on the phone." I wondered if Nina was big enough to strangle Greg or manhandle Lorna, but I didn't say anything.

"How had he gotten along with folks here?" Junebug asked.

"Fine," she said. "I mean, some people didn't seem keen on his development plans for the river, but I can't imagine someone would kill him over that. He told me when I got here that he'd met with some of the landowners already."

I supplied Junebug with the names of those who owned the land that Greg wanted. He jotted them down carefully and tapped his pencil again.

"Look, Lorna's been through hell. You've got the tape of her statement. Can't you let her get some rest and have her sign it tomorrow?"

"I—I can't go back there." Lorna's eyes pleaded with mine.

"Of course not. You'll stay at my house. You'll be safe there."

"One more question, Ms. Wiercinski, then we'll be done. I appreciate your effort in telling me all this." Junebug looked squarely into her gray eyes. "What kind of man would you say Mr. Callahan was?"

Lorna snapped, "Not the kind who deserved to die that way, Mr. Moncrief. He was smart, funny, confident of himself. He enjoyed life, and I can't believe he got taken this way." She dissolved into tears, and her statement was over.

It was nearly five in the morning when I got Lorna home. We let ourselves in quietly, trying not to disturb Mama or Sister. That was in vain; Sister was already up. She practically ran across the living room to me.

"Where the hell have you been? I wake up in the middle of the night to check on Mama and your bed's empty. I call Candace and she doesn't know where you are." She looked at Lorna. "You're not Candace."

Whoops. I made quick introductions, explaining in as few words as possible that Lorna had run into trouble and I'd had to dash out to render aid. At the news of murder, Sister's eyes widened.

"Well, of course, you can stay here, Lorna. I've heard so much about you, but you know Jordy doesn't talk much about Boston anymore. And I saw the lovely flowers you brought Mama. That was real kind of you." She herded her charge into the kitchen, giving me her patented we-*will*-discuss-this-later-little-brother look. "Jordy, you might want to call Candace. I'm afraid I've worried her sick by calling her."

"It's still awful early—" I started, but Lorna looked oddly at me.

"Call her, Jordan. She'll be concerned. Put her mind at ease."

Lorna didn't usually show solicitude for a rival. Wait a minute, I reminded myself, Candace and Lorna were *not* rivals. My heart was with Candace, wasn't it? Of course it was. I went back into the kitchen and tried to ignore the melting, little-girl looks that Lorna was giving me.

"I'm sorry to meet you under these circumstances, Arlene," Lorna said, staring down into a mug of decaf coffee.

"Don't you worry about it, Lorna." Sister glanced up at me. "I'll just get the guest bedroom ready for you. Clo's been using it when she stays the night—"

"Oh, don't put Clo out," Lorna began, but Sister interrupted: "Don't worry, I'm not. She's not here tonight. She doesn't usually work nights anyway. It's not a problem."

I picked up the phone and dialed Candace's number. One ring and she answered. She didn't sound exactly asleep.

"Candace, it's Jordy."

Silence on the other end, broken finally by: "Where are you?"

"At home. I had to go over to the Mirabeau B. Lorna—"

"I'm not sure I want to hear this, Jordy."

"Listen. Greg Callahan, Lorna's boss, got murdered." I explained what had happened to Lorna.

"My God. Do you want me to come over? Are you all right?"

"I'm fine. Lorna needs some rest. So do I. Sister's fixing up the guest room for her."

More silence. "Oh. How long is she planning on staying?" Candace's voice sounded just a tad arid.

"I don't know. Until the investigation is complete, I suppose. She can't very well stay where the murder happened, can she?"

Maybe Candace couldn't help herself. "I suppose not, but she seemed tough enough to handle anything."

"She's not so tough. I don't think any of us are at a time like this." I paused. "Greg was only a little older than me, Candace. To be cut down like that—"

"Go get some rest, sweetheart. I'll open up the library tomorrow and I'll talk to you later." The gentle click of her hanging up the phone was her only goodbye.

I slept like the dead, and the dead populated my dreams. I woke up around ten, my body slicked in sweat, my arms stretched out painfully in front of me, fending off some dream assassin who carried a twisted length of wire in gloved hands. I swallowed two Tylenol, took a shower, shaved, dressed, and maneuvered my sore arm into its sling. Wondering if I needed to have the doctor look at it again, I stumbled downstairs. Sister was working an afternoon shift, so she was sitting in the kitchen sipping late-morning coffee with Clo. Mama sat in her chair, staring at dust motes in the air. Perhaps they sang to her, or danced for her, in the closed theater of her mind. Lorna, I was informed by Clo, was still asleep.

Clo and Sister demanded more details. I told them everything I knew. They jumped on the case, using deductive abilities garnered from watching too many bad mystery movies on TV.

"Strangled with barbed wire. Sounds like something an Eye-talian would do," Clo theorized.

"Well, all those Yankee businessmen probably have mob connections," Sister opined. "Wait, though, he was from Boston and had an Irish surname. Maybe it was a union hit, like Jimmy Hoffa. If they'd had enough time with the body, they would've dumped him in the river."

Clo made a noise of sad agreement.

"I don't think someone would follow him all the way down to Texas for a hit," I said, pouring myself a cup of coffee. "Clo, a death by garotting, that would be quick, wouldn't it?"

"I would think so. Cut the blood and air off real fast. But I don't know." Clo sipped at her coffee. "You better hope it's not no mobsters, Arlene. They might want to hit that Yankee gal next."

Sister's eyes widened in horror. "Good Lord. I never thought of that!"

"This was not a mob hit!" I insisted. "You two are just trying to scare each other. And please, do not refer to her as *that Yankee gal*. Her name is Lorna. L-O-R-N-A."

"Did you make sure that Candace knows how to spell it, too?" Sister snapped back. She's never been one to skirt an issue, although I might wish she'd show a little interest in shyness now and then.

"What does that have to do with anything?" I sputtered.

"Plenty! That Yankee gal comes to town, sets up her hoops, and you just start jumpin' through them like Clyda Tepper's poodle. I'm real sorry her friend got killed, but it does seem that she's leaning on you awful hard. Why didn't she move to another room at Chet's or to another motel? I just wonder what Candace thinks of you being so sweet to Miss L-O-R-N-A."

"She's fine with it," I said in a low voice. "She understands that Lorna needs me."

"Jordy, you're as stupid as you are tall. No woman understands an ex-girlfriend needing her man." Sister sat back in her chair with grim satisfaction. "You know, lots of men sure would like to date Candace. She got chased plenty before you moved back to town, and I bet if you wander out of the picture, that race'd be back on in no time. Some men appreciate her, even if you don't."

Sister was spared the sizzling reply I was busily working on by the doorbell. She leaped up to answer it. "Clo, talk some sense into that boy."

"No way. I'm staying free and clear."

I heard Sister's muffled voice at the front door, and

she walked back into the kitchen frowning. "Your father is here," she said coldly.

I couldn't blame Sister for not particularly warming up to Bob Don Goertz; after all, our mother had had an affair with Bob Don. And her adjustment to Bob Don's presence in my life had not been smooth. However, she was at least grateful to him for saving us all during that last bit of unpleasantness in town and for helping with Mama's care. Bob Don paid Clo's salary.

I went out into the living room and found Bob Don talking gently with Mama. He knelt by her, a big blond man with a small-town haircut. He was dressed in his usual uniform of short-sleeved shirt, tie, khaki slacks, and brown, weathered cowboy boots. He was holding Mama's hand and using a soft voice he didn't use out on his car lot: "How you doin' this morning, Annie? Sure is a nice morning and you look real pretty today. Clo must be taking good care of you."

"She is, Bob Don," I said so he'd know I was there. He stood up, absently patting Mama's hand. She'd hardly looked at him. She doesn't always register presences. "How you feeling today?"

"Fine, son, fine." He calls me son every now and then, but I'm still not used to it. "I understand you had a helluva night."

I shrugged and indicated my arm. "Between the semimad bomber, an ex-girlfriend coming back to town, and a murder, I don't know why people say they get bored in small towns."

Bob Don shook his head and sat on the couch. I offered coffee, but he declined. I could hear that the chatter in the kitchen screeched to a halt; no doubt Clo and Sister were more interested in other folks' conversations. We won't have to send Sister to old-biddy school to get her ready for her golden years.

"You heard about all this?" I asked.

"Yep. Got a phone call early this morning from

Junebug. Wanted to know if I'd heard from this Greg Callahan fellow about selling him my land."

"Had you?"

"Hell, yes, he came by the other day, offering good money for my stretch of riverfront property. I figured he'd come see you, too. I was gonna call you about it, but then you got hurt and I didn't want to mention it to you while you were in the hospital."

I shrugged again. "He sent in reinforcements." I told him about Lorna's visit and last night's events. I had discussed Lorna with him a few weeks back, during our first attempted father-son dinner at the Sit-a-Spell. "Were you going to sell to Callahan?"

"I wanted to, but Gretchen thought we should hold out for more money," Bob Don said.

Let me digress for a moment about Gretchen Goertz. Gretchen is Bob Don's wife and they've had about as happy a marriage as the Royals. Gretchen used to drink pretty heavy, but after it came out that Bob Don was my daddy I guess she decided to clean up her act so Bob Don wouldn't leave her. She'd checked herself into a clinic in Austin, dried out, and had been sober for the past several weeks. She'd also been cloyingly sweet to me. I didn't believe for a second it was because she'd been dying for a stepson and was just showing her appreciation for my debut in her life. I couldn't tell, though, if her kindness was because she was finally sober for the first time in years or because she wanted to stay on Bob Don's good side. Either way, I avoided her as much as I could.

"Well, it doesn't look like Gretchen will get any money now," I said. "Who even knows if Intraglobal will still be interested in building here after this mess?"

"Good morning," a voice came from the stairs. It was Lorna, her hair a bit disheveled, dressed in some old pajamas and a robe of mine. God, I hoped Candace didn't see her in that. Bob Don leaped to his feet.

"Hello, there, darlin', you must be Lorna. I'm Bob

Don Goertz, Jordy's daddy. It sure is nice to meet you, but I'm just sick that it's under these here unfortunate circumstances."

Lorna wasn't quite awake yet and in full command of her etiquette. She stared, I mean *stared*, at Bob Don. From the helmet of carefully coiffed hair to the scuffed tips of his well-worn cowboy boots. "You're—you're Jordan's father?"

"Yes, ma'am, proud to say I am. He's just the best boy a man could hope for, you know, he is as smart as a whip and got his mama's good looks and of course he's all educated—"

I didn't want Bob Don quoting my résumé for the remainder of the day, and he will do so given the opportunity. "Bob Don, I bet you Lorna could use some coffee. Lorna, that sound good?"

"Wonderful." She wiped sleep from her eyes, regarded Bob Don anew, and offered her hand. "Forgive my rudeness, I'm not quite myself this morning. I am delighted to meet you, Mr. Goertz. Jordan told me all about you last night and it's obvious he thinks you're a remarkable man."

Bob Don's eyes lit up like he'd won the lottery and his mouth worked as he smiled at me. All right, so I'm not the most affectionate soul around. He knew I cared, didn't he? I frowned and fled, going to get Lorna her coffee.

Sister crossed her arms and grimaced at me as I came in. "Well, those two ought to get together like a house afire. They're both into trying to bust up relationships." Clo quickly excused herself to go use the rest room.

I poured a fresh cup for Lorna and turned around. "Let's get this straight, Sister, right here, right now. I don't care if you like Lorna. I don't care if you hate Lorna. But she is a guest in this house, and I think Mama would be ashamed of you for talking trash like you are."

Sister opened her cavernous mouth to respond, but I

didn't give her a chance to spew further venom. "And as for the other side of that little crack, I will remind you—once and just once—that you are talking about my father. Now his presence in my life may not set well with you, but this is my house, too, and I will not have him bad-mouthed in it." She shut her mouth and I paused for breath. I'm not really used to giving my big sister that much sass and I waited for the imminent explosion.

I'd miscalculated. "I'm sorry," she said, and she sounded it. "I'm mad at him, and I don't know how not to be mad at him. I appreciate what he's done for us. I do. But when I see him, I don't think about the good things he's done, I think about all those years ago when he must've tried to steal away Mama from Daddy—"

"Daddy is dead. Mama is dead in nearly every way. You have me, you have Mark. We aren't going anywhere, okay? And enough craziness is going on without you and me bickering."

She nodded, unable to look at me for a moment. I could've hugged her and had a real Kodak moment. It got spoiled, though, by another ring of the doorbell. I patted Sister's hand, went through the kitchen, and out to the front door.

It was Junebug, which wasn't a surprise. The surprise was that he was accompanied by a dark-haired woman I didn't know, a smiling Gretchen Goertz, and a frowning Billy Ray Bummel, Mirabeau's pride and joy of the legal system.

CHAPTER SIX

"JORDY, DARLING!" GRETCHEN SQUEALED, throwing her arms around me. It was so unexpected I sniffed her neck, wondering if I'd smell a daub of bourbon.

"Junebug just told me about what happened last night, you poor angel." Gretchen pulled back and patted my cheek. "You must've been through hell, but of course, you've *seen* a dead body before. Still, one just couldn't get used to it."

"What's going on here?" I managed to say.

"Well, Jordy darling, I was trying to track down Miss Wiercinski because I understood she might be continuing to represent Intraglobal's interests. I thought she might still want to make an offer at our land—Bob Don's and mine." It was actually Bob Don's land, not hers, but Gretchen's always been a big believer in community property. She glanced over at Bob Don's white Cadillac. "Chet Blanton told me she was staying with you. I had no idea Bob Don was already here. Is he meeting with Miss Wiercinski?"

"Not exactly." I smiled. "I think he came to see how I was."

She smiled back so she wouldn't look irritated. "Of course, Jordy, you would be his first concern."

"Excuse me," Billy Ray Bummel interrupted. "Just where is this woman?"

I looked down on Billy Ray with as much disdain as I could muster, which in Billy Ray's case is a great deal. He's the kind of prosecutor who's an embarrassment to the legal world. If Billy Ray had been prosecuting the Nazis at Nuremberg, there'd be even more old men speaking German in Uruguay today.

He puffed out his very small, unimpressive chest and lifted his briefcase. (I would lay odds the only briefs it ever contained were Fruit of the Looms.) He ran a hand through overoiled hair and adjusted his glasses so he could scowl at me better. We've never been friends. "I'm here to see Ms. Wytryski and I don't aim to put up with interference from you, Jordy."

"It's Wiercinski, Billy Ray, and I wouldn't dream of interfering. I don't need to. You always manage to shoot yourself in the foot just right."

"Jordy, please," Junebug said, sounding tired. "We do need to talk to Lorna." He indicated the dark young woman standing next to him. She was short, a little heavy, and had a look that hinted at deep intensity at whatever she did. "This is Sergeant Teresa Garza, from the Austin Police Department Bomb Squad. She's assisting us in dealing with the bomber. She wanted to talk to you, too, Jordy, about the mailbox incident." Sergeant Garza shook my good hand.

I surrendered quickly. "Fine. She's in here." I brought the entourage into the house with me. It made for quite a crowd. Gretchen made a beeline for Bob Don, doing her best not to glare daggers at Mama. Clo quickly whisked Mama upstairs and stayed with her. I don't believe I'd leave Gretchen alone with Mama, not with all the pillows in the house.

Against my will, I introduced Billy Ray and Gretchen to Lorna. At hearing that Billy Ray was the local prosecutor, Lorna flared. "Good. Have you talked to Nina Hernandez yet?"

"Not yet," Billy Ray purred, walking in a circle around Lorna. She shot me a quizzical look and I just shrugged. He turned to Bob Don, who was sitting on the couch with Gretchen.

"And how convenient that you're here, Mr. Goertz. I'll be wanting to have a word with you as well."

Bob Don looked surprised. "Me?"

"You knew Greg Callahan, didn't you?" Billy Ray asked. "You had business with him."

"Well, yes, I'd met him. He wanted to buy my land. He came by the car dealership day before yesterday, told me about the development plans he had, and offered me a price. I told him I wanted to wait and see if Jordy was selling his land, too."

Billy Ray rocked back on his heels. "Well, Mr. Goertz, I just find all that *highly* interestin'."

I wasn't about to stand mute while Billy Ray auditioned for Lear's fool in my own living room. I also didn't care for the accusatory stare he was favoring Bob Don with. "Do you have a point, Billy Ray?" Other than the one on your head, I added to myself.

Junebug said, "Hey, Jordy, why don't you go outside with Sergeant Garza and talk about—"

"That'll keep," I snapped back. I don't usually bark at the local constabulary, but I wasn't about to leave Bob Don or Lorna to Billy Ray's tender mercies. Sergeant Garza looked pissed, but I didn't care. This was about murder, not blowing up mailboxes or canine châteaux.

Junebug harrumphed. "Listen, Billy Ray, I think that—"

Billy Ray didn't give Junebug a chance to cogitate. Undoubtedly our local paean to jurisprudence thought he was hot on the trail of a career-boosting case, and he wasn't about to let common sense or decorum get in his way. Billy Ray's what folks around here call booksmart. He must've had one lobe working to get through law school (even if he got his certificate by mail, as it was rumored), but he didn't have enough common sense to fill a thimble. He's the type of fellow that'd poke his finger between a cottonmouth's fangs to see if the mouth really was all soft inside.

"You keep some of your land over by the river fenced off, don't you, Mr. Goertz?" Billy Ray continued, holding up a hand to fend off Junebug's protest.

"Excuse me!" Gretchen stood and looked down on Billy Ray imperiously. "Are you interrogating my husband? Or accusing him of a crime? Because if you are, you haven't informed him of his rights and I will not stand for it!" I could have kissed the old battle-ax.

"Gretchen, for God's sake," Bob Don interrupted. "Billy Ray's just asking questions. He doesn't suspect me. I don't have a solitary thing to hide."

"Not anymore," I thought I heard Sister mutter behind me, but I didn't turn around to check.

Bob Don nodded at Billy Ray. "Yes, I keep barbed wire on that property to keep out Dee Loudermilk's cows. I don't have fencing on the side of the property that's next to Jordy's." He beamed at me. No fences between this father and son, I thought to myself.

"That's *highly* interestin'." Billy Ray loved that pet phrase. "Thin barbed wire, ain't it?"

I saw where this was going and felt myself go pale. Bob Don shrugged. "I guess. Why?"

"Because, Mr. Goertz, the wire that was in Greg Callahan's neck matches a length of wire that's missing from your fence. Same length, same type."

"Wait a second!" I said. "How do you know this?"

"The wheels of justice move quickly, Poteet." Billy Ray Bummel smirked. "The lab over in Bavary identified the type of wire that killed Callahan last night. And this morning, Junebug got a call from the mayor, complaining that Dee's calves were getting loose because Bob Don hadn't fenced correctly on one section. We checked out that section and there's a big old yank of wire missing. Isn't that a coincidence?"

"Probably not," I retorted. "Maybe the killer cut that wire, maybe he didn't. But Bob Don didn't cut that wire and he didn't kill Greg. It's ridiculous! What motive would he have?"

"Jordy, you stay out of this—" Sister began, but she hushed when I scowled at her.

"Well, a little bird told me that Miz Goertz here was seen having lunch with Mr. Callahan yesterday. Maybe Mr. Goertz didn't appreciate having his wife wined and dined by a good-lookin' young feller like that."

Gretchen gave Billy Ray a glare that would've frosted a fire-ant mound. "I don't know who your little bird is, Billy Ray, but it's chirping the wrong song. Yes, I did have lunch with Mr. Callahan yesterday, at his invitation. He wanted to talk to me about the land purchases. He hoped I would be able to convince Bob Don to sell to him. It was purely a business lunch and he conducted himself like a gentleman the entire time." Gretchen took Bob Don's hand. "And I ought to whack you one for suggesting different, Billy Ray Bummel. Why, I've half a mind to call your mama and tell her how you've been treating decent folks, with your snide accusations!"

Billy Ray Bummel did for once look a little pained. Probably no one he'd tried to browbeat had threatened to call his mother on him—and if you've ever seen Mother Bummel, you know that's not an idle threat.

"Excuse me, Mr. Bummel." Lorna had finally decided to get involved in the fracas. "I don't see what motive Mr. or Mrs. Goertz would have. You know that Nina Hernandez loathed Greg. Why aren't you off questioning her?"

Billy Ray, repulsed by Hurricane Gretchen, turned his own bluster on Lorna. "It's real easy to keep pointin' fingers at Ms. Hernandez, when *you're* the one who knew the deceased best. I'd like to know more about your relationship with Callahan, Miss Whychintzy."

"Wiercinski," Lorna corrected. A nervous tongue darted out over her lips. "I don't know what you mean about a relationship. I worked for Greg. He was my employer and that was it."

Know when someone you know intimately is lying?

There's that subtle shift in the air, like when the air-conditioning comes on in a house that's been closed up too long. You can't always tell when a loved one is lying right to your face (because you want to believe whatever garbage they're feeding you), but it's a damned sight easier to tell when they're misleading some other fool. I caught my breath, sure that Lorna was fibbing.

Billy Ray wasn't deterred. "Mr. Blanton seemed to think that perhaps there was a bit more to it."

Lorna iced. "Mr. Blanton is mistaken." She glanced over at me. Her eyes played along my face.

"Just what is the purpose of all this, Billy Ray?" I demanded. "Are you just spending your time going around blindly accusing people of charges? How industrious of you."

"I've got to ascertain the facts of this case, Poteet," Billy Ray answered, a sudden odd pleasantness in his tone. "I want to know just what Mr. Goertz, Mrs. Goertz, and Ms. Wiercinski know about this case, and I don't intend to put up with interference from you." His little eyes (they don't need to be big because his brain can only handle limited information at any given moment) focused on me. "You knew the deceased as well. Care to comment on that?"

"I met him once, last night, very briefly. He never called me or contacted me about my land. He was letting Lorna handle that."

"Did you think he and your ex-girlfriend were having an affair?"

"Good Lord, of course not," I stormed. Would I have cared? I wasn't sure. I wondered if the sudden pang in my stomach was what Lorna had felt when she'd learned about Candace and me.

"So you say." Billy Ray smirked again. "But I already know what kind of temper you have, Poteet."

"Junebug, put him on a leash," I said. "I'm not going to have him come into my home and make totally unfounded accusations against my friend and my"—I nearly said *father*, but some internal editor cut me off—"other friend." I tried not to look at Bob Don. I didn't want him to think I was ashamed of him, but I also didn't want to share my paternity with a trashmouth like Bummel.

"I told you, I wasn't having an affair with Greg." Lorna shot me a look. "Is this what your judicial system is like down here? They'll never catch Greg's killer."

"Come along, Billy Ray," Junebug said with a touch of resignation and infinite patience as our assistant D.A. began to bristle. "Let's go talk with Miss Twyla and her houseguest." He nodded at Sergeant Garza. "Jordy, would you ride over there with us and answer some questions for Sergeant Garza?"

"Sure, as long as I don't have to listen to Billy Ray's exercises in fiction," I said. Bob Don and Gretchen quickly said that they had to be going, Lorna looked lost, and Sister stared at me with her arms crossed. I sighed and headed out the door.

Being interrogated by Teresa Garza was a sight nicer than being questioned by Billy Ray Bummel. First, Teresa Garza acted like she knew what she was doing. Second, she was polite. Third, she didn't conjecture—she just asked. Finally, she had a soothing voice. On the drive over to Miss Twyla's house, I answered Sergeant Garza's questions as best I could. Sitting in the back of Junebug's cruiser with her (and Billy Ray up in the front, being unusually quiet), I provided as many details as I could muster.

"You're the only person that's actually witnessed an explosion," she told me. "No one saw Mr. Boolfors's shed or Mrs. Tepper's doghouse blow up." She made me go over the details of what each blast looked like, the pop of the mailbox, the flash of light, and the concussive noise that trumpeted the detonation.

She gently touched my sling. "You're very lucky,

Jordy. If you had been by one of those mailboxes, you could have been more seriously injured or even killed."

Billy Ray coughed.

"I know. If Candace hadn't pulled me inside when I fell, I would have gotten a back load of shrapnel." I paused. "What kind of person does this, ma'am? Why would they blow up mailboxes on Candace's street?" A cold thought touched me. "Could someone on that street have been a target?"

Garza shook her head. Her hair was cut professionally short and mousse stiffened it into immobility. "I doubt it, although it's hard to say. But this has all the classical marks of a prankster. The explosives are homemade, are put in places that don't have high traffic, and are set off when people generally aren't about—although this last incident certainly came close to violating the pattern." She frowned. "That bothers me."

"Where would someone get explosives around here?"

Junebug cleared his throat. "Parker Loudermilk's a partner in that construction company over in Bavary. He knows all about explosives," he observed quietly as he turned into Miss Twyla's driveway.

This charge against authority was too much for an eggsucker like Billy Ray. "Chief Moncrief, I'm shocked. And the mayor being your boss! Why, I ought to—"

"It was just an observation, Billy Ray," Junebug said innocently. Made me wonder if perhaps Junebug wasn't going to seek higher office next election.

To my great annoyance, I was not invited in to see Billy Ray grill Nina Hernandez. Junebug handed me over to Sergeant Garza, and I walked with her, examining where the exploded mailboxes had stood. Garza told me the blackened posts of wood and twisted metal had been sent to her office in Austin for analysis. A total of six had exploded.

"Isn't blowing up mailboxes a federal offense?" I asked.

"If they blew up post office property, yes," she answered. "But I don't think we'll have to get the FBI involved yet. My worry is that no one in Mirabeau is turning up as having purchased explosives."

"You can check that?"

Garza nodded. "Yes, the ATF has all the records of explosives purchased in the country. They've been running the names of everyone in Mirabeau through our systems, and the only ones that have been coming out are people with legitimate commercial reasons—like Mr. Loudermilk—for having explosives. We're checking them out, but none of them seem to be good suspects."

"I still can't believe this is happening in Mirabeau."

She shook her head. "Most small towns never have to deal with this kind of activity. For that matter, neither do most big cities." She pointed at where Candace's mailbox had stood. "Blasting cap, I think, with a battery attached and definitely with a timer. From your description, someone wanted them to go off in a row, like firecrackers. You're lucky it wasn't one of the pipe bombs. Our boy's been packing those with potassium chlorate, sugar, and powdered aluminum. That would have taken your head off." I was only half listening; instead, I was staring at Candace's shrapneled front door. One windowpane had been broken and she hadn't gotten it fixed yet. I thought she'd come out and see us, but then I remembered she was at the library. Doing my job while I was holding Lorna's hand. I blew a long breath between my lips. What a mess.

"No, Sergeant Garza, we don't have to deal with explosives," I said. "We just have to deal with the Billy Ray Bummels of the world."

"He is a piece of work," she agreed politely.

"I wonder—" I stared down Blossom Street at the six empty spots where mailboxes should have stood.

"Wonder what?"

"If there's any connection between these ... pranks and Greg Callahan's death." I squinted into the after-

noon sun and rubbed my sore shoulder. The two Tylenol I'd taken earlier were wearing off and Billy Ray
had given me a headache.

"Why would you think that, Jordy?" Garza's tone
sounded guarded.

"Well, just 'cause Mirabeau is a small town and we
don't usually have murders or bombings. But now
we're besieged by both. Seems kind of an odd coincidence, don't you think?"

Teresa Garza favored me with an indulgent smile.
"Junebug warned me. He said you have a tendency to
stick your nose into crimes around here."

"I can't help it if I've gotten involved in some unfortunate incidents. And I don't have any intention of trying to figure out who our mad blitzer is." I shrugged. "I
just wondered if odd events that happen close together
were related. Don't they teach you wild-haired imagination at the bomb squad, ma'am?"

She laughed. "Yes, Jordy, they do. But they also
teach us to deal in facts. I don't know enough about the
Callahan case to see any connections."

I shrugged again. "I suppose I just like for everything
to be in its place. Or maybe I just find it a tad more
comforting to think we've got one nut running around
town rather than two."

Any further conjectures were silenced by Miss Twyla
joining us. She was carrying a tray of freshly made lemonade and she invited us to sit with her under the shade
of her back porch. I watched Sergeant Garza eye the expanse of Miss Twyla's backyard, amused at her reaction. There were a flock of plastic pink flamingos
herded around a birdbath, an odd sculpture that dated
back a couple of Oudelle generations, an old-fashioned
tornado shelter, and a lush garden of vegetables and
herbs.

We thanked her and drank heartily. Say what you
will, lemonade that comes out of a can just can't com-

pare with the real stuff. Tart and sweet like Candace when I've teased her a little too much.

"Sergeant Garza, it's just awful that Jordy was hurt." Miss Twyla looked mournful. "Do you think the police will be able to catch the—what is it you call them on TV—the *perp*?"

Garza shook her head. "I'm sure that Chief Moncrief will get to the bottom of this. And I'd like to talk with you as well, Ms. Oudelle. See what you can tell me about this incident."

Miss Twyla sipped her lemonade. "I'd be delighted to help. People think old ladies are nothing but nuisances, and I'd like to prove 'em wrong. Ask away. My, Jordy, all these questions flying about my little house. Poor Nina is just being hounded by that dreadful Mr. Bummel."

I shook my head. "Look, Miss Twyla, I know you're fond of Nina and all, but she did have the best motive to kill Greg Callahan. And I, for one, have never considered you a nuisance."

"Someone who nurtures the earth the way that Nina does could not cavalierly take a life," Miss Twyla answered. She refilled Garza's glass from a beautiful cut-glass pitcher. The ice popped as the cool liquid poured over it and Miss Twyla paused, as though listening to her lemonade. "Besides, Nina and I were up late plotting our strategy to defeat Intraglobal's land purchases. Nina suggested if the town is against the development, the landowners who are inclined to sell might be less likely to do so. My garden club is going to donate at least ten thousand dollars, and although I loathe the idea of using the profits of trashy literature, Eula Mae has generously offered fifty thousand. The Women's Guild is planning to hold car washes and bake sales to help raise money."

"That's a chunk-a-change, Miss Twyla," I said, "but I don't think it's going to be enough to counter Intraglobal's coffers."

"We were also going to appeal to the honor of our citizens who owned that land," Miss Twyla intoned. "I thought it most likely that your uncle Bidwell would sell that land to Intraglobal. I hoped you and Bob Don would at least listen to our side of the story. The Loudermilks—well, they'd find it politically unattractive to sell if we roused the town against the project. If they didn't sell, and I didn't sell, and if you or Bob Don didn't sell, then their project would fall apart and they'd leave Mirabeau alone."

"You were saving that money for Bid," I said, laughing despite myself.

"Well, you're right. We couldn't match whatever obscene amounts of money Intraglobal would offer. But we could turn the town against the development using that money. Educate people about why we need the river more than we need a bunch of silly condominiums. Money's the key to stopping Intraglobal, Nina says. Anyhow, as to your suspicions of Nina, she and I were up late discussing our plans and we went to bed around eleven. I am a very light sleeper and I didn't hear her leave during the course of the night."

"Maybe she left very quietly," I suggested.

"Oh, I even hear you and Candace coming and going at times," Miss Twyla answered and I started blushing before she'd finished her sentence, then realized she meant arrivals and departures.

"Besides"—and her old-maidish face made a pout of distaste—"I understand the poor Yankee was strangled with barbed wire. Most gruesome, don't you think, Jordy, and certainly not very ladylike. Sounds like a crime a man would commit."

I'd been so involved in trying to help Lorna I hadn't given the various aspects of the crime much consideration. Strangulation with wire. Death closing around your throat implacably, mercilessly. When I thought of what Greg must have suffered, the lemonade in my gut threatened mutiny. Once before I'd had hands closing around my windpipe. I recalled Tiny Parmalee trying to squeeze the life out of me on that long-ago playground.

"Jordy, you okay?" Teresa Garza leaned toward me. "You look sick."

"I'm fine," I said. I struggled to regain my composure. Tiny Parmalee had been sticking to Nina Hernandez's side like a familiar to its witch. No woman in town would have much to do with him. If she gave him the slightest encouragement, would he do her bidding? Or even do her dirty work? Killing a man with barbed wire didn't seem to fit Nina, but the idea of it slipped onto Tiny like a well-worn glove. God, Nina might not even have encouraged him. He might have taken it onto himself to remove anyone who annoyed Nina. I imagined the faint little neurons in his dense brain firing off the clever idea to get rid of Greg Callahan and win Nina's heart. Tiny saving the fair environmentalist damsel from the fire-breathing developer. I could just see it.

"Tell me, Miss Twyla, did Tiny come over last night after the library meeting?" I made my voice sound what I hoped passed for normal.

"Oh, yes, Jordy. He's been so helpful and dedicated. I know that not everyone in town likes Tiny, but he has really a good heart inside. I think the poor soul is just misunderstood. He's become terribly fond of Nina." Miss Twyla proffered the pitcher to me, but I shook my head. There was already a sour taste in my mouth. She continued: "He came over for a little while and just sat while Nina and I talked. Poor Nina was sure he was getting bored, so she told him to go home and—well, I'm sure she didn't mean it cruelly, but that she'd call him when we had, ahem, 'something you can do, like stuffing envelopes.' I'm afraid the poor dear didn't take it very well. He left in a bit of a huff."

To go prove his worthiness by crushing the life out of Greg? I thought, then chided myself. I sounded like Billy Ray, grasping at straws. But it was far easier to imagine Tiny committing a brutal murder than it was Bob Don or Lorna.

I was quiet, so Garza finally got the opportunity to inquire about the destruction of the mailboxes. Miss Twyla had no details to add to my account.

When they finished talking, Billy Ray, Junebug, and Nina came out onto the porch. Nina looked exhausted as she leaned against the wide white wicker chair that Miss Twyla sat in. Today she wore a faded Greenpeace T-shirt with the logo of the famed Rainbow Warrior vessel on it and snug, well-washed khakis. Her hair had the look of having nervous fingers run repeatedly through it, and she appeared tired.

"Nina, dear!" Miss Twyla said.

"Now that I've helped the authorities, I'd like to take a nap, if you don't mind, Miss Twyla." Nina glanced at me, no doubt wondering why I was there.

"Of course, dear. Would you like some lemonade before you lie down?"

"No, ma'am, I'm fine." Nina glanced over at Billy Ray. "Unless you have any more questions for me?"

"No, Miz Hernandez, I don't believe I do. Not just at this moment." Billy Ray flipped through some notes. "But you won't be leaving town without telling Chief Moncrief, now, will you?"

"Of course not. Greg Callahan being dead doesn't mean that Intraglobal won't still be after that land. Lorna Wiercinski's still here, so Intraglobal's still here. And I'm staying as long as this river is threatened."

"Then we'll know where to get in touch with you," Junebug countered.

"She'll be here," Miss Twyla interjected, her voice just a little sweeter than her lemonade. "Jordy, Sergeant Garza, if y'all will excuse us." She got up and herded Nina into the house.

The rest of us headed for Junebug's cruiser. Junebug slowed me down a bit, letting Garza and Billy Ray get ahead of us. He leaned in close against my sore arm. "I don't want you to run straight home. I need your help at the station and I don't want Billy Ray to know about it. Okay?"

I nodded and silently got into the cruiser, wondering what I had just volunteered for.

CHAPTER SEVEN

WHEN WE GOT TO THE STATION, BILLY RAY Bummel didn't tarry long; he sallied forth to terrorize other suspicious residents of Mirabeau. Teresa Garza said she needed to head back to Austin and asked Junebug to give her a call if he needed more help or if another prank occurred.

"Thanks, Teresa, for coming out here," Junebug mumbled. He seemed suddenly embarrassed, and I noticed Sergeant Garza was smiling at him in an enigmatic way. The air was charged between them. I stood there in glee, watching Junebug redden slightly under my gaze. Teresa Garza gave his hand a quick squeeze, thanked me for my time, and headed out the door. We watched her drive off.

"My, what was that all about?" I inquired.

"Nothing," he said, "let's go inside and talk."

This was simply too good to resist and in many ways I'm a slave to my lower drives. "Why, Junebug, one might think you were setting off these charges yourself, just to get her down for these little visits—I mean, investigations."

"All right, Jordy. I've known Teresa for a long time. She requested this assignment because she knows I need the help. Besides, the Austin Bomb Squad provides assistance to several surrounding counties. And don't tease me. You know better than anyone that these bombings aren't any laughing matter." We went back into his office and I watched him try to putter away his embarrassment by shuffling large piles of papers.

"She has lovely eyes," I observed to myself.

One pile of papers tumbled into further disarray. "Damn it," Junebug muttered under his breath. "I always end up paying for being your friend, don't I?"

He hadn't called me a friend in years and I sat for a moment, enjoying it. Men aren't always big on acknowledging who their real friends are when they're sober. I decided I'd tortured him enough and stopped short of asking him to bring Teresa to have dinner with Candace and me.

"You wanted my help with something?" I asked.

He scratched his brown burr and gave me a look of utter resignation. "You know a lot about computers, don't you?"

"I guess. I mean, I know how to use one and most of the common software packages. I can't write programs, though. Why?" I leaned back in my chair.

"Well, I don't know diddly about computers. Nelda and Franklin use one for office administration, and we got the TLETS system tied in with DPS, but I've never learned much about 'em. I need your help. I didn't want Billy Ray to know about it because he just got a home computer and he's been bragging plenty about how much he knows about 'em."

"They haven't yet made the computer Billy Ray can figure out," I said. "It would have to have buttons for chimp fingers and a built-in drool cup. What do you want me to do, teach you the basics? What kind of computer does Nelda use, or do you want to learn a different one?"

"What I want," Junebug answered, "is your help and your silence. I want to find out what was on Greg Callahan's laptop computer."

It took longer than I would've imagined it would. Namely because I had to explain to Junebug each and every step. He knew a little more than he gave himself credit for, but not enough to make himself useful.

We started off in his office, with the door shut. Greg's dark laptop and the pile of 3.5-inch diskettes that I'd seen in Greg's room sat there.

"Can you find out what's inside all this?" Junebug asked.

"Well, let me ask you a question. Have you dusted the keyboard?"

"No. Franklin Bedloe, one of my deputies, he knows about them, he said we'd damage the hard part."

"Hard *drive*. The fingerprint dust might very well do that. But I need to type on the keyboard to see what's inside. Why don't you want to have Franklin or Nelda do this anyhow?"

"Because I told 'em I'd do it," Junebug snapped back. He usually talks in this languorous drawl so you forget he has a temper. "I'm gonna catch the son of a bitch who killed that poor man that awful way in my town. Anyhow, you can teach me the basics while you do this. Kill two birds with one stone."

I shook my head at his foolish pride. "Okay, so how do I avoid getting my prints on the keyboard?"

He left and returned with evidence gloves, those clear kind you see cops handling the murder weapon with on TV. I slipped them onto my hands. "Damn, they're tight. Of course my hands are enormous anyway."

"Bull. You got the hands of a hamster. I never saw such a tall man with such little hands, and you know what they say about men with little hands."

"Yeah. They have to help their friends with little peckers figure out computers," I answered. "Okay, why don't we see what's on these diskettes first. Have you dusted these?"

"Nope."

"Okay. I'll make copies of the diskettes so you can dust the originals." I thumbed through Greg's diskettes. "Oh, this is interesting. One's marked LOUDERMILK FILES 2.

What do you imagine could be on there? And where's Loudermilk files 1?"

"That's what I want to know," Junebug said, sounding just a tad impatient.

I glanced through the rest. There were six diskettes in all, three unmarked, the one marked LOUDERMILK FILES 2, another labeled MIRABEAU PROJECT ESTIMATES, and another titled FINANCIAL.

Junebug followed me like a puppy while I found some blank 3.5-inch diskettes in a box in the supply office. He seemed calmed when I pointed out that Greg's diskettes were made by one manufacturer and were colored blue, while the station's were colored tan. No danger of getting them confused.

On Nelda's machine, I quickly formatted my disks so they could receive data, then copied Greg's six disks. I carefully labeled each of the copies so it matched the original. Junebug watched, fascinated by this simplest of computer tasks. He slid the originals back into an evidence bag as I finished with them.

"Okay, let's snoop," I said as I loaded up the first of the copied disks, choosing LOUDERMILK FILES 2. Nothing. I tapped keys, then turned back to Junebug. "Sorry. It looks like the disk is blank."

"What did you do wrong?" he wailed.

"No, listen. I didn't do anything wrong. There's just no information on this disk. Zilch." I sat back in the chair, rubbing my arm. I'd taken it out of my sling to type faster, and it felt rebelliously painful. Better than yesterday, but still not well. "Maybe he'd labeled it but didn't format it. It might have been that he was planning on putting files on it he hadn't created yet."

"Or maybe it was erased," Junebug mused. "Can you tell that from the disk?"

"Someone probably can. I can't. If they just erased the stuff on the disk, it would still be formatted to receive information. Or, they could have formatted over the information. That would completely destroy whatever was on the disk."

"Crap. Can you tell if someone reformatted it to ruin whatever was on there?" Junebug asked.

"There's probably a way, but I don't know it," I confessed. "You'd have to send the original to a business that specializes in data recovery. They have programs and means of getting back stuff that gets accidentally—or maybe on purpose—deleted. But there's only so much they can do."

Junebug gave a long sigh. "Let's check the others."

The story repeated itself five times. Each of Greg's diskettes was blank.

"So what happened to them?" he said, half to himself.

"One, Greg or someone put these labels on perfectly okay blank disks but never put information on them. To me, that doesn't seem likely. I never label a disk until I've put information on it. Or the disks did have stuff on them—at least the ones that were labeled—and someone has either erased or destroyed the information." I stopped and turned to him. "But if someone wanted to get rid of the information, why not just steal the disks and destroy them later?"

"Maybe they didn't want them on their person. And if they can destroy them by using the computer, they don't need to steal them."

"There might be the risk that the data could be recovered, though." I scratched my nose with one plastic-sheathed finger. "But, like I said, I don't know how much the data-recovery folks could do. Maybe it was enough to destroy the stuff on these files."

"You said that there would also be information on the hard disk on his machine," Junebug said. "Let's look at that. God, I hope it hasn't been erased."

"I can copy what's on the hard disk onto diskettes, if you like, or we can look directly onto his hard disk."

Junebug considered. "Better make the copies."

I did so. There were plenty of files on the hard disk, so at least it hadn't been erased. We both confessed to skipping lunch, so Junebug called the Dairy Queen and ordered two country baskets, with strips of fried chicken, peppered cream gravy, buttery Texas toast, and french fries. Cholesterol's not something we worry about, what with all the fresh air we get.

I finished up the copying while we waited for the food to arrive. (Dairy Queens don't usually deliver, but Junebug's a special customer, what with being the law.)

When the food came, we wolfed it down like a couple of good bachelors. The feeding frenzy completed, we took the several disks that held the contents of Greg's hard drive and went back to Nelda's computer.

I slid the first disk in and accessed its contents. There were a lot of spreadsheet files and word-processing files, and I went to those first.

"You're sure we're not breaking the law by doing this?" I said. "I mean, if you find evidence in here, you'll be able to use it, right?"

"Yes. Don't you worry about it, just don't erase anything." He leaned over my shoulder as I typed.

"Unless he's passworded the files, I should be able to see everything here," I said. "If he's put a password on any of them, they'll be locked."

He made a noise in his throat, and I got to work. The first files I looked at were word-processing files; I preferred to deal with language over numbers first. The files were organized into directories: LETTERS; MEMOS; REPORTS. I peeked first in LETTERS and looked at the contents, then began opening each file to read it.

"Couldn't we print out copies?" Junebug asked.

"Yeah, but let's skim through the stuff first and see what's most interesting. Then we can print hard copies."

There weren't many letters, and they all seemed to do with the condo project in Mirabeau. There was a letter to the Lower Colorado River Authority, asking for a list of any environmental requirements that developments on the river had to adhere to (regardless of any local or county regulations); a letter to Chester Blanton at the Mirabeau B. Lamar Bed-and-Breakfast, requesting reservations for Gregory Callahan and Lorna Wiercinski; a letter to Frederick Jacksill of Rivertown Real Estate of Mirabeau, confirming him as their commercial real-estate agent in Bonaparte County; another letter to Martin H. Noone, Attorney-at-Law, in Bavary, seeking a bid on legal services for land purchases in Mirabeau. The letters were written in a no-nonsense corporate style I'd become awfully familiar with in my days in the business world.

"All square and boring," Junebug murmured over my shoulder.

I nodded and opened another file, marked ZADICH1. Junebug and I had each read about three sentences into the letter when we said "Oh, shit," in near synchronization.

The letter read:

> 1213 Brennan Street
> Boston, Massachusetts 02114

Mr. Gary Zadich
Chem-Solutions, Inc.
1600 Port-of-Call Road
Deer Park, Texas 77536

Dear Mr. Zadich:

I believe that the purchase of land in Mirabeau, Bonaparte County, Texas, will proceed according to our timetable. The land is zoned for both commercial and residential use (private homes and commercial farms are already side by side) and there are very few controls set on which businesses may operate on the river. The land is ideal for your needs as a chemical waste storage facility. Labor in the area is cheap. The

slow economy and local unemployment should prevent
any grass-roots campaign against your facility. Of
course, I will be reselling you the land as soon as title
clears. Undoubtedly some environmentalists will be
deeply upset at the idea of a chemical waste storage facility on the river, but I think the community will welcome business of any sort. These bumpkins need the
money.

I will contact you again as soon as the purchases are
complete, or if I run into any difficulties.

Sincerely,

Gregory Callahan

"Holy shit!" Junebug crumpled back and collapsed in
his chair.

"Bumpkins? Bumpkins!" I exploded. "That smarmy
little bastard. Does he think we all just fell off the tur-
nip truck? We are not idiots, Junebug. He doesn't know
who he's dealing . . ." My voice trailed off as I remembered that the source of my ire was in the past tense.

"Shit! He was going to buy up that land then resell it
to some chemical dump. How could he do that?"

I took a long breath. "I don't know—maybe declare
insolvency, say that his other investors pulled out of the
project and he had to sell the land. Voilà, here's this
chemical waste company that needs some land and oh,
I just had to sell it to them. Maybe it's not even the
chemical company itself, but another company owned
by them so the folks who want to protect the river don't
know."

Junebug nodded grimly. "And then, that company
dangles the promise of new jobs. God knows we need
'em, what with so many family farms having troubles.
He's right. Some folks would even be willing to put up
with a chemical site on the river if it meant food on the
table." He paused and rubbed his chin. "But others

would do anything to keep a chemical dump off our river."

I heard everything that he was saying, but I had my mind elsewhere. Lorna. Did she know about this? Had she lied right to my face, telling me all about their delightful little condominium development while knowing they were going to sell the land right after they got it? I felt a slow burn of anger.

"Oh, lordy," I heard Junebug say. "If anyone here found this out, they'd have a helluva motive to kill him."

I blinked at Junebug. "Well, this should clear Lorna, right? This gives a lot of folks in Mirabeau a motive, and if she knew about this, what motive would she have?" I was babbling and I knew it. I fought back an urge to push my fist against my mouth. God, if she had lied to me about this for the sake of profit—

Junebug saw my vexation. He put a steadying hand on my shoulder. "C'mon, Jordy, let's look at the rest of the files."

Believing in the innate goodness of people (most of the time), I kept hoping we'd find another letter from Greg to Mr. Zadich, calling off the collective lie to Mirabeau. Greg, apparently, was not innately good. There were drafts of letters to the city council in Mirabeau, explaining that the condo deal had "fallen through due to investor withdrawal" and that he was actively seeking new investors, followed by another draft that claimed he couldn't find any investors, and so was selling the land to another "commercial concern." That commercial concern was no doubt Chem-Solutions, near Houston, but the letter didn't state that.

The financial files lent heartbreaking support to the letters. There was a set of spreadsheets for the condo project; this was probably what Greg planned on showing the landowners. Another set worked out Greg's profit on selling the land to Chem-Solutions, with money thoughtfully laid aside for any messy legal actions. As we read each file I felt slightly ill. I'd felt sorry for Greg Callahan at first, but my sympathy was now tempered with the knowledge that he must've been a supreme bastard.

There was only one other file that was on the disk, and it didn't work with Nelda's spreadsheet or word processor. It was a calendar program, the kind that businesspeople use to set up appointments. I donned my gloves again, went back to Greg's computer, and copied the entire calendar program over, along with the associated files. I then installed the program on Nelda's machine, and we began to look through Greg's last days.

The past week and a half were all that were there. Apparently he'd spent most of those days in Boston, in a few meetings with names that meant nothing to us. He'd taken one side trip to Houston, apparently the day before he came to Mirabeau. That day was marked 9:30–12:00: MEET WITH ZADICH. CONFIRM DEAL. Junebug busily jotted down all the information into his notes.

He'd spent three days already in Mirabeau, not counting today. His schedule, at least as marked down in his calendar went like this:

Tuesday, July 19
10–10:45 Meet with Noone @ Bavary
11:00 Go to county courthouse @ Bavary
12:00 Lunch with Mayor Loudermilk @ Mirabeau
1:45 Meet with Twyla Oudelle (landowner)
3:00 Meet with F. Jacksill @ Mirabeau
5:00 Meet with Dee Loudermilk (landowner)

Wednesday, July 20
11:00 Meet with B. Poteet (landowner)
1:00 Meet with B. D. Goertz (landowner)
4:00 Meet with J. @ Bavary

Thursday, July 21
[reminder—call Gary with update on progress]

[reminder—Lorna arrives @ Austin airport, coming in with rental car—leave J. Poteet to her.]
9–11 Meet with F.
12 Lunch with Chamber of Commerce @ Mirabeau
2:00 Meet with B. D. Goertz
8:00 Meet with Lorna after her meeting with J. Poteet
10:00 Meet with J.

Thursday had been his last full day in Mirabeau before he died. His plans for that day had been:

Friday, July 22
8 Breakfast with L. and F.
10 Close deal with B. Poteet
12 Lunch with Mayor, solve any problems with T.O. and N.H.

He hadn't lived for that breakfast with (I guessed) Lorna and Freddy, or presumably to give a bunch of money to Uncle Bid, or to "solve any problems with Miss Twyla or Nina." I scanned back over the list and Greg's penchant for abbreviations. Some were obvious: J. Poteet being me (and I wasn't very pleased at the idea of "being left to Lorna"), F. being Freddy Jacksill, T.O. being Twyla Oudelle. But who was J.? Another abbreviation for Freddy? Or someone else altogether? A name or a profession? Maybe even Junebug? I thought for a moment, then dismissed it.

We finished and I felt a craving for a cigarette. I used to smoke a pack a day, but then I got into running up in Boston, so I quit (repeatedly). I'd started up again with all the stress I'd felt when I moved back to Mirabeau. Candace hated cigarette smoke, so I'd sworn off for the past three months. I needed one now, though. I borrowed two cigarettes and a book of matches from the dispatcher, and Junebug and I sat outside in the late-afternoon shade of a live-oak tree behind the station, having ourselves a good old think. The summer air, heavy with humidity, draped over us. My shirt started clinging to my back.

"Well, Nina's reasons for killing him certainly have gone up, if she knew about that letter," I said, blowing smoke above my head. Nasty habit, I reminded myself, but it did make me feel better. As soon as my arm was healed, I'd have a good solid run to make up for my vices.

Junebug scratched his chin. "But why kill him over it? If she knew about the letter and the plot with this chemical company, why didn't she just blow the whistle? She could've humiliated him and exposed him for a crook. I think Nina would find that a sight more fulfilling than killing him."

That made sense. I pictured Nina and Greg bickering at the library meeting and her smugness when she challenged him. I thought that she might rather see him squirm than see him dead. "But she'd do just about anything to help protect the river." I considered the ember at my cigarette's end.

"Including murder? That's a bit of a stretch, don't you think?"

"She'd faced off against him before, and lost." I paused. "I wonder if he tried this same scam somewhere else. But she had confronted him over this same chessboard; wouldn't she know his tricks?"

Junebug shrugged. "That bears looking into. But maybe he's done regular land development before this and just decided to turn crooked with this deal. I think we better try and find out more about Greg Callahan's business deals. I gotta go make some phone calls." He stood and dusted off the back of his blue uniform pants.

"So who do you suspect?" I jumped up to my feet.

"Everybody and nobody," Junebug said. "I don't suspect you, though, you'll be pleased to know."

"My gratitude knows no bounds."

"Well, neither does mine. Thanks for helping me with the computer. I think I'll quietly sign up for one of those introductory courses over at Bavary Community College now that you've got me on the basics. Can I call you if I need more help with it?"

"Sure, Junebug." We shook hands and he went back into the station. I stomped on what was left of the cigarette, picked it up and thumbed it in a trash can and headed to my car. Lorna had a lot of questions to answer. I tore off down the street, ready to go confront her. But as I drove off I caught sight of Tiny Parmalee's battered red pickup truck coming up quick behind me.

CHAPTER EIGHT

TINY'S PICKUP, RESPLENDENT WITH ITS BAT-tery of dents, smoke-spewing pipes, and oversized Confederate-flag decal in the back window (along with what looked like a deer rifle) stayed close behind me all the way home. I felt a childish fear. I'd never forgotten how Tiny had nearly crushed the life out of me at little provocation. My fear, though, quickly changed to anger as his truck followed barely two feet behind my own back fender. I took a deep breath. I wasn't a little kid who could be pushed around again. And I wasn't about to let a blunt-headed bastard like Tiny Parmalee intimidate me. I'd seen too much pain in life, and backing away never got a soul anywhere.

His grimy truck finally backed off as I pulled into my carport and he stopped in front of my house. I wondered for one moment if he'd come out swinging and how I was going to handle that with only one good arm. If he did attack me, I'd be at a serious disadvantage. I decided then and there that the best defense would be a solid kick to his beer gut, followed by another boot to the groin and a judicious retreat into my house. Not a polite way to fight, but mannered combat takes two gentlemen.

I'd just emerged from the car when Tiny slammed his door shut and came lumbering across the lawn at me. His whitish hair gleamed like a bald dome in the summer sun. His eyes were a thin, watery blue, but they were narrowed in anger. One hand was already in a fist.

114

"Hey!" he yelled, stopping a few feet ahead of me. "Get something straight, you shithead. You leave Nina alone!"

"Excuse me?" I answered, pulling my arm close against my body and tensing my legs. "I haven't even talked to Nina today. What's your problem?"

"My problem, Poteet, is you. You think Nina killed that Yankee son of a bitch. You told Miss Twyla that." Obviously one had to be careful what one suggested to Miss Twyla.

"I never said that she did." Well, not exactly. "I just asked Miss Twyla where Nina was last night, and she told me. If you think someone's bugging Nina, you need to go see Billy Ray Bummel and Junebug." I wanted to take a step back, but I didn't. You don't do that to a bully, and Tiny Parmalee had changed very little since those schoolyard tussles. He had been angry then, with no outlet for releasing it other than torturing other kids; he was angry now, and still hadn't learned how to deal with wrath. "Look, Tiny. It's obvious that you care about Nina. I understand that."

"What the hell do you know about me?" he asked, drawing a heavy hand across his lip. "You don't know shit about me, mister. Or about what I think about Nina." He shook his head. "You think you're so smart, Poteet, you always have. Always looking down on me, always thinking I'm just nothing but a big stupid shit. I'm not. I'm a hell of a lot smarter than you'll ever give me credit for."

"Okay, you're smart. Who killed Greg?"

He took one step forward and pushed a finger toward my face. I smelled the nauseatingly sweet odor of a thick wad of chewing gum he had in his mouth and I saw the bulge it made in his unshaven cheek. "Just stay away from Nina. Stay out of this whole mess. Just ship that Yankee bitch of yours back where she belongs and keep out of mine and Nina's business."

Since I didn't know what constituted his and Nina's

business and I hadn't interfered in any way that I knew of, I very much disliked his jabbing his finger at my nose. Not to mention him calling Lorna names. "This is not a joke, Tiny. This is a murder. Someone killed Greg and whoever did that is going to pay for it. Nina and Greg didn't get along at all, so she's going to be investigated by the cops. Don't take it so personally. I mean, you're sure she's innocent, aren't you?"

He wasn't expecting that. The finger receded from my personal space. "Yeah, I am," he said slowly, as though I'd asked a trick question.

"So then you and Nina have nothing to worry about." I didn't add my thought: *Unless you strangled him, you animal.*

Tiny blinked repeatedly. "She didn't do it. Maybe I'll find out who did, if the cops keep suspecting her." I didn't think Tiny would make much headway as a detective, but I kept my mouth shut.

"Is that all?"

"Yeah. Just stay away from Nina and quit fillin' folks' heads full of foolishness about her." Back on the familiar territory of threat making, he regained his confidence. He turned his back on me and headed back for his truck.

"Tiny?"

He paused while climbing into the truck. "Yeah?"

"Don't ever follow me that close again, or I'll shoot out your tires. Understand me?"

He wasn't expecting that I'd threaten back in any way and to my surprise he smiled. Coldly. "I'll remember that." Slamming his door hard enough to shake the truck, he started the engine and roared off, leaving a bloated cloud of exhaust in his wake.

I exhaled a long breath. He'd been pissed, but he hadn't beaten me up. Unless, of course, he was out to seek vengeance against Junebug and Billy Ray for suspecting his inamorata of being a bloodthirsty garroter.

I went into the house, quietly. It was nearly three in

the afternoon and I felt exhausted. I needed a nap. I wasn't going to get one. Eula Mae and Lorna sat on the couch, smiling tightly at each other. I felt I'd walked onstage halfway through a death scene.

"Hey, y'all, what's going on?" I said. Those tight smiles of theirs didn't budge an inch.

"Hey, sugar pie. I just thought I'd stop by and see how Miss Lorna here was doing." Eula Mae got up, her layers of necklaces tinkling as she moved, and gave me a perfunctory kiss on the cheek. I was not swayed.

"You sure y'all aren't squabbling over that land deal?" I asked.

Eula Mae pressed a well-manicured hand to her violet peasant blouse (showing her freckled cleavage to best display). "Honey, we haven't even talked about that stuff. It's so trivial in the light of poor Mr. Callahan's murder."

Lorna's smile faded as soon as Eula Mae wasn't looking at her. "Ms. Quiff was kind enough to invite me to come stay with her. She thought I might be underfoot here."

Eula Mae rolled her eyes at me before turning them, glistening with kindness and sympathy, toward Lorna. "Sweetie, the way you phrase things! I simply thought that it might be nicer for you to have a little more room, what with this house being so full of Jordy, and Arlene, and Mark, and Anne, and Clo being over so much."

I frowned slightly at Eula Mae, who did not appear to notice, being busy closely examining the setting of one of her many rings. I decided on the gentlemanly approach. "How kind of you, Eula Mae. And how unusually generous of you." She bristled a tad at that and I grinned. "But I think Lorna's just fine right here."

Eula Mae shrugged, the field of battle abandoned. "You're right, Jordy. I mean, you are spending most of your time at Candace's, so there *is* plenty of room here for dear Lorna." Well, nearly abandoned. She leaned down and patted—or lightly slapped, depending on your point of view—Lorna's leg. "If you change your mind, sweetness, you just call Eula Mae. You'll always be welcome at Chez Quiff."

I steered the Unwelcome Wagon firmly to and out the door. The full blast of the afternoon humidity and sunlight hit us and we both blinked against the glare. She shrugged off my light touch and frowned at me when I'd shut the front door. "Jordan Poteet. Are you thinking with your loins these days?"

"What's wrong with you? Have you totally forgotten your manners?"

"You could strip the flesh from my bones," Eula Mae hissed, "and I'd still have more class than that nasal-voiced little minx in there."

"Good Lord!"

"Turning down my heartfelt invitation in her hour of need. And not even nicely, telling me she was sure Candace had sent me over here." She was near fake tears.

"Did Candace send you over here?"

"Of course not!" Eula Mae stomped her foot. "I *am* capable of independent thought, mister. You forget I've made my money from knowing all about love." That was a tempting statement to twist around on her, but I kept my mouth shut. I wouldn't have gotten a line in anyway.

"I know exactly what that woman's up to. You don't give a man the *Kama Sutra* if you just want to be pen pals. Especially the new edition," Eula Mae continued. "And it's the way she looks at you. I saw it last night at the library when she came in. She only saw you, Jordy. The way her eyes narrowed, I figured the poor child was astigmatic or in heat. And she don't wear glasses."

"Eula Mae. I appreciate your concern, honestly, but you're getting carried away."

"Jordy, darlin'." She took my arm. "Listen to me. That girl's still in love with you. It's as plain to me as it is hidden to you. You're sweet as pie, but dense as fudge when it comes to women sometimes."

"I know she has feelings for me, Eula Mae." I wasn't about to tell the Human P.A. System here about last night's after-dinner kiss.

"Forewarned is forearmed," she intoned.

"I've made it clear to her I'm not about to tumble back into her bed. She knows I have feelings for Candace."

Eula Mae raised one plucked eyebrow. "And does Candace know?"

"Of course she does!"

Eula Mae made a noise in her throat, fished her keys out of her denim skirt pocket, and sauntered off to her purple BMW with the ROMWRTR vanity license plates.

I watched her roar off. Eula Mae was obviously not spending nearly enough time in front of her word processor and was inventing romantic fictions in real people's lives as compensation. Of course Candace knew I loved her. And I wasn't going back to Lorna. Nosireebob.

Lorna was stretched out on the couch, the back of her hand resting gently against her forehead. Her long legs lay along the cushions, ideally formed and with the beginnings of a tan. Her khaki shorts were snug and short, her neon-aqua T-shirt pulled taut across her breasts. She'd been sweating and there was just a hint of a sheen at her throat. Her waist, which had always fit perfectly against the inside of my arm, was encircled with a colorfully stitched cloth belt. She'd pulled her thick yank of hair back and fastened it into a ponytail with a bit of ribbon, and a lank of it lay on her shoulder. I watched her breathe and she kept her eyes closed. I'd stormed in, ready to confront her about Greg's lies, and now I found myself not wanting to have this conversation—just wanting to watch her doze, the way I used to on lazy Sunday afternoons in New England.

"Has the Wicked Witch of the South ridden off with her flying monkeys?" Lorna asked.

"Hey, there. Eula Mae's harmless and she's my friend." I sat down on the end of the couch, pushing her feet up to make room. Her skin felt annoyingly good.

"I get the distinct feeling she doesn't want to be my friend, despite her oh-so-kind invitation to stay with her."

"What was all that about?"

"Your harmless little friend sauntered in like she owned your house, told me in nice—but no uncertain—terms that you really didn't want me here, and just seemed flabbergasted I wasn't packed and ready to go. I think she even hinted that your mother might be inclined to go into homicidal spells, without reason, at any given moment."

"Eula Mae's bark is worse than her bite."

"Well, mine's not."

"Where is everyone?" I asked.

"Your sister has gone grocery shopping. She made some comment about not expecting another mouth to feed." Lorna sounded a little cross and I couldn't blame her.

"Sorry about that. Just ignore her, she's basically decent when she isn't being catty."

Lorna shrugged. "I have far more to worry about than being on Arlene's shit list. Your mother's upstairs taking a nap; I checked on her a few minutes ago. I did meet your nephew Mark, by the way. He stopped by for lunch and he's off swimming with some friends." She opened one gray eye and watched me past her raised knee. Probing my ribs with her wriggling toes, she said: "You don't want me to go, do you, Jordan?"

I took a long breath. "That depends on how you answer my questions." That got both those gray eyes open.

"What?"

"Did you know that Greg was running a land scam?

That he was planning on reselling the land he wanted to buy for condominiums to a chemical dump site?" I watched her face as I spoke, for any betraying flicker.

Her mouth worked, her jaw closing and opening on empty air. "What do you mean?"

I told her again. She pulled herself into a sitting position. "How do you know this?"

It wasn't an answer to my question, but I told her about finding the files on Greg's laptop.

"Jordan, I swear to you—I swear on our friendship—that I didn't know anything about this."

We exchanged stares, then she lowered her eyes. "I feel like an idiot, and you don't believe me," she said.

"How could you not have known, Lorna?"

She shook her head, her eyes staring off into her memories. "I didn't know."

"I felt that you weren't being entirely up-front this morning with Billy Ray and Junebug when they were asking about Greg. You'd better tell me everything you know."

"I did tell you," she said, her eyes still watching something in her mind and not me. Absently she picked at the bandage on her finger.

"No, Lorna. I know you well enough, and I don't think you did. Now, what exactly did you do for Greg?"

"I handled—I did—research for him. On properties around the country that met certain criteria that he had. I'd—identify the properties and then he'd see about acquiring land there, and investors to build on the land. I didn't deal with any investors—I never met them."

I felt a sudden anger. "So you just happened to identify Mirabeau as the town to fit Greg's needs. How convenient."

"I didn't do it just to see you again, despite what your enormous ego might say," she retorted, then looked contrite. "I'm sorry, I don't mean to be a bitch. I'm just shocked." She swallowed and went on: "I set up these databases for him of towns all over the country. Then I'd run queries on the database, finding out which ones had the attributes he looked for—river site, slow economy, proximity to a major metropolitan area. Lots of towns qualified, and he'd go check them out. He just—picked Mirabeau."

"And you didn't help him make that choice?"

"You know, if I'd still wanted you, I would never have let you leave Boston. I didn't have to get a job with Greg to try and get you back." Her voice grew sharp. "You're just so full of yourself, Jordan."

"I can afford to be a little arrogant," I snapped back, letting the pain talk before my brain edited. "I'm not the one who looks like a land-scam artist. What he was doing was horrible, Lorna, and you were helping him."

"I didn't know! Honestly!"

"I want to believe you. Desperately. I don't think you're a liar, but right now—"

"I'm not a liar!"

"Then what were you hiding when you were talking to Billy Ray? Maybe you knew about the land resale all along? What else was going on? Maybe you and Greg were lovers?"

"Fine, I'll tell you." Her voice took on a strained, sad tone. She coughed once, as though the words were slabs in her throat. "Greg and I *were* lovers. For a short while after you left. But I cooled it down, because I knew it was a mistake to get involved with my boss. It was the stupidest thing I'd ever done, but you broke my heart when you left and I was entitled to make stupid mistakes. Satisfied?" She bolted off the couch, in tears, and stormed out of the room.

"Hello!" Sister trilled as she came into the kitchen, laden with groceries. I quickly offered to help and she looked at my bad arm with a raised eyebrow. "Don't bother, Jordy. Where's Lorna?"

"She's resting upstairs. She's not feeling well." I didn't feel too hot myself.

"Oh, dear." Sister's voice just dripped concern. "I

think she needs a little company to brighten her day. That's why I invited Candace over for dinner." I whirled to face her. Sister smiled like an angel just getting her wings.

I spent the rest of the afternoon lying on my bed, hearing Lorna's vague movements in the next room, thinking about all the hell that'd broken loose.

Greg might not have done anything outright illegal—that would be for a court to decide—but he was obviously an unsavory character. He didn't deserve what had happened to him, but he'd obviously chosen a bad path. (Even now, thinking about his savaged throat made my bile rise.)

I closed my eyes and images danced behind my lids. Wire taken from the fence that bisected the Loudermilks' property from Bob Don's ending up in Greg's neck. Gretchen in Greg's company. That mysterious phone number on the pad in Greg's room. Greg being Lorna's ex- or maybe-not-ex-lover. Greg's long-standing animosity toward Nina. Tiny's fury at the thought that Nina could be accused. The erased diskettes. Greg's neatly arranged files that indicated he was out to defraud the people of Mirabeau with this condo development. The letters he'd already drafted to send to the city council, even before his deals were done. His many meetings with people in the town: Miss Twyla, the Goertzes, Parker and Dee Loudermilk, Freddy Jacksill, Uncle Bid. He hadn't met with me and I felt pert near left out. And who was the J. he met with at the end of each day? It hadn't been me. I wondered, idly, if it was Jenny Loudermilk—she'd come in right behind Greg at the library meeting. Or another abbreviation for Freddy Jacksill. They were the only people connected to the case that I could think of. Of course, it could be someone else entirely. And to add to all this, the bombings. Tomorrow, I decided, I'd have to talk with Mr. Freddy Jacksill and the Loudermilks.

I took some more Tylenol, wondering if you could get addicted to the stuff, and rewarded all my hard thinking with a predinner nap.

I could have killed my nephew Mark. He'd ended up getting invited to stay at a friend's for hamburgers for dinner, leaving me alone with three women, all of whom had their eyes on me for different reasons. It was really more than any one man should be expected to bear.

Sister was the congenial hostess, being as sugary to me and Lorna as two-day-old sweet-potato pie. She'd insisted on doing all the cooking, while leaving Candace, Lorna, and me out in the living room with a life-preserver-shaped tray of cheese, fruit, and chips. (I felt like the dip.) She brought in our beers and patted Lorna on the shoulder.

"Lorna, I know you're probably not feeling like partying very much, but trust me—a relaxing evening with friends will make you feel better. Try and put all this dreadfulness behind you for just a few hours." Good thing Lorna wasn't diabetic—Sister's cajoling tone would have put anyone into a sugar coma.

Lorna wasn't fooled for an instant. "That's awfully sweet of you, Arlene. And inviting Candace, too, so I can make a new friend here in Mirabeau, well, really, you shouldn't have."

I managed to choke down a chip. I could see the evening unfolding like a bad horror movie. Candace and Sister (or at least, Sister) had connived not to leave me alone with Lorna, not knowing that right now I was a bit tiffed at Lorna. Sister wasn't about to have her baby brother get into a mixed marriage (and marrying a Yankee would be considered just that in Mirabeau—we didn't trust genes that hadn't been in nearby pools for several generations) and she was kind of stuck on the idea of me and Candace staying on a steady course. Candace had either gotten dragged into this or was a co-

conspirator, but she was the person I was happiest to see.

And Lorna, God help me. Lorna saw right through Sister's charade and had determined to be as affable (at least outwardly) as Sister was being. She wouldn't look at me, given her latest confession, but when she'd come down to dinner she'd given me a sideways hug and patted my shoulder. I admit I had no clue as to where I stood with her, or whether I believed she didn't know about Greg's fraud. I shouldn't be mad that she and Greg had been lovers, but I did feel a vague tug in my gut at the thought. Had she felt the same when she'd found out about Candace? At least, I comforted myself, I'd had better taste in companions. Far better, I thought with a smile as I glanced over at Candace. She was wearing an outfit of hers I'd always liked, a simple blue-and-white-stripe tanktop dress. I glanced over at Lorna. She'd changed into a Boston Marathon T-shirt, deliciously snug over her chest, and long navy walking shorts. Both these women were beautiful, in different ways. Any man should have delighted in their company, but the tension hung in the air like a hanged man's ghost. They'd spend the whole evening fighting over me. A slight grin touched my mouth; I'd never had two women fight over me before. It'd be hell to sit through, but it might also be kind of fun—at the least, a boost to my benighted ego.

I sat on the couch with the tray of food before me. Lorna had gracefully maneuvered to sit by me and Candace had retreated to a nearby wicker chair. Sister had already fed Mama and put her to bed, so she wasn't there for me to talk to. I find it a comfort to talk to Mama sometimes even if she's not paying me a bit of heed.

"You must stay busy here in Mirabeau, Candace," Lorna purred. "I mean, what with helping Jordan out at the library."

"That takes a lot of my time, yes," Candace concurred. "And I do volunteer work for the Daughters of the Republic of Texas chapter, and the Bonaparte County Literacy Program, and the Mirabeau Historical Society."

"How sweet," Lorna said. "Of course, that's not really like having a career. Don't you get bored?"

"Not really." Candace smiled tightly. "And you're right, it's not like a career. I'm not shackled to it."

"But then you don't get all the rewards from a career."

Candace leaned over and patted my knee in a most proprietary way. "My work brings me all sorts of rewards."

God, they were just going to snipe at each other all night. Over little old me? I tried not to smirk.

After delicately arranging some cheese on a cracker, Lorna eyed Candace and me. "So what do you guys do for fun in town? If it's just having sex, spare me any gruesome details."

Candace might have taken slight umbrage at being referred to as a *guy*, but she wasn't put off by Lorna's ribaldry. "Oh, no. We watch TV—cable is a necessity if you live out here. We go into Austin to shop, sometimes go over and eat in La Grange or Smithville."

"TV, huh? Does he make you watch all those old spy shows with him?" Lorna asked, leaning forward. This had been a particularly annoying habit of mine; foreplay had often consisted of wrenching the remote control out of my hand.

"Oh, yes." Candace laughed. "He still loves to watch *The Avengers*. I think he'd like me to go as Emma Peel for Halloween and he could be John Steed. I just told him I wasn't about to cavort around town in a black leather jumpsuit with a Sixties hairdo, no sir."

"He tried that on me, too! Like he wouldn't look ridiculous in a bowler." Lorna giggled. "Plus, you know Jordan, he can be clumsiness personified. He'd poke someone's eye out with that umbrella Steed always carried." She sighed. "No, I always picked out our Halloween costumes, and every year he was an absolute baby about it."

"I don't think this is really—" I began, but Candace cut me off: "What did y'all go as?"

"Sex toys," Lorna whispered back, shooting a cautionary glance toward the kitchen, where we could barely hear Sister humming a Trisha Yearwood song with no regard to key.

"Lorna, really—" I tried.

Candace exploded in laughter. "Oh, my God!"

"I know. Isn't it horribly tacky? But, Candace, you have to understand the crowd we ran around with up there, they were awfully full of themselves. Jordan and I liked to let a little of their stuffy air out. So I went as a vibrator—basically I wore a long silver gown, with speed settings on my front and an old football helmet with halves of golf balls glued on it."

"Oh, my God!"

"And Jordan was a dildo!" Lorna managed to finish. She was howling as hard as Candace. I wasn't howling at all. I started a very detailed examination of Sister's cheese tray. This had ceased to be amusing.

"How?" Candace wanted to know.

"Just basically put a phallic-shaped cylinder around him and he was set. I did make him wear a beanie on his head, for that 'special pleasuring sensation.' You wouldn't believe how cute he looked, I think I still have a picture of him back home—"

The cackles followed me as I escaped into the kitchen. So much for their bickering over my studly form. Sister glanced up from her chicken-fried steaks, sizzling in the skillet with a heavenly aroma.

"What's all that screeching?" Sister obviously anticipated a catfight between my two paramours.

"I hope you're satisfied," I snapped. "They're laughing at me!"

I managed to make it through dinner, but more than

once I wondered if my steak knife would provide me with a fast death if I fell on it. I did enjoy Sister's food: chicken-fried steak surrounded by a delicate, golden batter, topped with rich cream gravy; black-eyed peas, cooked with peppers and bits of bacon; steamed summer squash from Sister's own garden, with just a hint of rosemary; thick slabs of homemade jalapeño cornbread, with butter melting inside each slice. For dessert we had warm, gooey homemade pecan pie with Blue Bell vanilla ice cream on top. The ladies drank iced tea with lime slices and I stayed with beer, hoping to numb the conversation between Candace and Lorna.

It almost didn't matter who was saying what.

"How long did it take you to get used to the snoring?"

"Ages, even though he claims he never snores."

"Yeah! Right!"

"I hope he picks up after himself better."

"Actually, no. He still believes that clothes that land on the floor have life and walk to the hamper under their own power."

"I know. But he says he's tidy at work."

"Well, he is. Usually. Of course he's the worst flirt at work with all the old ladies. They just love him."

"Didn't you ever want to snip out that tongue, though? I got tired of always having to engage in repartee. Not to mention what you just said, his innate need to flirt. Really!"

"Oh, but you got used to it, didn't you? I always thought that it was kind of cute."

Sister tried to dam the flow: "More dessert, girls?"

"No, thanks."

"No, Arlene, thank you."

"God, and have you ever dated a guy that liked war movies so much? I always wondered if that meant Jordy really wanted a military career."

"But he's not good at taking orders."

"Or at giving them." Laughter from both sides. I

started counting the nuts in my pie, hoping to find a big one I could choke on.

"And did you ever see a man with so many damn books?"

"No. It's like having another library at home. And God help you if you interrupt him when he's wanting to read. He gets awful moody."

"Lord, and those depressing books. All those murder mysteries. That actually scared me when we started dating. I thought it was a little morbid."

"At least he wasn't in a Civil War phase. God forbid he starts reading Bruce Catton again. You won't see him for weeks."

"Sounds like football season when the Cowboys are playing. You better not talk during a Cowboy game."

"Or laugh at him when the Cowboys score and he does his little victory dance."

"I have never minded being laughed at for that!" I exclaimed, finally rousing to defend myself. I looked at Sister for help. She seemed unduly interested in the crust of her pie, picking at it like an archaeologist clearing dirt from an artifact.

"He's not a bad dancer, as long as the music has a *very*—strong—beat."

"And you'll need steel-tipped shoes to protect your feet."

"Well, he did do a little striptease dance for me on my birthday that was just adorable! All he kept on was a rose in his mouth and his Cowboys baseball cap—"

I hoped that all the blood in my body was not rushing to my face; I wanted enough left to have a proper heart attack. I wondered what it would take to shut them up.

The explosion shushed them, a few moments later. The roar of a blast maybe two streets over, a faraway chorus of screams, and moments later, the cry of sirens.

CHAPTER NINE

IT WAS EASIER TO RUN ACROSS THE LAWNS TO the smoky haze in the sky than drive; it was only two streets over. Sister stayed with Mama; Lorna, Candace, and I dashed through the darkening yards, the summer sun just setting to the west, the early-evening moisture sticking our clothes to our skins. Folks were pouring out of their houses—children, scared but excited; parents with frantic looks; the elderly with worn eyes and unsteady limbs.

Candace and Lorna followed me as I made a shortcut through a couple of backyards and came out onto Mockingbird Street, a block down from the bed-and-breakfast. One room-sized portion of the beautiful old house was gone from the second story, as though a hand had come down from space and torn it free. Smoke gouted from windows on the top floor. Broken glass and hunks of burned brick lay scattered across the yard. One Mirabeau Police Department cruiser was already in front, its siren blaring at the burning building like a dog barking at a stranger. In the distance I heard the whine of our one fire truck.

"My God!" Lorna exclaimed. Reflexively, she grabbed hold of my slinged arm. I hardly noticed the pain.

"Chet! Oh, my Lord!" Candace cried. She ran toward the police cruiser and we could see Chet huddled in the backseat, coughing.

One of Junebug's officers, Franklin Bedloe, was barking into his radio, calling for backup fire trucks from Bavary. I glanced back at the house. The fire was spreading and my heart sank. That house is one of the most beautiful in Mirabeau, and one of the oldest. I looked up at the smoldering chunk that wasn't there anymore. If I figured right, the room that had been blasted into oblivion was Greg's.

Lorna, beside me, saw it, too. "My God," she yelled. "What the hell is going on in this goddamned town of yours?"

We didn't have a chance to discuss it. There wasn't much of a summer wind, but one burning shingle sailing in the sky could destroy other homes, touching them with the plague of fire. Lorna and I helped Hubert Moore, a neighbor of the bed-and-breakfast, hose down his little antiques shop to keep it from burning. (Even with only one good arm I can still aim a garden hose.) One fire truck arrived and began containing the blaze, quickly joined by two others from Bavary. Junebug and his officers began clearing people back from the heat.

Exhausted, I sat down on the curb, Lorna next to me. I didn't see Candace in the milling crowd in the street. I did see our honorable mayor, Parker Loudermilk, and his wife Dee, watching the fire. Dee looked cold despite the heat, her hands hugging her elbows.

"Back in a sec," I said to Lorna. I went over to approach the Loudermilks and barely caught a hiss from Parker to Dee: "You just keep your mouth shut and get Jenny home."

What was that about? I wondered as I tapped Parker on the shoulder. He fairly jumped, whirled, and put on his best political smile—tempered, you understand, by the unfortunate circumstances.

"Jordy. Terrible shame about the Mirabeau B., isn't it?" Parker wiped a sooty hand across the back of his mouth.

"It's awful." I glanced back over at the blaze. "I know Junebug's doing the best that he can to stop this bomber, Parker, but people are getting really scared now. Someone could've been killed tonight."

Dee made a noise in her throat and looked away from the heat and smoke. "I'm going to go find Jenny," she said in a strangled voice, and turning, she wove into the crowd.

Parker didn't look happy and he glared back at me, his politicking forgotten. I was, after all, his subordinate on the governmental food chain. "Are you questioning my commitment to catching the bomber, Jordy?" His voice held the faintest threat of malice and there was a rigidity in his expression that I didn't like.

I blinked. "Of course not, Parker. I'm just telling you that people are frightened out of their wits. Just look at them!"

He glanced around at the crowd with annoyance. "They're like vultures on a dead coon," he grunted.

"They're your voters, Parker, and if you don't remedy this situation, they're going to vote someone else into office." Notice that I would not make a good politician with such blunt statements.

His lips thinned, and he glanced down at the ground, but when he looked back at me, the public mask was securely in place. Parker pointed at my sling, smiling beatifically. "I know you've already been hurt by all this. We are going to catch whoever's responsible. Assuming that this is the work of the bomber and not just a regular fire or a gas explosion." His eyes traveled back to the dancing flames. Even in the fading light, I could see a fascination in his eyes as the blaze flickered. "It's losing its battle, Jordy. Do you see it? The fire's dying." There was an odd tone to his voice; almost remorseful.

I snorted. "A gas explosion now would be an awful coincidence, Parker. I think that—"

Parker Loudermilk wasn't particularly captivated by my thoughts. He squeezed my shoulder in the fatherly way favored by small-town politicians (I think they all must be sent to a school for that) and said, "Appreciate your citizenly concern, Jordy. Don't worry, we're on top of this." He spun on his heel and headed for the police cruisers.

"I'm sure that will be a great comfort to Chet!" I hollered after his back, but he ignored me. Childish of me to do that, I suppose, but I didn't really think that Parker cared too much about what happened to anyone but himself. Despite the summer warmth and the heat from the fire, I felt a tremor of cold watching him leave.

Abandoned by the gentle patronage of our mayor, I plunged into the crowd, searching for Candace and Lorna. I saw Miss Twyla, Nina, and Tiny, all sitting in Tiny's pickup truck, watching the crowd. I thought of waving at Miss Twyla but didn't want Tiny to fancy I was waving at him.

I found Lorna standing with Dee and Jenny Loudermilk. I could see Jenny was crying. Unless she had an unsuspected emotional attachment to antebellum architecture, it wasn't the destruction of the Mirabeau B. that had reduced her to tears. Lorna looked lost, so I collected her and headed up the road. I glanced back at the Loudermilk women; they both appeared upset as hell. What was going on in that family?

Candace was sitting on a porch two houses up, holding Chet's chubby hand. Eula Mae, never one to be away from the excitement, was holding his other hand. He was fighting back tears as the main chimney in the house shuddered and fell apart, scattering soot and brick and a hundred and sixty years of history.

"Chet, what happened?" I squatted across from him.

His heavy face glanced at me, as though he hadn't known me for years. "I—I don't know. I mean—" He coughed again, as though trying to clear his mind and his throat. Candace patted his back. Lorna came up to us, kneeling next to Candace. Eula Mae stared daggers at Lorna, but Lorna ignored her.

Chet wiped tears from his eyes. "I'd just gone out to

the backyard to put seed in the bird feeders, and there was this horrible explosion. I ran back into the house, I tried to get up the steps, there was all this white smoke, but suddenly fire broke out and the heat, the smoke—they drove me back. So I ran. I just ran."

"Chet, was anyone else in the hotel?"

He shook his head. "I've only got one couple staying, and they went over to Bavary about ten minutes before-hand, to eat at one of the German restaurants. I haven't had any other guests check in since Mr. Callahan died and Lorna left." He broke down, crying now, holding Candace's hand. "Why, why? Why would someone do that?"

I stood, staring up at the charring building. The fire-fighters seemed to have it under control now, but the old house looked gutted. The fire was retreating, but already sated with a diet of fine antiques, expensive fab-rics, handwoven carpets, and the dark memory of Greg's murder. I noticed that one of the fire trucks was maneuvering for a position closer to the west side of the house, and several people were moving a car out of its way. The car was a teal Ford Taurus with RIVERTOWN REAL ESTATE emblazoned on a magnetic sign on the driver's door. Debris from the explosion covered the car, having thoroughly dented its hood and starred the windshield. I watched the volunteers move the dam-aged car and I wondered where its owner was. I'd been meaning to talk to Freddy Jacksill about his deals with Greg.

We sat for another hour, watching the fire die. Neigh-bors offered Chet a place to stay and he accepted mutely, taking a flask of whiskey from one fellow and disappearing into a house across the street. The cop cars and fire trucks stayed, their lights whirling in a red-and-blue dervish. It was as though no one quite wanted to go home.

Lorna and Candace decided to head back to the house; I told them I'd be there shortly. I thought they might not enjoy talking about me so much when I wasn't around, but they'd have to make do.

Junebug was talking with the firemen and Franklin Bedloe, watching the house. A few heavily suited firemen came in and out of the smoldering remains. I wondered how compromised the structure was, if the timbers would give way and collapse at any time. Much of the house still stood, but it looked weak behind its smoky veil.

Junebug nodded at me as I came up. "Hey, Jordy, I guess you heard it all, huh? Were you at home?"

I nodded. "Yeah, and Chet told us what happened. You think it's the bomber? I mean, couldn't it be a gas leak or something?"

"It was a gas fire, but we think the gas line was ruptured by the explosion. That in turn caused the fire." He sighed. "This doesn't exactly fit the bomber's pattern, though, does it? He's just been blowing up little diddly things, not taking out buildings."

"Maybe," I said. "I remember reading about pyromania in college in a psych class and I wonder if the impulse to blow up things is connected to a pyro's impulse to set fires. I remember that they said they tend to start off small and work their way up to bigger targets."

"They say that about serial killers, too," Franklin Bedloe offered helpfully.

"Goddamn it, that's all I need," Junebug muttered. "I already got a killer and a terrorist-in-training. All I need's a serial killer."

"I guess Sergeant Garza should know about this," I suggested quietly.

Junebug didn't smile. "I don't care much for seeing Teresa under these conditions. I'm just thankful no one was hurt."

"Yeah," I answered, then glanced back over at the fire trucks. "You'd think Freddy'd see about getting his car out of here. His insurance agent's going to have a hissy fit when he sees all that damage."

Junebug shot me a look, then followed my pointing finger toward the wrecked Taurus. He glanced back at me. "Have you seen Freddy?"

I shook my head. "No, not today." I paused, then looked back at the remains of the bed-and-breakfast. "Oh, God, you don't think—"

The blaze had died down long enough for some of the firefighters to try to go up to the second floor. It held; they built houses to last back in the olden days. The search was short. They found Freddy at the top of the stairs. And along the second-story hallway. And in Greg's room. And on what was left of the ceiling. Whatever caused the blast, Freddy Jacksill had been right next to it.

When I got home, Candace and Lorna had filled Sister in on the explosion. Sister was nearly frantic and had called my nephew Mark home to stay. Mark's thirteen, a bright independent boy who's never quite recovered from the desertion of his daddy, who vamoosed to play cowboy in the rodeo all those years ago. He's dark like his daddy, but smart-mouthed like Sister and me. We've had a rocky relationship at best, but he'd finally grown to accept me as a more or less permanent part of his life. When I came into the living room, thirsty and wanting a beer, Mark was animatedly telling Lorna how I'd saved his life a few months ago.

Lorna raised an eyebrow at Mark's highly embellished story. "I had no idea you were such a hero," she said.

"Big hero. I nearly got a bunch of folks killed, including myself. Try scared-shitless hero."

"Uncle Jordy was cool!" Mark bragged. "He was in the newspaper and everything." He was obviously still hoping that Nintendo would take heed of my adventures and fashion a video game on me. We still hadn't heard from them.

I told them about Freddy Jacksill being torn apart in

the explosion and the blood drained right from Sister and Lorna's faces. Lorna was quiet, but Sister didn't hold back. "That does it, Mark. There are some extra loonies in town and you're not going anywhere. You're staying right here where it's safe."

"Maybe it's not safe, Arlene," Lorna said quietly. She stood and looked at us all, a wild fear in her gray eyes. "My God. First Greg, now Freddy. Is someone killing everyone that had anything to do with the land deal? What if they come after me next?"

That was a distressing possibility. Several terrified looks crossed the room. I felt the tug of panic at my heart. Candace, as always, was the rock.

"Look, Lorna, we'll get you some protection, okay? Jordy, why don't you call Junebug and see about getting an officer to stand watch here. I'm sure it'd make Lorna feel better."

Lorna gave Candace such a look of gratitude that I felt like hugging them both. "That's a great idea, Candace. I'm sure he can spare someone," I said, and went to make the call. Junebug said he'd send over Franklin Bedloe to serve as a guard. He also told me that Teresa Garza was going to come back to town tomorrow to look over the damage at the Mirabeau B. Lamar. He sounded exhausted, so I wished him a quick good-night.

I think he wasn't the only one worn-out. The folks in my living room looked like death warmed over. Candace announced that she was ready to turn in. She wished Mark, Sister, and Lorna a good evening and thanked Sister for the dinner. I offered to walk her out to her car.

She leaned against my good arm as we approached her Mercedes. The faint glow in the sky that had come from the burning antebellum home was gone, replaced by a smudge of smoke that stars shimmered softly behind.

"Thanks for the suggestion about getting protection

for Lorna," I said. She slid her hand into my back jeans pocket as we walked.

"Protection for all of you while she's in your house," Candace answered softly. She wasn't looking at me, but staring down the street. "I'm sorry Eula Mae decided to interfere and try to get Lorna to go."

"Eula Mae loves to get involved in her little causes. I'm just sorry I always seem to be one of them."

"Eula Mae would never admit it, Jordy, but she loves you like a little brother. She's always going to interfere—that's how she shows her affection."

I nuzzled her neck. "And how do you show your affection?"

She put a hand up to my chest and pushed me away, but gently. "I don't exactly feel like a public display of affection when you're going back into that house where you've ensconced your old girlfriend."

"Wait a minute, honey. You know that it's for her own good."

"I don't doubt Lorna does anything that's not for her own good," Candace said dryly. She slid her hand out from my back pocket, where it had felt oh-so-comfortable, and crossed her arms.

"You're not jealous of her, Candace. You can't be."

"She's funny. She's smart. She's gorgeous. She's loud, too, but I've seen the way that you look at her. You're still attracted to her, and please don't insult my intelligence by denying it."

"Okay, I won't. Yes, I find her attractive. But not as attractive as you." I'm not good at undying protestations of love and I felt coltish and awkward. "Lorna and I are past, okay. For God's sake, don't you trust me around her?"

"I trust you, but not her." She shook her head. "What is the hold she has on you, Jordy? She's conceivably putting your whole family in danger by staying here and yet you roll out the red carpet."

"If you trust me, then you shouldn't have a problem with this."

My heart ached at the pain on her face. "Okay. I love you enough to trust you around her. But I still don't have to like her staying here."

"She's my friend, and I'm not going to abandon her right now."

"That's right. Put everyone else ahead of your own interests." Candace yanked open her car door. I didn't have a decent reply, so I stayed silent. She stood on tiptoe, I leaned down, and we exchanged a quick, dry kiss.

"Sleep well," she said, and drove off.

I love you enough to trust you around her, she'd said. She told me she'd loved me, but I'd been unable to reciprocate the words. My front teeth gnashed on my lip, still warm from her kiss, and I turned and went back into the house.

Mark had been dispatched to bed. His complaints about being treated like an infant filtered down from upstairs. Sister, softening toward our guest in light of this latest trauma, had kindly offered to run Lorna a bath. The gurgling noise of the water in the pipes reminded me of when Mama had run baths for Sister and me when we were little. (This activity was usually followed by her chasing a naked me around the house and forcibly putting me in the tub.) Lorna was sitting, staring down at a colorful quilt that my grandmother Schneider had made decades ago. Her fingers traveled across the patterns and stitches, as though tracing a road on a map.

"This is really lovely, Jordan," she said, not looking up at me. "You're lucky to have such keepsakes in your family. The Wiercinskis were never big on keepsakes."

"Are you okay, Lorna?" I asked. Her voice had taken on a distance I didn't like.

"I am. I think I am." She looked up at me. I could still get lost in the whirlpools of her eyes. "I don't know what to think. Greg being dead, and all his lies.

Now Freddy being blown to bits in Greg's room. It makes no sense."

"We need to talk."

Sister came halfway down the stairs, peering over the railing. "I drew a bath for you, hon. It's nice and warm."

"We'll talk when you're done," I said. She nodded and went upstairs. The doorbell rang and it was Franklin, ready to watch over Lorna and the rest of us. I invited him inside.

"How does this work, Franklin? You want to sleep on the couch, or do you sit out in your cruiser and watch the house, or what?"

"I never guarded anyone like this before," he confessed. "I think it'd be okay if I stayed down in the living room, if that's all right by you." He didn't look pleased at the prospect of spending an entire night in his police car. I couldn't blame him.

Sister showed him where all the sandwich fixings were in the fridge. ("Now, you just help yourself if you get hungry, Franklin. I made that chocolate pie myself and you just can't get better.") Franklin looked pretty pleased at the provisions and promised he'd clean up any mess he made. Sister warned him repeatedly not to shoot Mama in case she wandered downstairs in the night. Franklin assured her he wouldn't.

I took two beers upstairs to Lorna's room when she finished her bath. She had toweled her long hair as dry as she could, but it still hung in a damp cascade around her shoulders. The hot water had pinkened her skin, so she looked more relaxed than I'd seen her since she'd got to town. She wore a simple white robe that fortunately went down to her knees. I remembered a red silk one she'd had, far skimpier, that used to fall off at my touch. I was glad she hadn't packed that one for this trip.

"We need to talk, Lorna." I handed her a beer. She nodded and sipped at her Celis bock.

"First of all, I believe you when you say you didn't know about Greg's plan to resell the land to the chemical company."

She gave me an unreadable look. "It means so much to me to have your trust, Jordan." Her voice wasn't unreadable; it dripped with sarcasm. That word *trust* again. I tried not to visualize Candace's wounded face in the moonlight.

"Look, I was upset. You can imagine how I felt, especially when it seemed you'd lied to me about using my land."

"I still don't see how you could have thought I'd lied," she snapped.

"Let's not argue," I pleaded. "We need to work this mess through. Now, what was your impression of Freddy Jacksill?"

Lorna paused and took a slow sip of her beer. "You know, I remember being surprised when I found out you were originally from a small town; you were worldly in certain respects. But Freddy was exactly what you expected from someone from a little town; he was anxious to be the biggest fish in the bowl. More blustery than self-assured. He was very eager to please Greg, keep him happy. I'm sure that Greg filled Freddy's head with all sorts of garbage about how much money was to be made when Intraglobal acquired the land."

"Who's going to take over Greg's assignments at Intraglobal now that he's dead?"

Lorna opened her mouth, then closed it again. "Well, no one. I mean, maybe me, but the company's nothing without Greg. Unless Doreen Miller wants to keep it going. I don't think Greg was working on any other deals right now."

"Surely there's another senior person . . ."

She shook her head. "Greg didn't like to discuss it when he was out closing a deal, but he's Intraglobal all by his lonesome. It's basically a one-man consulting service with a silent partner. Her name's Doreen Miller; she put up a bunch of the money for Greg."

"Good Lord, Lorna. The name *Intraglobal* makes it sound like they're two steps shy of world domination, not a one-man shop."

She smiled. "I know. I told Greg it was a little misleading, but he said it made us sound more professional."

"Have you talked with this Doreen Miller, told her about Greg's death?"

Lorna shook her head. "I don't know how to get in touch with her. Greg said she was old Boston money; I've never met her."

Odd and odder, I thought. Greg never said that he was a big company, but I'd always had the impression he was.

"We better see about tracking down this Doreen Miller. Junebug said he was going to be calling up to Boston; I'll tell him he needs to find Ms. Miller as well."

Lorna nodded. "Her number must be in a file on Greg's laptop somewhere." I didn't remember seeing it, but I'd double-check anyway.

"One more question. What was going on with the Loudermilk women when you were standing with them? Jenny looked like she was crying and Dee looked upset."

Lorna shrugged. "I don't know. I met them both briefly when I got into town; Greg introduced me to them. They seemed kind of twitchy." She paused. "There's an undercurrent of bad feeling between them; Jenny was sassy to her mother a couple of times while I was at their house, but Dee just ignored it. Typical teen-and-mom strife, I guess."

I didn't answer, lost in thought.

Until I noticed Lorna's hand idly playing along the bedspread, weaving through the two feet of space that separated us. "You've been exceptionally kind to me, Jordan."

I suddenly felt nervous. "Well, sure, Lorna. Glad to."

"I don't excel at playing the helpless female. Neither does Candace. Maybe that's why you like her—she reminds you of me."

I definitely wanted to skirt this discussion. I stood. "Maybe so, Lorna. Listen, it's been an exhausting day. Let's get some sleep." I moved to the light switch, raising one hand in a quick wave of farewell.

"Not going to tuck me in?" she asked coyly. She didn't sound so tired anymore. And her modest white robe had somehow shaped itself to the curves of her generous body.

I stared down at the floor. "No. Like you said, you're not the helpless female. Good night, Lorna." And with that, I made my escape to my own room, like a nervous teenager dashing home without a good-night kiss.

Sleep didn't come easily. I lay awake rehashing all that had happened earlier. First of all, why was Freddy Jacksill in Greg's room? Or near Greg's room? The room had been yellow-taped as a crime scene. Was Freddy simply curious? Or had he had some business in Greg's room he hadn't wanted anyone to know about? Could he have been involved in Greg's scam? Surely not, I thought. It would have ruined his business in town. I needed to know a little more about Freddy Jacksill.

And the explosion—if it was indeed the work of Mirabeau's mad bomber—suggested two possibilities. First, Freddy was the bomber and had planned to blow up the Mirabeau B. (or Greg's room, to be more specific) and the bomb went off prematurely. I thought I could dismiss that theory; Freddy wouldn't know squat about explosives. Second, the bomb had been placed in Greg's room and Freddy was just unlucky enough to be there. Why bomb Greg's room? Perhaps, because of its sudden notoriety in town, it presented itself as an appealing, attention-grabbing target. Why were the bombings happening anyway? Clyda Tepper's ridiculous doghouse, Fred Boolfors's town-famous shed without a single tool that belonged to him (not to mention that legendary collection of *Playboys*), a series of mailboxes exploding in a synchronized dance. There was a strong air of desperate theatricality about the incidents, like a child who throws a particularly creative temper tantrum so he'll be paid extra attention.

The Loudermilks troubled me, too; an air of unhappiness hung about that family, as though they'd recently suffered a loss. Dee's being upset, Parker's weird watching of the fire, Jenny's crying—perhaps I was conjuring up my own theories about the Loudermilks on flimsy suspicion, but my intuition registered that something wasn't right in the mayoral mansion. I gave up worrying about all these folks and finally drifted off to sleep.

I've never been a light sleeper, so I don't know how long Lorna had been lying next to me in the dark hollow of my bed. Her fingers awakened me, rubbing slowly in an arc from my waist up to the basin between my shoulder blades. A kiss touched the tender joint where neck meets back. I jerked awake, aware of her presence and my own involuntary response. I usually sleep in the buff, so I yanked the sheets up to protect my modesty. My arm throbbed when I leaned against it.

"Lorna, what the hell—"

"Jordy. Can I call you that, since everyone else does?" she said, her face very near to mine. "I can't sleep. I'm scared and I'm lonely. I need to feel you near me."

I resented the position she'd put me in—or wanted to put me in. "It's not a good idea, Lorna. Really."

"No one has to know. Candace is okay, I don't want to hurt her. But I have needs, too. I can't be alone right now. You know how good we are together." She was pulling at her own robe with one hand and pulling me toward her with the other.

I pushed back. "No! It's not true that no one would know. *I* would know. I'm sorry things haven't worked out between us. But I'm not risking what I have with Candace just because you want a roll in the hay. Now go back to sleep and we'll talk in the morning."

In the darkness I couldn't see her face clearly, but her silence spoke for her.

"Good night, Jordan. I hope you never need anyone the way I needed you right now." Her voice was like ice on my skin.

When she left the room, I rolled over—somewhat painfully. Until sleep finally claimed me again, I tried not to think of all those wonderful nights in Boston.

CHAPTER TEN

WHEN IT'S A PLEASANT MORNING, MAMA likes to sweep the back porch. The exercise is good for her, the doctors say, and I think she might get a vague comfort out of doing a job well. Alzheimer's patients use simple, repetitive actions as their own security blanket, as though cleaning a porch for six hours replaces having a life full of fear and love and joy and sorrow.

The next morning I found Lorna sitting on the back porch with an unusually dapper Mama, talking to her while Mama clenched her favorite broom. As I poured myself a cup of coffee I could hear Lorna's voice through the screen door.

"Of course Jordan isn't the easiest person to love. I guess you know that. He likes his own way sometimes, and he can get a little sharp-tongued. My mother never could stand him; she thought he was a real hick, despite his urbanity when he lived up north. I hope you're not offended by that, Mrs. Poteet." The gentle swishing of the broom against wood was the only answer. Mama had been unusually quiet since Lorna's arrival. I paused by the door, not wanting to listen—but not being able to help myself. This sounded like the Lorna of old, the one who lived behind the bravado, and the one I'd been missing.

"I think I understand now how Jordan felt when he lived up north. Missing home doesn't sound so silly anymore. Of course he had you and Arlene and Mark to come home to. I've got a sick fern and a pile of bills."

I coughed loudly in the kitchen and slammed a cupboard door, letting her know I was around. Suddenly I didn't want to hear much about Lorna's lonely life up north. Maybe it was lonely now only because Greg was dead.

She met my eyes as I came out onto the porch with the coffee, then glanced up toward heaven. "Gorgeous day, isn't it?" was all Lorna ventured by means of conversation. I had to agree with her. The Saturday-morning sky was a faultless blue, shimmering toward white in the early-morning warmth. It was going to be another hot summer day, without a hint of rain. Or at least for the next five minutes. They say if you don't like the weather in Texas, wait five minutes and it'll change. Summer afternoons often brought quick, drenching showers when moist air pushed in from the Gulf. Afterward, it was like being in a sauna, your clothes adhering to your skin in the heavy humidity. It wasn't raining now, though, and I blinked up at the fine blue sky. It offered a conversational refuge.

"Yes, it's real pretty." I stared down into my coffee cup. I wasn't going to ask her how she'd slept. "I'm going to have to go into the library. Can you entertain yourself for a while?"

"I'm quite good at that." Lorna tucked her feet under her bottom. She glanced over at Mama. "Maybe I'll just stay here and keep your mother company." She blinked at me. "I'm sorry I never got to meet her before she got sick."

"Me, too. I think y'all would have liked each other." I didn't know what else to say; I didn't believe that myself. Mama would have thought Lorna far too brassy, I feared. I finished my coffee. "I got to go. I'll talk to you later."

"Here you are." Sister strode out onto the deck, nodding a good morning at Lorna. "Are you ready to go over to the cemetery? C'mon, Mama, let's go. Mark's in the car."

I felt like I'd walked onto a stage and I didn't know my next line. "Cemetery? Freddy's funeral surely isn't today, is it?"

Sister's green eyes steeled. "Jordan Michael Poteet, you have forgotten that today is the anniversary of Daddy's death. Six years ago. I thought we'd go over this morning before work and put flowers on his grave." She glanced at Lorna. "I guess you've had too much on your mind."

"Oh, God, Sister, I'm sorry. I totally forgot. Yes, let's go and do that now." My face felt hot with shame and embarrassment. Daddy's death had just about killed me; he'd been my best friend, my pal, my mentor, until the cancer took him in a slow, agonizing embrace. I couldn't believe I had forgotten, especially in light of learning that Bob Don was my biological father.

"I've got an order waiting for us at Neuberg's Florist," Sister said, ushering Mama inside and pausing on the doorway. "Lorna, I'm sure you understand that the family needs some privacy right now. Franklin said he could stay on guard until eleven, then they'll have someone replace him."

"Of course, Arlene. You guys go on to the cemetery. I'll be fine." She forced a smile and followed us inside.

The Mirabeau cemetery, lying far from the river on the east side of town, is beautifully maintained—an expanse of clipped grass, marked by marble monuments to lives once lived. A gravel road cuts a circle through the middle; beyond it lie the oldest graves, those with solely German names, denoting the earliest Bavarian colonists who settled the river land. The dead here start in the 1830s, and in a back corner lie markers with only first names, those of the few slaves that lived in this section of Bonaparte County and only found equality in their cold coffins.

I parked my Chevy Blazer near the Poteet section; there were at least twenty tombstones with that sur-

name. My mother's people, the Schneiders, outnumber
the Poteets considerably and there are even some of
them in the old German section. I have not ever looked
to see how well represented Bob Don's people are.

"My, it's going to be hot today." Sister fanned herself
with a brochure from the florist as I struggled to pull
the wreath out of the back. She'd abandoned her earlier
frostiness to me, but I sensed I wasn't entirely out of
the doghouse. Mark stood, holding Mama's hand.
Mama seemed to know she was around old friends and
happily gossiped with the breeze.

We walked over to Daddy's grave, looking lonely in its
plot of Poteet land. His own parents were a bit farther
away, and the plots next to him—the ones reserved for
Mama, me, Sister, and Mark—were, of course, empty. I
wondered if he missed us as much as I missed him.

Sister and I set up the wreath, steadying it against the
granite marker. Sister inspected the grave, making sure
no fire ants had desecrated our father's rest. I stepped
back to admire our handiwork. Sister frowned at me, as
though I'd missed a cue.

"Well? Aren't you going to say anything?" she demanded.

"What? You want me to make a speech?" I pointed at
the wreath. "Doesn't that say enough?"

She stared at the flowers, and her tears came quickly.
She cried silently for several minutes, Mark leaning
against her in comfort, Mama watching a pair of bees
dance above her husband's stone. I crossed my arms,
stared down at my shoes, and kept my own thoughts. Finally Sister wiped her face, sniffled, and said: "Mark.
Take your grandmother to the car. I need to talk to Uncle
Jordy a minute."

"Aw, Mom, it's hot in the car—"

"Here. Turn on the air conditioner." I tossed the keys
at Mark and he went, knowing she would brook no argument. Mama laughed as they stumbled among the
graves, winding their way back to the road.

"Look, Sister, I'm sorry I forgot—"

"You just tell me, Jordy. I need to know. Are you forgetting about him? Does he not matter to you anymore, now that you've got a new father?"

I blinked. "Of course he matters to me. How could you ask that? I could never forget Daddy!"

"You did today. I realize that all this mess with Lorna has you distracted, but you don't ever talk about Daddy anymore. We used to laugh about his old Aggie jokes, the way he could impersonate Cousin Pearl, how he taught us to play baseball when we were kids. You don't ever mention that now."

I shook my head. "This is crazy."

"Is it? You've got a new father, one that's just chomping at the bit to be the World's Greatest Dad to you. I don't have that luxury. I've buried my daddy. I don't have a replacement waiting in the wings."

"No one—not even Bob Don—could replace Daddy, Sister. Bob Don may want to be a father to me, but hell, I'm still not used to the idea of him being my father. If you think this has been hard on you, you don't have a clue what it's been like for me." I knelt by Daddy's wreath and fingered the ribbon of blue—his favorite color—that hung from the circle of flowers. "And my having a relationship with Bob Don—*if* I choose to have one—doesn't mean I've betrayed Daddy."

"I'm not so sure I believe that, Jordy."

I stood. "Have you forgotten that Mama, Mark, and I would probably be dead if it wasn't for Bob Don?"

"No, I haven't forgotten. Have you forgotten that your precious Bob Don slept with our mother when she was married to Daddy?"

"Hardly." I patted my chest. "You wouldn't have *me* to torture if he hadn't."

"And that's the man you have as a father now." She wiped her tears and pointed down at the grave we stood arguing over. "I'm angry. I'm angry the man who could have broken up our parents' marriage wants to be in our lives. And don't say it's just your life. It's mine, too. You're my brother and I love you. But I'm furious and I've got every right to be."

I shrugged. "I don't know what to say to you. I don't know what I even want from Bob Don. I'm certainly not prepared to dismiss him from my life. You can't ask me to do that."

"No. I don't expect that."

I heard the distant whine of a car and saw a steel-gray Cadillac Seville churning dust along the cemetery road. "God, does he have radar?" Sister asked. We watched Bob Don's Caddy park behind my Blazer. He got out of the car, smoothing his crown of hair into place, carrying a large bouquet of flowers.

"My God, he remembered and you didn't." Sister walked in Bob Don's direction as he tentatively approached Daddy's grave. "Hi, Bob Don. I'm sure you and your son would like some time together."

He heard the hardness in her voice. "I'm sorry, Arlene. I didn't mean to interrupt."

"Give Jordy a ride to the library, would you? I have to take Mama home." She didn't wait for a reply.

I remained silent as he laid the flowers on Daddy's grave, the only noise the retreating engine of my car as my sister gunned it down the cemetery path.

"Thanks for coming," I said, at a loss for original conversation. "I'm a little surprised you're here."

"I'd planned to stop by today, but I called and Lorna said y'all were out here. I hoped you wouldn't mind me coming out while you were here."

"I don't mind. I can't speak for my sister."

He tucked his hand into the back of his well-worn khakis. "She still ain't used to me. That's okay. It'll take some time."

"Yeah, but she has to be willing to give you that time, Bob Don. She's not exactly comfortable with what you represent in our family's past."

"Boy, you are the biggest brooder I ever saw." Bob

Don smiled up at me, shielding his eyes from the morning glare. "I've always believed that a man should go on with what life dealt him and try not to fret about it so much."

The thought rose in my mind, unbidden: Maybe that's why you could wait until my mother was crazy and my daddy was dead to tell me the truth. It wasn't fair; he'd only been holding up his end of a damnably hard bargain. "I don't mean to be a brooder. I suppose I have more than my share to fret over."

"Arlene messing with your head?"

"No. Lorna and Candace." I kicked at the grass. "I got women troubles, Bob Don. I got one in my house that needs me and one that's pretty upset about the situation."

"You love that Lorna?" Bob Don has never been one for beating around bushes.

"I did once, I think. I'm not sure. I don't know what love is."

"Now that, boy, is unadulterated bullshit." Bob Don put his hands on his ample hips and shook his head at me.

"Excuse me?"

"Nobody who was raised with as much love as you could say they don't know what love is. Your mama loves you." He pointed down at Lloyd Poteet's grave. "And you can't tell me that man didn't love you. God, he loved you. And your sister and your nephew love you, and I do believe Miss Candace Tully loves you. You've known more love in your life than most, Jordy. So don't try telling me that you can't figure out what to do about them gals 'cause you don't know what love is. You're just goddamned lazy." He imitated a drawly rasp of a whine on the last few words that I was sure represented my voice.

I started to parry with a sharp reply, but ended up staring down at Daddy's grave. Bob Don'd scored a hit against me and I knew it. I ran a finger along the clay-red granite top of Daddy's marker, the stone beginning to heat in the rising temperature. "Do I love Lorna? I'm sure I did once."

"Once ain't now."

"No, it's not. A lot's changed. I'm not sure what I want. If I was back with her—"

"You could go on back to big ol' Boston town and not fret no more about having a new daddy and a sick mama." Bob Don, awkwardly, put a beefy hand on my shoulder. And as I looked into his face I saw that folks had been wrong; I wasn't the spitting image of my mother. There was a lot of his face in mine—the wide eyes, the gentle taper of the nose, the high cheekbones, and the ruddy skin. Standing over my daddy's grave, I nearly shuddered at the shock of the realization.

"I'm not interested in ducking my obligations, Bob Don."

"I wasn't suggesting you were. God knows I'm not one to accuse some soul of avoiding responsibility. But I think I know what that Yankee gal means to you. Your old life back, with none of these complications. You may love Candace and your mama, but they make life a little harder to live."

"Can you take me to the library? I'm running late now and if I lose my job, my life will be complicated for sure."

"Glad to, son." He glanced down at the double spray of flowers on Daddy's grave. "See, Lloyd? I'm doing my best to take care of him now. Just like I promised."

I spent the rest of that Saturday morning doing library business: drafting a grant application for more government money (the competition among rural libraries can be intense), ordering some new children's books (that's our fastest-growing section—we're a fertile bunch in Mirabeau), and getting advice on how to heal my arm from our elderly patrons, many of whom still believe that a shot of whiskey mixed in a dollop of honey will cure pert near anything.

I'd called Junebug earlier in the morning and told him what Lorna had told me about Greg's business and his silent partner, Doreen Miller. He hadn't called back with any news.

Eula Mae and Nina Hernandez stopped by to festoon the library bulletin board with colorful flyers that proclaimed JOIN SAVE OUR RIVER ECOLOGY (S.O.R.E.)! CONTRIBUTE AND PROTECT MIRABEAU'S FUTURE.

"I hope," I observed acidly while watching Eula Mae indiscriminately shoot the cork with a staple gun, "that those flyers are printed with nontoxic inks on recycled paper."

"Of course they are!" Nina retorted. She seemed to have recovered from her interrogation after Greg's murder and to be possessed of a new zeal to defeat the land-acquisition plans.

I winced as they stapled right over my poster for the summer reading program. "I don't think there's much chance of Intraglobal continuing with their plans for Mirabeau. Greg Callahan has one silent partner that no one can find yet, and she'll probably want to pull out."

"We aren't taking that chance." Eula Mae smirked. "If it's not Intraglobal, it'll be some other scum-sucking outfit of post-Eighties yuppies looking for one last frontier to ruin. Nina and I are amassing a good-sized war chest to fight development on the river."

"Just how big has this gotten, Eula Mae?" She is one, after all, to throw herself entirely into a project. Lucky she's never developed an interest in quicksand.

"We've raised nearly fifty-five thousand dollars," Eula Mae said, the pride evident in her voice. "With more pledged on the way. We're going to hold a big dance over at the Veterans' Hall, and we've got people going door-to-door to solicit contributions, and—"

"And you are about to staple those to the bricks. Give me that." I wrested the staple gun from her over-eager hand before she could attach the next notice to a spot beyond the bulletin board.

"Well, aren't you a mite grumpy? Things tense over at the Chateau de Yankee Amour?" Eula Mae asked sweetly, grabbing the staple gun back from me.

"Everything is fine," I replied. "Don't y'all have somewhere else to go? Or someone else to bother? I can't believe Miss Twyla is letting the two of you run this." I usually have a saint's patience with Eula Mae, but today I felt decidedly heretical.

"Miss Twyla has her mind on strategic matters. C'mon, Nina," Eula Mae said, shaking her head sadly at me. "Jordy is just upset he's not going to be able to sell that land of his now. Of course *he's* probably getting ready to go back to Boston anyway, where I'm sure they're used to having nasty polluted rivers." With that parting shot, she left the field, an equally haughty Nina in tow.

With the S.O.R.E. Sisters dismissed, I'd just finished eating a ham sandwich I'd fixed in our little back kitchen when Gretchen arrived.

I can't say I wasn't pleased to see Gretchen. She'd gobbled that annoying Billy Ray Bummel like a freetail bat on a skeeter, and I had to like her a little for that. Even if the rest of the time she could be a bitch.

She paused in front of my desk, dressed nicely in a chambray skirt and white dress shirt, turquoise and silver dripping from her neck, wrists, and ears. Her graying hair had that just-did look.

"Jordy, how are you?"

"Fine, Gretchen, and you?" I wiped away the last of the crumbs on my mouth. Since I didn't have a napkin, I had to use the back of my hand. One Gretchen eyebrow arched and I tensed myself for criticism. As though she could say anything about my bad manners; I'd seen her stinking drunk.

"Better than this morning. I thought you might like to know that oaf Billy Ray was just out at our house grilling Bob Don. He is absolutely fixated on that wire that the killer used to strangle poor Mr. Callahan."

I blinked. "He can't think Bob Don had anything to do with this. It's ridiculous."

"The ridiculous is Billy Ray's specialty," Gretchen snorted. "He's totally ignoring that the fence isn't just on our property. It's on the line with the Loudermilks' property."

"That's true." I nodded. "But maybe he's already questioned the Loudermilks about it."

"I seriously doubt that. Parker Loudermilk says jump and Billy Ray says how high. Even though Billy Ray doesn't work for Parker, he just can't stifle that suck-up reflex of his."

I thought for a moment. "Why are you telling me this, Gretchen?" She was coming to me as an ally, but she'd certainly never encouraged my relationship with my birth father before. I was suspicious; it would be just like Gretchen to pretend to make pleasant overtures to me then slap me silly when I let my guard down. If Bob Don had told her we'd had a heart-to-heart out at the cemetery, she'd be envious as hell. Gretchen is the kind of lady that if you had a heart transplant, she'd want one, too.

Her lipsticked mouth thinned into a red line. "That's a mean thing to ask. Obviously I want you to know that they're bothering your—Bob Don." She still couldn't say the words *your father*, hadn't been able to since the night she'd drunkenly, meanly informed me of my parentage. She set her blue leather purse on my desk. "I just thought you might like to know. So you can give him a call. Or maybe you can get Billy Ray to lay off him."

"Thanks, Gretchen, I will call him." I glanced around the library; on such a fine summer day we were nearly deserted, except for permanent-fixture Old Man Renfro in the corner, reading a collection of Wallace Stevens's poetry. "Can I ask you a question? I'm just curious why you had lunch with Greg Callahan the day he died. I understand he was supposed to have lunch with the Chamber of Commerce that day."

She measured me with a long stare. There was something dull still in her eyes, even if she'd laid off the liquor. I'm not sure after all those years of drinking that a person could just spring back to life. I had to admire Gretchen though; she could take up for herself.

"Yes, he did mention that he was supposed to have lunch with the Chamber of Commerce officers, but they'd had to cancel. I don't know why. He ran into me outside the Sit-a-Spell and asked me to lunch."

"You'd met him before?"

She smiled. "Why, yes, he'd come out to the house to offer Bob Don money for our riverfront land."

"Really? Bob Don said that he'd come and seen him at the car dealership."

"He was looking for Bob Don, so he came out to the house first." Her words spilled out quickly, too quickly. "So I sent him over to the dealership."

"I just wondered."

"It's really none of your business, though, who I have lunch with."

"But he didn't know many folks in town, and he ended up murdered. I'm sure the police have already questioned you—"

"Oh, that idiotic friend of yours, Junebug? Honestly. I do wish that Bob Don would run for mayor someday so he'd fire that incompetent."

"He's not incompetent. Or is he just an idiot because he's my friend?"

She smiled, back on familiar territory, with the battle lines drawn between us. "You, as always, have a high opinion of how much you bother me. You don't bother me, little boy." *Little boy* was her favorite nonendearment for me and I knew when she used it that I was hitting nerves.

She fumed on: "You think I'm the queen bitch in

town, anyway, no matter what I do. I come here to tell you that Bob Don might need some support and you attack me."

"No, I don't think you are the queen bitch, Gretchen, and I didn't attack you." I forced myself to take a long breath. "Can't we try and make peace, please? I know you don't like me being in your and Bob Don's lives much and I'm sorry that it upsets you, but I am here. I'm here to stay." The words came easily, far more easily than they ever could talking to one father over another father's grave.

"If you're so proud of having Bob Don as your daddy, why haven't you announced it to all the world?" Her bottom lip curled. "You sorry hypocrite. You accuse me of interfering with your relationship with my husband, and then you don't have the nerve to own up to what you're defending. You really are just a little fraud." She leaned down into my face and I could smell the vaguely unpleasant odor of sweat under powder. "What did that Yankee gal see in you, anyhow? What does someone who counts in this town like Candace Tully see in you?"

"I know what Bob Don sees in you, Gretchen. Someone to feel sorry for." She stiffened and drew back. I felt bad for taunting her about her problem, but she'd hit a raw nerve with me and I'd lashed back without giving much thought.

"As long as you're casting aspersions, why don't you look in your own house for someone to grill?" Her voice had a hollowness to it, like her throat had been drained of blood.

"Yeah, right, like I'd believe anything you say." She'd rip Lorna to shreds if she thought it would hurt me.

She shrugged. "Makes no never mind to me, little boy. But you might want to be more careful about who you have taking care of your precious mama."

"What did you say?"

"That snooty nurse of yours. I saw her talking three

days ago with Greg Callahan, in his car. I didn't know who he was then, of course, but I recognized him when I met him. 'Cause I wondered why Clo Butterfield was sitting in a car down in the town square with a rich-lookin' white fellow."

"You're making this up."

Her smile was pure enjoyment. "I'm afraid not. He was probably wantin' to know just how poor you are so he could entice you to sell him your land. I mean, Clo Butterfield could probably tell him just how much financial strain you're under. You got to depend on Bob Don to pay her measly old salary."

"If Clo was talking with Greg, I'm sure there's a good reason." I couldn't think of one, though. And why hadn't she mentioned it?

"Ask her," Gretchen suggested unhelpfully. "But if you fire her, don't be expecting Bob Don to hire you another one. You're lucky he's even willing to put up the money for your crazy old mother anyway."

I stood, feeling heat in my hands. "I think that's enough, Gretchen. Maybe you should go."

Gretchen tucked her purse back under her arm. "I'm sorry I even tried to talk to you about Bob Don. I can only tell him that I once again made an effort to be friendly to you and you pushed me away." She turned on her heel in a way I'm sure she'd mastered from watching soap operas and took her leave, whisking arrogantly out of my office.

I could only imagine what sort of version of this incident Bob Don would hear. Gretchen was right on one point, though. I hadn't publicly owned up to Bob Don being my dad. And he was caught between two people that he cared about who obviously had nothing better to do than snipe at each other.

I made myself sit down. Clo with Greg? What the hell was that about? Or was it just a lie on Gretchen's part to rile me up?

I picked up the phone and dialed Bob Don's number.

He answered on the first ring, his drawling voice sounding tired.

"Bob Don? Hey, it's Jordy."

"Hi, son, how are you?"

"I'm fine. Listen, Gretchen was just by and said that Billy Ray was giving you a hard time about that wire. You okay?"

"Oh, I'm fair to middlin'. I think he's figgered that I didn't have anything to do with that poor feller's murder. Once he saw that Callahan was going to offer me fifty thousand for that land, he realized I would have been a sight happier with Callahan alive."

"Fifty thousand? Wow." I wondered if my land, somewhat smaller in size than Bob Don's lot, would have fetched such a high price.

"Gretchen told you they were bothering me? That was decent of her to come by and see you." His voice held a shred of hope that there'd be peace between his wife and son.

I opened my mouth to tell him how charmed I'd been by sweet Gretchen's visit, then shut it. "Yes, it was thoughtful."

"You are trying, aren't you, Jordy, to get along with her?"

"Sure, Bob Don."

"Good, 'cause I've been awful worried about her. I been wondering if she's been nippin' a bit when she gets upset."

I cleared the stone from my throat. "You mean drinking?"

"Yeah. I don't have proof, but after Callahan got killed, she seemed a little tight. But I couldn't smell it on her breath, and I couldn't find a bottle anywhere, so I couldn't say anything. It might've been nothing; she just might've been upset. It's unnervin' when someone you just met dies."

"You're right about that," I murmured. Great, Gretchen might be leaning back toward the bottle and here I was giving her a little shove. I hoped I hadn't upset her too much with our bickering. The last crisis Bob Don needed was Gretchen tumbling out of sobriety.

Bob Don asked about Lorna and Mama; I assured him they were fine. He invited me to have lunch with him next week and I accepted.

"Well, goodbye, son. I enjoyed our talk this morning. You call me if I can help," he finally said.

"I will. Thanks. Goodbye." I hung up. He called me son all the time, and I called him by his Christian name. I couldn't call him Dad; I'd already had a father I'd loved and lost. I abhorred the prospect of hurting Bob Don, but I couldn't help myself. Bricks walled in my tongue anytime I thought of referring to him in fatherly terms. I went back to my work, rolling my eyes at the administrivia involved in grant writing and wondering if robbing banks would be simpler.

Junebug called me later, sounding bone weary on the other end of the line. "Teresa examined the house today. She's pretty sure that Freddy was holding the explosive when it went off. It was about a 14 ½-inch pipe bomb, and we think it was in a briefcase." He paused. "Chet might be able to rebuild, but it's going to be a long process. He might just tear the Mirabeau B. down and start again."

I swallowed; that house had been a part of growing up for every native of Mirabeau, and I couldn't imagine some new building in its place. I concentrated on what Junebug had said about Freddy.

"So what the hell does it mean that Freddy was next to the bomb?" I asked. "He's the mad bomber and he blew himself up? I can't see Freddy doing anything to hurt real-estate prices, and terrorism does have that effect on the market. Unless he wanted to blow up the Mirabeau B. to build a fast-food restaurant."

Junebug didn't laugh at my tasteless humor. "I don't know. I also am trying to track down that Doreen Miller Lorna told you about. Haven't found her yet. I got the

Boston police going through Intraglobal's offices, but they haven't found anything. Doesn't seem like Mr. Callahan kept too many records."

Odder and odder. "Well, what about Greg's lawyer, that Martin Noone fellow? Or this Gary Zadich that Greg was going to sell the land to?"

"I talked to Zadich today. He says he never even heard of Greg Callahan or Intraglobal, but I'm not sure I believe him. He sounds like a Houston wharf rat to me. I got the chief over in Bavary talking to Mr. Noone, but he says he only met once with Callahan to discuss being the attorney of record on the deal. He doesn't know anything about Callahan or Intraglobal."

Junebug paused. "I did learn a singularly interestin' fact, though. Did you know Tiny Parmalee worked with explosives when he was in the army?"

"Now I know the Department of Defense needs more careful monitoring," I muttered. "Are you serious?"

"Yep. I think Sergeant Garza and I may have to have a few talks with ol' Tiny."

Tiny Parmalee as the bomber? It'd never occurred to me; frankly I didn't think he would know lickety about pipe bombs or blasting caps. Apparently I was wrong. I suddenly remembered his gibe at me at the library about nearly getting blown up. My mouth felt dry and I switched topics.

"I'm wondering something, Junebug, if you can tell me. There was that phone number written on the pad in Greg's room. Did you find out who that belonged to?"

There was silence on the other end. "Yeah, but I think I better keep that close to my vest."

"Oh, come on! I helped you with that computer stuff. I'm just curious as to who Greg was calling." If he'd been having little tête-à-têtes with Clo, God only knew who else in town he'd been visiting. Perhaps he and Sister had gone canoeing on the river, or he'd taken Mama to the movies in Bavary.

"I'm counting on your discretion, Jordy," Junebug warned.

"You got it." I practically leaned into the phone.

"Which is why I know you won't ask me again. Goodbye." The phone clicked in my ear, which was good. I didn't want Junebug to hear what I called him. I finished my day's work on writing the grant request and left the library in the hands of Florence Pettus. (On an incredible summer day like today, it was as empty as last year's bird nest.) Then I headed toward Freddy Jacksill's office. He'd ended up dead as well, and I wondered if I could piece any of this jigsaw together if I started in his corner.

Rivertown Real Estate stood in a corner spot in Mirabeau's downtown block, right off Mayne Street. It occupied the bottom two floors in a faded red-brick building. Like several of the other buildings in downtown Mirabeau, it had 1844 carved into its stone, signifying the year the town began its one and only major growth spurt. Being a Saturday, there wasn't much activity going on in the business district, except for a few old men sipping cold Dr Peppers in the shade of the hardware store. A CLOSED sign hung lopsided on the door, but I could see Freddy's partner, Linda Hillard, on the phone at the front desk. I tapped and she waved at me, still speaking into the phone. Trying the doorknob, I found it unlocked and stepped into the welcoming coolness of air-conditioning.

Linda was practically barking into the phone, in her raspy smoker's voice: "Yes, Miz Tyree. I understand that you were supposed to close on your house this Monday. But Freddy's dead, ma'am, and we may just have to push it back. I haven't been able to find your file." A moment's silence. "Yes, Miz Tyree, I know that life goes on." Linda made an obscene gesture toward the receiver while still keeping her saleswoman's smile firmly in place. "Yes, I'll call the title company and see if we can proceed on schedule. Yes, Miz Tyree, I'll call you back later. Goodbye now." Linda slammed the phone down and muttered, "Mean old bitch!" She didn't seem to notice that I'd come in for a moment as she ran her hand through her short red hair and adjusted her tortoise-rim eyeglasses. Then she glanced up at me and managed a smile. Linda keeps our romance section at the library circulating pretty well. "My favorite librarian. How are you?"

"Fine, thanks. I wanted to stop by and say how sorry I was about Freddy."

"Oh, thanks, Jordy. I shouldn't even be here, but Freddy had so much business going on all over the county that I've been on the phone all day calling his accounts. I just can't leave 'em dangling; my competitors over in Bavary might pick them up, and I can't afford that. Don't I sound awful?" She blinked back tears behind her thick glasses. "Freddy's dead and I'm worrying about stupid old land. I have just become every negative real-estate stereotype."

I sat down next to her. "No, you haven't. All you can do right now is cope and do your best."

She gestured to the back of the office. "I got some coffee brewing, and my mama brought me a fresh peach pie this morning. Want a piece?"

I nodded and followed Linda back to the small kitchen area of the office. "I suppose you're here for the same reasons that Miss Twyla and the Loudermilks have been bugging me all morning. Not to mention that crazy tree hugger from Austin."

"Uh . . . I don't know. I did want to talk to you about Greg Callahan."

Linda made a face as she cut two good-sized wedges from the pie. The crust looked that perfect brown you only get with home-baked pies and my mouth began to water. "I'm tired of hearing about him. I'm starting to think he was nothing but a crook."

"Why do you say that, Linda?" I asked carefully. Obviously Junebug hadn't yet spilled Greg's land scam.

She placed a plate of pie, a dessert fork, and a linen napkin in front of me (Linda is a details person), then turned back to the coffee machine. "Decaf okay with you? I'm too hyper to drink octane."

"Fine," I said. "I think Greg might have been a crook, too."

"He tried to buy your land, right?"

"Well, his colleague Lorna Wiercinski made a pitch to me about it. I knew her in Boston." No need to tell Linda more; she was a gossip. That's why I was talking to her.

"Oh, that tall girl. She's a looker. I thought Callahan might be chasing after her, but I didn't know. Lord knows Freddy would've liked to get to know her better." Linda's hazel eyes misted. "Poor Freddy. I guess he won't get to annoy any more women. Old sweet thing never did get flirting down right. And poor sugar thought this Intraglobal deal was his lucky ticket. He kept hinting about how much money he'd make, even after poor Mr. Callahan got killed."

I sipped at my coffee. It tasted slightly smoky and stale. I tasted the peach pie—perfection: sweet and sticky and crisp. "Did you spend much time around Callahan?"

It was a simple question, but it seemed to require ample consideration from Linda and several chomps of pie. "I didn't see too much of him—he was Freddy's pet project. Freddy had this image of getting some huge commission off the land sales and didn't want me horning in." She coughed, as though attempting to dislodge further information from her throat.

I pulled. "I thought there was something shady about him, too, Linda."

It didn't require much of a yank to get her talking again. She leaned forward, as though the remains of the peach pie might have ears. "Not as much shady as lecherous. I think he was stirring up a mess at the Loudermilk place."

I bit my bottom lip. It had been obvious during the fire that Jenny and Dee Loudermilk were both unusually distraught, and Parker had seemed angry with Dee, telling her to keep her mouth shut.

"I thought something was going on between all of them when the Mirabeau B. was burning down," I confided. "Parker seemed awful mad at Dee, but I didn't know why."

My tidbit sparked Linda's interest. She toyed with a slice of peach on her plate. "Well, he ought to be mad at that daughter of his, too. She's nothing but a conniving little slut."

"What, you mean Greg was chasing after Jenny *and* Dee?" I forgot to lower my voice, and although the office was empty, Linda shushed me.

"Chased and caught, I do believe. But I'm not certain."

"Wait a second, Linda, he wasn't even here that long. And he wasn't even that good-looking." I was still irked that Lorna had taken Greg for a lover, so my memories of him were not kind ones. "How on earth did he seduce a mother and a daughter in that short time?"

Linda shrugged. "Well organized? Or well something. I don't know. I just know that I caught Freddy admonishing him to stay away from Dee and Jenny if he didn't want to sour the land deal."

I slumped. "Well, that's hardly evidence of an affair, Linda."

"Give me more credit than that, Jordy. Callahan was using the phone plenty to sweet-talk Jenny Loudermilk. I, well, accidentally"—the word was ever so slightly emphasized—"picked up line four when I was trying to hit line three last Monday morning and heard Greg asking Jenny to meet him."

"How do you know it was Jenny?"

"He kept calling her Jen babe. As soon as I heard that petulantly whiny voice, I knew it was her."

"And what were they meeting for?"

"To talk." Linda made it sound like it was illegal. "And they had to be careful so they didn't get caught, he said that in particular."

I mulled this over; Linda took my silence as judgment.

"Look, I don't usually eavesdrop. I was just protecting this agency. I didn't like Freddy being so involved with Greg anyhow—we hardly knew anything about him. He seemed too polished, too perfect in how he presented himself. Not a wart on the man." She sniffed. "I mean, you could ask Jenny or Dee. They might know if he had any warts."

"Have you told all this to Junebug?" I asked.

Linda glanced down at the remnants of her peach pie. "Yeah, but he didn't seem too interested in it."

I leaned back in my chair. Assume, I told myself, for one moment that what Linda says is true. Greg sleeps with Jenny. Greg sleeps with Dee. Does either woman know about the other's involvement? And what about Parker? What would he do if he thought either his wife or daughter had been seduced by this Yankee interloper? And if Freddy found out about Greg's alleged misconduct with the ladies Loudermilk, could that give Parker a motive to silence both men? Freddy had said he'd make money even *after* Greg was dead. I remembered Parker Loudermilk's dark eyes, the consuming blaze dancing in the black ballroom of his irises, his comment on the fire's momentarily satisfying beauty. And I felt a chill in my heart.

CHAPTER ELEVEN

JENNY LOUDERMILK ANSWERED THE FRONT door and no one could lean more provocatively into a doorway than she did. She seemed determined to live up to Linda's image of her. She was real pretty, like her mother, except darker like her dad. A lock of luxuriant brown hair hung down over one eye. She was wearing a T-shirt one size too small, and beneath the fabric, the swell of breasts looked perfect. Snug jeans finished her wardrobe. Her feet were bare and her toenails were immaculately painted a shade of dark scarlet. The whole stance had the air of not-so-subtle calculation.

"Hello, Miss Loudermilk. Are your folks at home?"

She regarded me with a bored eye. "Mom's out back, throwing a pot. Daddy's not here, though. You're the library fellow, right?"

"Yes, that's right. Jordan Poteet." I offered her my hand. She took it limply, gave it a shake, and then trailed her fingertips along my fingers when she let my hand go. My fingers felt itchy, but I kept them still.

"I was just having a drink. You want one?" I thought she meant drink of water, but I realized with a jolt that she meant alcohol. The glassiness of her eyes looked like it had been poured from a bottle of wine.

"I don't think that I should drink with you. I doubt your parents would approve." I'm sure I sounded like a total prude, but what else was I supposed to say? Call me old-fashioned, but I don't hold with teenagers getting drunk in the middle of the day. And I would hazard a guess that drinking with my boss's daughter is not de rigueur in Mirabeau government. (Yes, I'm a hypocrite. I drank beer as a teenager, but I only did it while sitting in the back of a pickup truck. I certainly didn't invite folks in for cocktails.)

She opened the door wider. "What would you know about what they approve of? Believe me, there's not much." She turned and walked away, her gait slightly unsteady. I stepped inside the foyer and shut the door behind me.

My first sensation was of antiseptic; even the air smelled as if it'd been scrubbed. The Loudermilk place was big; Parker's construction company was one of the most successful in the tri-county area, and Loudermilk money was old money. The foyer I stood in had a fancy, swirled marble floor in gray and white, and the wallpaper of gray, black, and silver stripes looked expensive. One entryway opened into a living room that hadn't seen much living; it was decorated with glazed pots of all shapes and sizes, no doubt the product of Dee's hands and wheel. She'd painted them with all sorts of figures—stylized antelopes in graceful leaps, Egyptian letters (I recognized the ankh, the symbol of life), and Native American totems. Lifted from other cultures, I thought, without a single symbol from her own heritage. Maybe our culture was just uninteresting to Dee, I reflected. Not even a pot with the Fighting Bees of Mirabeau High on it. I'd stepped away when I noticed the shards in the corner; one of the pots had fallen, smashing into bits on the hardwood floor. It was a shame; it looked like it was a real pretty one, with geometric shapes in red and green painted on it. I wondered why no one had cleaned it up, in this immaculate house.

Jenny saw my eyes staying near the shattered pot. "What can I say?" She shrugged. "I'm a klutz."

I glanced elsewhere; the other entryway opened into

a formal dining room with an impeccably tasteful cherry dining table and a huge china and silver cabinet.

"You coming or you just gawking?" Jenny Loudermilk bleated back at me. I cut through the dining room and found her in a spacious kitchen. It gleamed white—the appliances, the floor, the lights. Jenny perched on a bar stool, elbows leaning on the spotless Formica kitchen counter, a fashion magazine open in front of her. A tall, clear drink with ice and a fat wedge of lime sat in front of her, sitting in its own puddle of condensation.

I picked up the glass and sniffed it. Gin and tonic, and good gin from the smell. "Aren't you a little young for Tanqueray?" I asked, trying to sound jovial but undoubtedly sounding like a stern nerd.

She shrugged. "I'm a little young for a lot of things, but that never stopped me." She took the glass back from my hand and sipped, pretending not to watch me over the rim.

"I'm very impressed with how adult you are," I said.

She ignored the sarcasm, or maybe she just didn't give a shit what I thought. That seemed a distinct possibility for this little poseur. She sucked on a piece of ice, then dropped it back into her glass. "So why do you want to see my mom? She overdue with those Dr. Seuss books she borrowed for me?"

"Actually I was curious as to how you were doing. You seemed awful upset at the fire last night." I pulled up a stool and sat down.

She examined the free-floating morsels of lime pulp in her drink. "It was upsetting, seeing that beautiful old house burn down."

"I didn't think you were the type to care much about antebellum architecture."

It was the wrong thing to say. "What the hell do you know about me, anyhow, Mr. Poteet? Where do you get off coming in and telling me what I care about? Jesus,

I get enough from the King and Queen!" Her dark eyes flared in outrage, flinting like struck stones.

I raised a hand in pretend surrender. "Hey, look, I'm sorry. I didn't mean anything."

Jenny snorted and sipped at her drink again.

"I thought maybe you were still upset about Greg Callahan," I ventured. Or your mother and Greg Callahan, I added silently.

Her fingers had been sliding up and down the cool wet length of the cocktail glass and they braked. She stared at her hand and did not look at me. "What is any of this to you?"

"I don't want my friend Lorna getting hurt. Whoever killed Greg and Freddy might come after her next. You'd gotten to know Greg Callahan, right? Someone here killed him and we have to find out who."

She was quiet again, as silent as a statue. "Look, Mr. Poteet, just leave it alone. Okay? I'm not going to weep anymore for him. I—"

"Weep for him? What was he to you?" The words tasted terrible in my mouth, but I had to know.

"He was just a friend, a business associate of Mom's. He wanted to buy Mom's land."

"And you got all worked up over a man you hardly knew?"

"I—I cried because I'm just not used to death, okay? It shocks me. Older people get jaded about it, but us kids, we're different."

It nearly rang true; I remembered my first funeral, my grandmother Schneider's when I was twelve, and fighting back unexpectedly hot tears simply at the sight of her closed coffin. But a tone in Jenny's voice was too calculated; she would not have made for a good actress, despite her poses.

"Your father didn't seem too upset." I remembered the excited glow in Parker's eyes as he watched the fire.

"He likes burning." Jenny shrugged. "He gets a boner lighting a fire in winter."

If it was intended to shock, it did. I didn't go around talking about my folks' sexual responses much when I was a teenager; I was too interested in my own. I suddenly didn't want to be around Jenny Loudermilk anymore. She looked unutterably sad to me, sitting alone in this huge, cold house, a little girl drinking hard liquor to show how mature she was, trying to engage in witty repartee that she was sadly ill-trained for.

"If you'll excuse me, I'll go have a word with your mother." I stood and pushed the stool underneath the counter.

"She won't like being interrupted when she's throwing pots," Jenny warned me, coming a little unsteadily off her stool. "You better not—"

"I think I better. And I think you better go sleep off this little afternoon drunk you've enjoyed." I went out the back door toward a small potting shed, decorated on the side with fanciful paintings of children gathering mushrooms. Bright beds of wildflowers surrounded the shed, bestowing a rustic charm they usually only talk about in magazines. As I knocked on the door I could see Jenny Loudermilk watching me from the curtained breakfast nook.

I rapped again on the door. I could hear a gentle humming noise from within, and then Dee Loudermilk's hard-edged drawl: "Come in."

I entered the dark pottery studio. Dee Loudermilk sat hunched over a whirling wheel, shaping a mound of clay into something that looked like a cross between a vase and a lozenge. Her hands moved with infinite patience up and down the spinning clay, and I saw they were very like her daughter's hands moving up and down on the glass of cold gin. I stared spellbound, and Dee, one lock of light hair hanging in her face, glanced past her errant strand at me.

"Shut the door, please, and push the hair out of my face, if you don't mind," she said, and I obeyed. It was an oddly intimate moment as I gently moved her hair

back behind the delicate shape of her ear. I stepped back,
uncomfortable with the sudden closeness between us.

She wasn't bothered. "Thanks, Jordy," she said with
a workman's bluntness. "I usually wear a kerchief, but
I couldn't find mine today."

The humming I'd heard was the whirr of her potter's
wheel, powered by electricity rather than her sandaled
feet. I watched in respectful silence as she finished
molding the small pot, its gentle curves taking shape
under her clay-smeared fingers. Finally, when it had
spun long enough, she slowed the wheel to a stop then
pried the new vase free with a flat-edged knife. She
stood and began to wash her hands at a soapstone sink
that sat in a corner.

"How is Ms. Wiercinski holding up? I heard she was
staying at your place." She kept her back to me and I
could appreciate again what a fine figure of a woman
she was, attractive in her dirty chambray shirt and argil-
smeared black jeans, with the smell of wet clay and
light sweat about her. It wasn't hard to see why Greg
might've liked her.

"Yes, she's there. She's holding up well."

"I hope she's more likable than Callahan," Dee said,
still soaping her hands clean.

"Didn't you like Greg?"

One bubbled hand found the faucet and turned the
water on higher. She didn't look up at me. "I didn't
know him very well. He tried to get me to sell him land,
but I wasn't interested."

"How often did he meet with you about your land?"
I asked, sitting on an empty stool.

"Now, why would that be any of your business?"
Dee asked, reaching for a clean towel. Her hands, free
of dirt and soap, looked as though they had been freshly
sculpted from some rare pink stone.

I didn't feel like pushing Dee Loudermilk. She'd tell
me in no short order to get the hell out if I stepped over
the line. I tried not to fidget on the stool, stared into her

dark blue eyes, and decided on the direct approach. "Gossip around town suggests that Greg Callahan was chasing after you. Did you know that?" I decided to leave Jenny's name out of it for the moment.

"Funny, I used to enjoy gossip. I don't find it nearly as interesting these days." Dee leaned against the gray soapstone sink, surveying me with eyes that betrayed nothing.

"I don't usually listen to rumor, either. But someone has killed two people here, Dee, and they were both on one side of the riverfront development deal. My friend Lorna might be the next target. If you know anything about Greg Callahan or anyone who might have wanted him dead, and you're not telling, I'll have Junebug over here so quick your head'll spin faster than your potter's wheel."

She surprised me by laughing. "My goodness. Threatening the boss's wife? You've got more guts than I gave you credit for."

"I'm not trying to be impertinent, Dee. I figured you'd appreciate me not beating around the bush."

She smiled. "Does Candace know you feel so strongly about protecting Lorna Wiercinski? She might keep a closer eye on you if she did. Look, I barely knew Callahan."

"He'd already offered you money for your land, right? In the area of fifty thousand?" I guessed that her land, close in size to Bob Don's lot, would fetch the same price.

"Yes, that's right. It wasn't going to be enough to make me sell."

"And how did Mr. Callahan take that?"

"I didn't tell him my decision. He was dead before I got a chance to." Dee stared away from me, at the smears of white clay on her workbench. She moved away from the sink and got out some liquids and brushes. Pulling a stool over to the workbench, she began to apply a glaze to a bowl.

She glanced back up at me. "I don't know why you're wasting time here. None of us had a reason to kill Greg Callahan. You should be off talking to that nutty Miss Twyla or that oaf Tiny Parmalee. They're the ones who were against him."

"You don't know anything about Freddy's death, either?"

"No, I do not," Dee answered in a measured, nearly soft tone I had to strain to hear. The sweep of her brush made a delicate mark on the bowl's surface, like an angel's fingerprint.

"You seemed terribly upset at the fire."

"That's a stupid comment, Jordy; we all were upset at another bombing taking place." She glanced at my arm in its sling. "I mean, when we think we nearly lost you to that lunatic." Her tone didn't sound like my loss would be a grief for her.

"Parker seemed to enjoy watching Chet's house burn."

Her brush hesitated over a dark crescent of watery glaze she'd just applied to the pot. "Parker has a strange sense of humor. You really shouldn't pay him mind." She completed her glazing and went over to another workbench with a cabinet next to it.

"Jenny seemed terribly upset as well."

"She's a teenager," Dee answered, pulling on a heavy pair of rugged work gloves, "and she gets upset easily." Flexing her fingers inside the gloves, she opened the cabinet and rummaged inside.

I was about to tell her how upset—and drunk—her daughter was, when Dee turned back to me, her hands spread apart like she was measuring a caught fish, and metal sparkled like stars between her palms, the length of silvery barbed wire glinting in the bright sunlight from the studio's window.

"Isn't it lovely, Jordy?" she asked, a half smile on her face.

I stood quickly, nearly falling over and toppling the

stool, staring at the strand of death in her hands. It was just like the wire in Greg's throat.

"Don't be afraid, silly. God, but you're jumpy, just like Parker." She moved over to the pot she'd thrown, sitting down again. I stayed on my feet.

"Where did you get that?" I managed to ask.

"At the store, just like everyone else," Dee answered. She began to wrap the wire around the pot itself, pressing the barbs into the material so the wire held.

"That's—that's an odd decoration for a pot," I croaked. "And not in very good taste right now, Dee."

"It'll be lovely when it's done."

"You have a lot of that wire on hand?" I cleared my throat, knowing that it wasn't about to be ripped (at least for the moment), and righted the chair I'd knocked over.

"Sure. I do lots of Southwestern-style pots for that crafts store over in Bavary. Barbed wire's a big decorating item there. You can get pottery, sculptures, all sorts of stuff like that."

So the killer wouldn't necessarily have had to cut the wire from the fence that bisected Dee and Bob Don's land. He or she could have filched a length from Dee's studio. Dee knew it was here, and presumably so could Parker and Jenny—or anyone who bought Dee's ceramics. Of course, it wouldn't be filching if Dee herself took it to wrap into Greg's neck like soft clay.

"I'm sure you mentioned to Junebug that you had that kind of wire on hand, didn't you?"

She shrugged. "He didn't ask. I didn't volunteer."

I shook my head. "Are you just trying to make yourself look bad? Is this some game to you?"

She finished setting the sharp wire into the pot and stepped back to admire her handiwork. "Of course it's not a game, Jordy. A man's dead, isn't he?"

"Two men. Don't forget Freddy."

"Poor Freddy. He was really an oaf, wasn't he?"

"You're ice, do you know that?" I suddenly wanted

to be away from Dee Loudermilk. "You make that pot right after a man is strangled with wire. I think that's sick."

"Aren't you the sensitive boy? Then leave, Jordy. No one asked you here anyway. Why don't you run back to your little friend Junebug Moncrief and tell him what I've been up to?" She smiled hollowly at me. "I'm a Loudermilk. See if he'll do anything about mean ol' me."

I opened my mouth, then closed it. "Not cooperating with Junebug in his investigation isn't going to help your husband."

She laughed. "I'm not a good political wife and Parker knows that. I could frankly not give a rat's ass about him being mayor. If I did, I'd have him fire your ass in a minute. You're not exactly behaving like a loyal employee. But maybe it's good for old Parker to have a thorn in his side."

"Do you give a rat's ass about your daughter? She's in there—" I didn't get a chance to finish my sentence as Parker Loudermilk barreled into his wife's studio, looking for all this world like his senses had fled him. He stared hard at me, venom contorting his face.

"Jordy. What are you doing here?" The breath that powered his voice was ragged with fury. His eyes slid to Dee, who stood calmly by her wheel, arms crossed over her breasts.

"Just talking with Dee about all the goings-on in town," I offered. It sounded idiotic, but I frankly didn't have a witty excuse available.

"Would you mind leaving?" he asked, the politician in him kicking in belatedly. "I mean, I need to talk with Dee privately. And I'm sure you must have work at the library to do." His dark eyes darted to her and lingered. I saw the folds of flesh in the corner of his eyes crinkle in annoyance when he saw her standing disinterestedly watching us.

He might be the mayor, but I'd had enough. "Yes, I

think I will leave. Y'all are just too strange today for me. First Dee makes a big production of letting me know that she's got a bunch of the same kind of wire that killed Greg"—he swallowed hard at that little announcement—"and your daughter's got a solid drunk on in the house. I've had my fill of Loudermilks today, thank you kindly." I turned to go.

"Goddamn you!" Parker roared, and I whirled back, thinking he was coming after me. But he wasn't. He was after Dee, seizing one of her arms and shaking her hard. Her eyes were frozen on him, unblinking, like marbles left in sand.

I had no wish to get involved in their domestic squabble, but I couldn't very well walk out when it looked like he might hit her. I grabbed his shoulder, said, "Hey, Parker, calm down—" That's when he spun around and belted me, hard.

I landed on the floor. You don't know how much getting hit in the face hurts. It's a lot, trust me.

"Parker!" Dee shoved past him to kneel by me. I was busy working my jaw; it seemed okay. My eye, though, sure was sore.

"Oh, aren't you tough?" Dee spat at her husband, who stood staring down at me with a look of utter blankness. "Hitting a man who's got his arm in a sling! And he's a librarian, too."

I decided to ignore that implicit slur against my profession and my manhood as I got to my feet. My left eye tingled, as though announcing that its skin would soon darken like an overripe plum. I was still so surprised that I hadn't even gotten ticked at Parker. I just thought: *The mayor hit me.*

Dee steadied me. "What the hell is wrong with you, Parker?" she snapped. "Have you just totally lost your mind?"

Parker Loudermilk continued to glare at me, but his fingers unfolded out of fists. Finally his well-worn mask of local government slipped back into place. He smiled, nearly beatifically at me, then walked out of the studio.

"Tell me he's not going to get his gun," I said to Dee, holding my good hand up to my eye. This investigating crap could get you damaged if not outright dead.

"No, he's not going to get a gun," she answered, but I saw her delicate teeth biting the top of her lower lip. She looked worried, which did nothing to reassure me. "Let's get a cold compress on your eye."

Dee helped me into the kitchen. We heard the squeal of tires in the driveway; Parker leaving, I guessed. Jenny wasn't in the kitchen. I sat on a stool while Dee wrapped a baggie of ice in a dish towel and pressed it against my eye. I was feeling better—so well, in fact, that I wanted to kick Parker Loudermilk's ass for him. Dee pressed the coldness to my face. Another lock of her blonde hair dangled before her face and I wanted to push it back behind her ear, the way I did back in her pottery shed. I didn't.

"I'm sorry, Jordy. But maybe you shouldn't go around asking so many questions." I saw her eyes dart around the kitchen again, as if looking for something.

"She might be passed out, but I don't think she'd drunk that much," I answered, guessing that she was looking for her daughter.

"Jenny's much like her dad. Prone to stupid decisions. But I really don't want to talk about my daughter with you." She pushed down hard on the ice over my bruised eye. "Does that feel better?"

"Not when you're trying to drive it through my skull like that," I answered. I pulled on her hand to ease the pressure and she let go of the compress entirely. I took hold of it and watched her walk to the sink.

"You know, it's not like I barreled in here, guns blazing and accusations flying," I said. Well, maybe I did, but that was beside the point. "Your daughter's drinking heavily and your husband—a public figure—is belting city employees. What are y'all trying for, a guest spot on *Oprah*?"

"I'm sorry that Parker hit you. He doesn't deal well with anger." Her back was to me and I saw her chambray shirt wrinkle and smooth as her back tensed.

"No, I guess not. But never mind his behavior to me—that I can figure out. Why's he so mad at you?"

"He's not mad at me, he's mad at the world." She ran water in the sink and rinsed her face.

"No, he's mad at us." Jenny's voice came from behind me. She walked slowly and steadily around me, pulling the ice down from my face. "That'll turn cool colors. It'll go with everything." Her words didn't slur, but I could see the effort in her face to enunciate.

"That's a real comfort," I answered.

Jenny watched her mother, who had turned to face us. "Is this how the end starts, Mom? I'd like to know so I can get my front-row seat."

"Jennifer Louise, go upstairs. You're drunk. You and I will talk later." Dee's voice was as hard as fired clay.

"No," Jenny said, not even looking at her mother but staring at me. "Greg's friend, she's your ex-girlfriend, right?"

I nodded.

"Jenny! I said go upstairs!" Dee yelled.

"That's where I hide the liquor now, Mom," she retorted. "Are you sure that's where you want me to be?"

I stood up, keeping the ice pressed to my swelling face. "This has all been charming, ladies, but I'm frankly tired of this bullshit. I've already gotten my eye punched, so I might as well go for broke. Rumor has it that you were both sleeping with Greg Callahan." I turned to Dee. "Now he's dead, and your family is falling apart. Your daughter's drinking and your husband's pissing mad and beating up innocent librarians. What am I supposed to think, Dee? Maybe that hunk of wire in Greg's neck did come from your studio." I sounded cruel, but this dancing around the sour core of what might have happened with them had grown tiresome. I held my breath, waiting for her reaction.

Dee's mouth, pale and unlipsticked, worked as though trying to form words. A vague smile haunted her face.

Jenny didn't wait for her mother. "Leave her alone. She didn't kill Greg."

"Jennifer Louise, hush, right now!" Dee came forward in a burst of motion like a runner exploding from the block. She seized her daughter's arm. "I told you to go upstairs."

"How long are we going to protect him, Mom?" Jenny screamed. "I can't do this anymore! I can't—" The slap against Jenny's face reverberated in the tiled kitchen. She stared at the hardwood floor, and a thin dribble of blood formed on her lip. She shuddered. "Mommy—"

Dee whirled on me. "You. Out. Now."

I lowered the ice from my face. "Y'all are, without a doubt, the most screwed-up family I've ever seen." I glanced over at the stunned teenager. "Jenny, you okay?" She didn't answer.

"If you don't leave, I'm calling the cops," Dee said, taking a step toward me.

"Good idea. Let's have them all over." I shook my head at her, Jenny's words ringing in my ears. *How long are we going to protect him, Mom?* "Whatever the hell mess y'all have gotten yourselves into, Dee, get out of it now. Let me help you—"

"I don't need help. I need for you to go. Goodbye, Jordy." She put her crying daughter under her arm like a bird protecting a wobbly nestling and escorted Jenny out of the kitchen.

I left, keeping the bag of ice and the dish towel it was wrapped in. They owed me that much, surely. And I drove to the police station just as fast as I could.

CHAPTER TWELVE

"JUST WHAT THE HELL DID YOU THINK YOU were doing, Jordy?" Junebug barked, shaking his head at my black eye.

"Never mind me," I said, wincing as Dr. Meyers probed at the bruise. "Why don't you go talk to our fruit-headed first family? I swear those Loudermilks redefine dysfunctional."

"You'll have a nice shiner for a few days, Jordy, but there's no permanent damage." Dr. Meyers shook his gray head at me. "Honestly, aren't you too old for this?"

"My behavior is beside the point," I stressed, keeping my voice polite. "It's our mayor who's the threat to society."

Dr. Meyers smiled. He'd been Mirabeau's favorite doctor for nearly thirty years. "You look more like you've been threatened by society, what with your arm and your eye."

"You're gonna be the poster boy for people who stick their noses into police business," Junebug snapped. "Hold still while I get my camera. Doc, see if you can knock out a couple of his teeth for completeness."

"All right! Are you going to do anything about what I told you about the Loudermilks?"

Junebug sat down across from me. "Depends. You want to press charges against Parker? Jesus, this is going to be a mess. The mayor smacking around his staff. He's probably going to lose the next election over this."

"You sound heartbroken. As to pressing charges, I'm not sure. Right now I'd just like to give him a shiner and call us even."

"I don't think that'd solve anything." Junebug coughed. "Not to mention that a boxing match between the mayor and the chief librarian could lower civic morale."

I ignored his feeble attempt at comedy. "Look. He went after Dee, he went after me. He's beyond his boiling point, and we need to know why."

"Maybe he and Dee are having problems." Junebug stood to look out the window.

"And maybe that problem was Greg," I said. "Have you found out where any of them were the night of the murder?"

"Dee says they were all at home."

"Well, I'd ask Miss Jenny again if I were you. She made some remark about protecting him and I think they're covering for Parker. My guess is that Jenny thinks her father was involved with Greg's death and she's incapable of keeping up the charade. Dee I don't get. If she's covering for Parker, why'd she show me that wire?"

Junebug kept staring out the window. "Maybe she's tired of covering for him—but she wants us to figure it out so she doesn't have to tell on him." He looked back at the window.

I stood. "What is it, Junebug?"

"You've given me a lot to think about, Jordy. Now you go on home. Let me know if you want to file assault charges against Parker."

"Go home? Listen, I think that—"

He turned to me like a father admonishing a wayward lad. "Go home, Jordy. Or go to the library. Someplace that's safe. I think you've gotten into enough trouble for the day."

I tried the library first, because on the way home I'd remembered a resource I should have remembered before, when I was begging Junebug to tell me whose phone number was scribbled down in Greg's room. The library was still open and Florence Pettus yawned at the counter, looking surprised to see me and my shiner.

"Jordy! What happened to—"

"I'm fine," I lied, hurrying toward the reference stacks. "I walked into a door." I found the book I was looking for next to a collection of Mirabeau phone books that went back to the first telephone in the town.

I pulled down the reverse phone book and found the slip of paper in my wallet where I'd scribbled down the number from Greg's notepad. If you haven't seen a reverse phone book, they're great fun; they list phone numbers according to the number, not by the person. You can look up any phone number and find out who it belongs to. I felt like an idiot for not remembering sooner that we had this reference book in the library, but what with all the emotional confusion going on between Lorna and me and the subsequent bombing, it'd slipped my mind.

555-3489. I found it: Edward and Kathy Johnson, over on Heydl Street. I didn't know them. I went back up to the front counter and checked our Rolodex of library-card holders. No Edward Johnson, but there were two Kathy Johnsons that had cards, and one had the Heydl Street address. I quickly flipped through the rest of the Johnsons and found two other cardholders at that address. Brice Johnson, age seventeen, and Becca Johnson, age sixteen.

I sat back. Who were the Johnsons and why on earth did Greg have their phone number?

I was reaching for the phone to call home when I saw Nina Hernandez come in. She eyed me warily and walked over to the counter.

"I take it you and Eula Mae have covered every square inch of town with y'all's flyers?" I asked.

"Hello, Jordy. You look a bit worse for wear." She studied me. "I do hope Tiny didn't do that to you."

"Hardly, Nina. But I suppose it's not an unlikely guess. He's already threatened me once about you."

She shook her head. "Tiny's sweet. Just overprotective. And I'm afraid he's a bit smitten with me."

"Very. It makes one wonder what lengths Tiny would go to to win your affection."

She frowned. "Sorry?"

"Tiny. He's a doer, not a thinker. Did you know he nearly strangled me once, in a rage when we were children?"

She gestured at my slinged arm and my black eye. "You seem to be very beloved in this town. Maybe if you kept your nose out of people's business, you wouldn't need higher health-insurance premiums." She had a wicked grin.

"I'm not the one who came from out of town to stir up trouble, Nina. You are."

"I'm not jousting with you, Jordy. I didn't come to stir up trouble, I came to stop it."

"But you weren't counting on Tiny. He's not stable, Nina. You should know that before you get involved with him." I nearly blurted out that Junebug suspected Tiny of being Mirabeau's munitions marauder, but I bit my lip instead.

She sniffed disdainfully. Her motto of loving all of earth's creatures apparently didn't extend to Tiny Parmalee. "I'm not involved with him. But I can't help what he feels or thinks about me. I've made it clear to Tiny that I'll be leaving Mirabeau soon and I'm not interested in a relationship with him."

I almost felt sorry for Tiny. Notice the *almost*. "So what can I help you with?"

"Miss Twyla's not feeling well, and she asked me to return these books for her." I glanced at the stack— older Phyllis Whitneys, with the latest potboiler thrown in for a modern touch, and a Stephen Hawking to appeal to her scientific side. "She didn't want them to be overdue."

"Miss Twyla is very civically minded. Is she okay?"

"She's fine. And hopefully she can worry about overdue books more than the river being plundered, now that Callahan is dead."

I leaned back in my chair. "You must have hated him extraordinarily. I mean, to have fought him more than once."

"I didn't care about him, one way or the other. I just wanted to stop Intraglobal."

I remembered the rather surprising news of Lorna's that Intraglobal was a three-person shop. "Do you know who Doreen Miller is?"

Her lips thinned. "No, I don't."

"Well, she was Greg's silent partner in Intraglobal. You know that Intraglobal wasn't a big company, right?"

"Small companies can do a lot of damage to our ecosystems, Jordy. It's a lack of responsibility, not a lack of money, that plunders our environment."

"I just wondered if you knew who she was or where she might be found. Last I heard, they were having trouble tracking down this woman to tell her about Greg." And I'd forgotten to ask Junebug if he'd made any progress on that front. I'd call when I got home.

"Sorry, I can't be of help. The only person connected with Intraglobal I ever dealt with was Callahan, until he hired Wiercinski." She crossed her arms and looked down on me with her wire-rim glasses. "Speaking of her, is she planning on staying and developing the land in that same grossly irresponsible way that Greg suggested?"

Junebug had asked me not to say anything about Greg's fraud to buy the land and then resell it to the chemical waste company. I didn't want to tell Nina anyway; she would have just crowed over her moral superiority in opposing Greg.

"No, Nina," I said, my voice sounding tired. "Lorna

won't be trying to develop the land. I'm sure the whole deal's off."

"Really? I wouldn't be so sure. Wiercinski strikes me as the type of woman who won't quit easily."

Nina was right enough there. I forced myself to shake my head at her. "I don't think Lorna will have any interest in land development in Mirabeau."

"Pardon me if I—and the others, like Miss Twyla, who are concerned about this—don't exactly relax our vigil. We've raised a substantial sum to stop them in no short order, thanks to Miss Twyla and Eula Mae. Even if Wiercinski leaves town, we'll be ready for any other unscrupulous developers that try and ruin the river."

"Whatever, Nina. But the deal's dead, as dead as Greg. As dead as poor Freddy."

"I'll tell Miss Twyla you asked about her. Good night, Jordy. Don't get hurt anymore." Her beaded necklace jangled as she left. I watched her leave, the faint smell of her citrusy perfume lingering on the air.

I thought that seeing my bruised eye would elicit shock from Lorna. What I wasn't expecting was the absence of a cop car in front of our house, and then seeing Lorna and Candace sitting in my living room, in front of a laptop computer that appeared to be hooked up to my phone in some crazy way, and Lorna crying while Candace handed her tissues and patted her shoulder—a bit reluctantly, I thought.

After exchanging a "what the hell happened to your eye?" and "why the hell are you carrying on so?" I sat down with a Dr Pepper and heard what they'd been up to.

"I feel like an utter fool," Lorna wailed, blowing her nose loudly and liquidly into a tissue. Candace gave her another reassuring pat but frowned at me. I know Candace has a big, sweet heart, but she looked right then like she'd rather be swallowing glass than comforting my ex-girlfriend.

"Why?" Not to ask would have been anticlimactic.

"You're right. Greg must've been a huge fraud." Lorna gestured at the laptop. "Candace was kind enough to bring over this computer from the Mirabeau Historical Society. It's got a modem, so I tried to dial into Intraglobal's files in the Boston office from here. I wanted to go through all Greg's home-office files and see what I could find out—see if maybe there was something that'd point us to Doreen Miller or to how he was planning on unloading the land he was going to buy here. But nothing. I'm locked out of everything! Files that used to be there are gone, and files I used to be able to get into are locked."

"When was this done?" I asked.

"Who knows?" She sat back from the computer, a disgusted look on her face. "Greg must've done it after he and I came down here—or maybe Doreen did it after Greg got killed and she heard about it from the Boston cops. She must've wanted to be sure we couldn't find out about the land fraud. She must've not known about the files on Greg's laptop down here."

"I don't even know if the Boston police have found Doreen, Lorna," I said. If they had, I didn't know if they'd examined Greg's computer files—but surely they would have gone through his office. If Doreen Miller was a partner in the fraud, she could have destroyed the files to cover Greg's tracks. I bit my lip.

"Could someone have done this from Greg's laptop? Was it hooked up with a modem?" I asked. I became aware that Candace was staring at me, a pensive look on her face.

"I suppose," Lorna said slowly. "His did have a modem. I didn't have a laptop down here. But his machine's at the police station, and how would anyone here know the passwords?" She shot the finger at the machine. "This is so frustrating!"

"Would you mind telling me where your guard is?" I

asked. "I thought someone was going to be here to relieve Franklin."

Candace cleared her throat. Lorna stopped frowning for a moment and looked at my knees, standing next to her at the table. "I decided I didn't need a guard. Not with you here. So I sent him on his way. You're not mad, are you?"

"Lorna, honey, what you need is some nice, relaxing chamomile tea. Jordy, don't y'all have some in the kitchen? I know your mama likes a cup now and then."

"Uh, yeah, I think so."

"Good, we'll make Lorna some tea. Come help me find it." Candace seized my wrist in a death grip and pulled me along into the kitchen. I glanced back at Lorna; she was staring intently at the uncooperative screen.

I pulled free from Candace after she'd dragged me into the kitchen. She rattled the teapot under the faucet, turning the water on full blast. She jerked her head toward the living room and whispered, "She did it."

"Excuse me?" I wondered why we were whispering.

"She did it," Candace repeated. "She destroyed those files."

"Pardon me? What the hell are you talking about?"

"I saw her do it," Candace hissed. "I saw her select a bunch of files and delete them. I was getting us Cokes from the kitchen while she was trying to get into that Boston computer, and when I came back, there was this box on the screen that said DELETE SELECTED FILES? and she pressed OK. I saw it all over her shoulder and she nearly jumped out of her chair when I came up behind her. It was only after that that she started whining about all these files being missing."

"Candace, are you sure?"

"Yes, goddamn it, I'm sure." She switched off the faucet and banged open a cabinet, still speaking in a soft but smoldering tone. "I have been around a computer before, Jordy. She destroyed those files. Are you still going to stand by her side now and defend her to the death?"

"I can't believe this!"

"Believe it, Jordy. And now she's gotten rid of her guard. You think maybe that's so she can skedaddle out of here when she wants to? Or maybe she just wants to shame you into protecting her precious self."

Candace went back to the kitchen door and stuck her head into the living room, now all smiles. "You want some cookies with that tea, hon?"

"Too bad Candace had to go," Lorna said, munching on a peanut-butter cookie, her head leaning back on the couch.

"Yeah, it is." I stared out at the early-evening haze of heat. Crickets and katydids raised their voices in the backyard, singing their midsummer oratorio, celebrating their brief lives. I tried to turn back to Lorna, but I was having trouble facing her.

Candace had left shortly after serving Lorna her tea. I'd walked her out to the car, still stunned by Candace's accusation. She wasn't very happy with me for not throwing her testimony in Lorna's face and seeing what stuck to those gray eyes and high cheekbones.

"Why don't you confront her?" I had demanded.

"I'm not the one protecting her," Candace had snapped back. "God, what does she have to do? Commit a crime in your presence? She is trouble, Jordy, and I am sick and tired of you taking up for her. I only loaned her the computer to help her, since you believe in her so much. And what does she do? Possibly commit another crime with it. I only get played for a fool once by Lorna, Jordy. You ought to adopt that motto for yourself."

"This is awfully circumstantial, Candace."

"Please. I think Lorna could climb up on the water tower with a rifle, blow away half the town, and you'd still cling to her innocence." She got into her Mercedes, slamming the door. "You come see me when you've decided what to do. I'm washing my hands of this whole affair, Jordy." And that had been the end of the conversation. I'd skulked back to the house, feeling the slow throb of a headache in my temples.

Assume Candace was right. Why had Lorna destroyed those files? To get rid of information. What kind? That she was in on Greg's fraud? That she'd been in touch with the chemical waste company in Houston that'd planned to turn Mirabeau into another Love Canal? She'd stoutly proclaimed her ignorance of Greg's duplicity. But maybe those files had been humming in computer memory in faraway Boston, and she'd had no way of getting to them until she'd talked Candace into getting hold of a laptop with a modem. And of course, suspecting Lorna of being a liar now meant I might have to suspect her of worse. Of far, far worse.

I forced myself to turn back to her. She was licking the crumbs from one of Sister's homemade peanut-butter cookies from her fingers. She caught my eye and smiled.

"Feeling better?" I heard my voice ask.

"Sure am. I think your sister's cookies have medicinal value. Let's put one on your eye and see if the discoloration goes away."

I nearly laughed. It was the old Lorna, the Lorna I could laugh with and tell my secrets to and trust. Surely Candace was mistaken. I knew Candace wouldn't have fabricated the story about the files; she was not a liar. Right now I didn't know if I could say the same for Lorna.

"Why don't you sit down, Jordan? You're going to pace a hole in that carpet."

"Sorry. It's been an eventful day. I'm restless."

"Well, I think I should call Junebug and let him know about those files. And see if he tracked down Doreen Miller." She lurched off the sofa and headed for the phone.

I sat down on the warm couch cushion she'd vacated. My arm hurt and so did my eye. And most of all I felt mad at my own inaction. I wanted to talk to Sister, but she was working the night shift at the truck stop again, covering for a friend who was taking care of a sick kid. Mark was upstairs watching TV with Mama. I was basically stuck here alone with Lorna.

Until the doorbell rang, followed by the gentle twisting of a key in the lock.

"Y'all home?" Clo's voice carried into the living room. Great. Now I had two visitors in the house that I had a ton of questions for, and no easy way to ask them.

"Hi, Clo," I called, feebly waving a hand from the couch. "What are you doing here?"

She hovered above me, peering down at my face. She wasn't in her nursing whites. "Good Lord. What happened to your eye?"

"The mayor slugged me."

This announcement would have elicited shock from anyone other than Clo. She examined the eye critically, muttered "fool boy" under her breath, and sat down.

"Arlene told me she had to go into the restaurant last minute, so I thought I'd stop by and see if y'all needed any help with Anne." She leaned close to me. "Lorna still here?"

I forced a smile on my face. "Yes, she is. Would you mind stepping outside with me for a minute, please?" A frown creased her face and she slowly rose to her feet.

"What's wrong?" she asked.

I didn't answer her as she followed me out onto the back porch. Thunder rumbled distantly, and I wondered if we were likely to get one of the tempestuous summer evenings that would keep a lightning show going the entire night, one to shake the floors and the walls. The air was heavy with the promise of storm.

I gestured to one of the porch chairs and she sat, still frowning. "Anne all right?"

"Yes, Mama's fine." I cleared my throat but didn't

say anything—I didn't know where to start. I decided with someone as blunt as Clo, the blunderbuss approach would work.

"I was told by someone that you were having a discussion with Greg Callahan, sitting in his car a couple of days before he died. I just wondered why."

Clo's face didn't betray any reaction to my announcement. I wasn't surprised; she would make a world-class poker player if she ever decided to take up the game. "Who told you this?"

"Does it matter? You're not denying it."

"I didn't think anything I did outside of this house was any concern of yours." Her voice held a grating edge that suggested I was on thin ice.

"Look, Clo. You've always shot straight with me before. Please don't stop now."

Her gaze rested on the newly mowed grass of the backyard. She wasn't going to look me in the face anymore. "I don't have to answer this, Jordy." She stood. "You'll have my resignation in the morning. Or should I send it to Mr. Goertz, since he pays my salary?"

I stood to face her. "Goddamn it, you are stubborn. Look. The man supposedly didn't know very many folks in town. He talked with you. Privately. I assume from your attitude he hadn't stopped you for directions to the Dairy Queen. Now he's dead." I held up my hands. "Wait, now two men are dead. You're in this house, taking care of my mother. I think I have a right to know why you were talking to him, Clo. Unless you've done something wrong, it's not an unreasonable question."

She sat, considering. Her fingers folded into the shape of a steeple and she rested her thumbs on her heavy chin. The chittering of the night's creatures rang in my ears, and sitting like that she looked like a statue of some forbidding, unforgiving goddess. If she couldn't tell me this, I could never trust her again with the simple duties I'd seen her perform so often: braiding

Mama's hair, coaxing her to rest during her fitful spells, washing her face with the gentlest of strokes.

The steeple of her fingers folded. She looked at me with eyes of complete candor. "He wanted to talk to me about you, Jordy. He stopped me on the street, introduced himself to me, said he knew you, and said he had a business proposition for me. I decided to listen to him.

"He sat me down in the car. I was kind of nervous about that, but I figured I could handle him. We talked for a long while. He wanted to know about my kids and he told me he knew times were hard for people, even honest hardworking folks like me. He wanted to know how much free run of your house I had. I got pretty suspicious at this point and started to leave. Then he offered me five thousand dollars. I decided to listen some more."

"To what?" I asked, my breath caught in my throat.

"He wanted me to put a bag in your attic."

"A bag? I don't understand."

"I didn't either. Till I looked in the bag. Had chemicals and wires in it." She didn't blink. "And rods that looked like sticks of dynamite."

"My God! He wanted you to put a bomb in my house!"

"Not a bomb—the makings of a bomb. It wasn't all hooked up together." She let out a long, unhappy sigh. "I told him no way, no way in hell. He offered me ten thousand. I said no, not any business of mine. He reached in his jacket, and I thought for sure he was getting a gun to shoot me dead, but he pulled out a thousand dollars. A thick wad, in twenty-dollar bills. He pushed it in my hand and said we'd never talked. He said if I did talk, keeping the money wasn't going to pay for the trouble I'd buy myself."

"My God. He wanted to make me look like the bomber." I stared at her. "What did you do?"

She surveyed the lawn again. "I kept the money. I

was afraid to say anything—he frightened me. There was something about his eyes, a blankness behind them that made me all shivery. And Jordy, a thousand dollars is a lot. I guess I can't buy back your trust with it. I thought he wanted to pull some mean prank on you because of you and Lorna's past. I thought maybe he was involved with her. Or maybe I thought he'd be gone soon and I could just take the money and put it in my granddaughter's college fund. But then he turned up dead, and no one at all had to know he'd given me that money. I figured it was okay, 'cause at least he couldn't hurt you like how he wanted to.

"I didn't have to say anything and I could keep the money. At least, I thought I could." She shook her head. "I ain't cut out for this shit. I can always keep other people's secrets but never my own."

I was hardly listening to her. Greg had wanted to frame me as Mirabeau's least favorite explosive personality. Why? What on earth did he have to gain? I looked over at Clo; I'd been staring off at the wall as she talked. A hot anger boiled up in me. This woman, who had cared for my mother, for me, our family—she'd taken money from a man who wanted to implicate me as a criminal, and not said a word.

"And if he hadn't died, I guess you would have just stayed quiet about it." My voice was cold.

Her stoic mouth trembled for a moment. "I don't know what I would have done, Jordy." She fumbled in her purse and drew out a roll of crisp bills. "I can't spend it. I can't put it in the bank, I can't even put it into Diane's college fund!" Diane was Clo's granddaughter, a pretty, precociously bright girl of ten. "It's like blood money. I wished I'd never stepped out of the car with it!" Her thick hand, closed around the roll, shook in anger.

I didn't feel much sympathy for her. "I think you better go, Clo. I'm sorry that our family wasn't worth more than a thousand dollars to you—"

She threw the money in my face; the rubber-banded wad of cash bounced off my forehead. If I hadn't been so numbed by her news, I imagine it would have hurt.

"I wish I had your smug superiority, but I don't." She was screaming now, and tears made her voice ragged. "Instead I got one son to support 'cause he can't find work and a grandbaby to raise 'cause her mama's dead. I don't get to sit behind a library desk all day on my ass. I have to take care of people that are going to die soon. And I try not to love them, but I do. People like your mama. I'm sorry I made a mistake, but I made it. Only you can forgive me for it. I ain't gonna forgive myself anytime soon."

I glanced up; Lorna leaned in the kitchen doorway, a shocked look on her face, and Mark stood stock-still on the stairs, his mouth gaping.

I didn't know what to say; I felt the molten pain of betrayal—in my gut, in my heart, in my head. My mouth was dry. "I—I suppose you should tell Junebug about this. Maybe Greg knew who the bomber really was."

"All right, I will." Her tears were gone, wiped away on the back of her hand. "I suppose you don't want me around here no more. Like I said, I'll send my resignation to Mr. Goertz."

Sister'd kill me if I let Clo go. But what was I supposed to do? This woman was caring for my mother, yet she'd stayed quiet for money, knowing that I or my family might be in danger from Greg Callahan. The trust I'd felt for her lay shattered.

"I think that would be best, Clo. I'm sorry."

"I'm sorry, too, Jordy. More than you will ever know." She glanced up at Mark. "Tell your Mamaw goodbye for me, sugar pie." She turned to Lorna. "You be glad that man's dead, miss. He was nothing but trash through and through." Lorna didn't answer. I didn't look up as the front door closed behind her. I was still staring at the thousand dollars at my feet. Lorna had more presence of mind than I did; she picked it up using a towel and dropped it in a paper bag. "Junebug'll probably want it," she said. I nodded, hating Greg, hating myself, and wondering if I should let Lorna keep a hold on that money. I took the bag from her and said, "I'll keep it for him." She nodded and went back into the kitchen.

Mark had vanished upstairs. I went to go lie down on my bed.

I closed my eyes. Try not to think about Clo. The sharp sting of betrayal still hurt. Was I being unfair? Could I forgive her? I rubbed my eyes through closed lids. If Candace was right, Lorna was betraying me in a way possibly worse than Clo—yet I'd given Clo, who had confessed, a tongue-lashing, and I'd given Lorna, who hadn't, a peanut-butter cookie. I wasn't being entirely fair by being understanding toward one and damning toward the other.

I rolled over and called the police station. According to Junebug, the Boston police had found an address for a Doreen Miller, but she apparently was no longer in residence. They were still looking for her. He had not offered an opinion about the passworded and destroyed Intraglobal computer files. I could only imagine what he would make of Clo's tale.

I tried to be analytical. Greg wanted me to look like the bomber. Why? What was his connection to the bomber? I drew two quick blanks, discarding the notion that he considered me a serious rival for Lorna's affections. Unless he'd been madly in love with her and we hadn't known it. Had he planned on blackmailing me into selling my land? That wouldn't have worked, him using some manufactured secret against me. It made no sense.

My black eye hurt and I resisted the urge to rub it. Greg asking Clo to plant phony evidence against me had nearly eclipsed my misadventures with Parker, Dee, and Jenny (I'd never seen a whole family of suspects before, but then I'm not a cop) and Candace's accusation against Lorna. Not to mention that Tiny Parmalee, with all things considered, was the only person vicious enough to do these crimes anyway and could not be eliminated from the running; and neither could his probable puppet master, Nina Hernandez. And how did poor Freddy Jacksill, getting blown to smithereens in Greg's room, tie in? He must've known something about Greg and gotten killed for it. Something Greg did here in town and no one wanted known—was there a reason not only that Freddy got killed, but that he was murdered in Greg's room?

My headache was not ebbing with all this arduous speculation. I kept thinking about Lorna and those files. A rap at the door interrupted my completely chaotic train of theories.

"Uncle Jordy?" Mark stuck his head in. "Lorna wants to know if you want some dinner."

"Yeah, I guess. I'll come down in a minute and fix something."

"You better. She's talking about cooking something called bread dressing, but it doesn't have cornbread in it. Sounds real gross."

"It is, trust me. It's not like dressing you're used to. I'll be down in a minute." A stray notion, hovering on the edge of my speculations, crowded to the front of my brain for attention. The odd phone number in Greg's room that I'd traced to the Johnson family. "Hey, Mark, do you know two kids at the high school named Brice and Becca Johnson? A little older than you?"

Mark nodded. "Brice is a geek. He's going off to major in chemistry at A & M this fall." Chemistry. Interesting major. You could blow up a lab if you're not careful. I shook my head, chastising myself for chasing at shadows.

"What about Becca Johnson?"

Mark shrugged. "She's real pretty, usually nice. She can be a little stuck-up."

I bit my lip. "You ever see either of them with Jenny Loudermilk?" It might make sense; she was the only other teenager in the stew.

"Oh, yeah. She and Jenny Loudermilk are best friends. They're always hanging out together."

I rolled over and reached for the phone. I drummed my fingers against my cheek and then decided. I dialed the Johnsons' number.

It barely rang before it was answered. A young man's voice, slightly nasal: "Becca? Is she okay?"

I was taken aback. "Um, no, this isn't Becca. I take it she's not there."

"No, she's not." The boy hesitated. "Who's calling?"

"Um, Brice?"

"Yeah?"

"This is Jordy Poteet. I was calling for Becca because I'm a friend of Jenny Loudermilk's and—"

"They're all at the hospital. I'm manning the phone here in case folks call."

"The hospital?"

"Yeah. Hey, sorry to be the one to tell you. Jenny took an overdose—they think it's Valium and booze. She's in the hospital."

"Oh, my God! Is she okay?" I gripped the phone harder. Mark stared at me, his dark eyes wide.

"I don't know. I don't know if she's going to make it or not. Becca's down there now."

"Thanks, Brice. Thanks very much." I hung up without further ado. In the middle of this sweltering evening, I felt cold down to my bones.

CHAPTER THIRTEEN

THE CROWD TO WATCH OVER JENNY LOUDER-
milk's life had gathered in front of the malfunctioning
television in Mirabeau Hospital's second-floor waiting
room. Mostly teenagers, with a scattering of parents, sat
watching the distorted colors on the screen. You could
see the shameful thought in the adults' faces: *Thank
God it's not my child.* The kids themselves looked
numbed, as though shocked at the thought of their own
mortality. Parker and Dee were not there.

I wavered in the doorway that led into the waiting
room, hesitant to intrude on their grief. I felt terrible.
That girl—her drinking, her attitude, it was all a cry for
attention, a cry for help. I could have tried harder to talk
to her. Instead, I taunted her, watched her mother slap
her, and left.

I didn't know a soul in the room; believe it or not, I
don't know every person in Mirabeau. Gingerly, I approached one of the parents, a portly woman who kept
wringing her hands, as if wanting to rub the flesh off
her fingers. She watched me walk toward her; no doubt
I looked a sight with my slinged arm and my black eye.

"Excuse me, is there any news on Jenny?" I asked
softly.

The woman shook her head, the corners of her lips
tugging downward. "I'm afraid not. Dee is in with the
doctor now. We're just hoping that Dee found her in
time."

"Could you tell me which of the girls is Becca Johnson?"

She nodded and pointed at a girl sitting on the dingy plaid sofa, a *People* magazine open and unread in her lap. The girl rested her chin on her hand, staring off into space, ignoring the other kids around her. She was strikingly pretty, with a thick mane of black hair and wide-set green eyes that penetrated like light shining through an emerald. Her skin was flawless, the kind that most teenagers only dream of, and her lips were full without being comic. She was already beautiful and had the promise of even greater, deeper loveliness as she aged. I could almost wish to be sixteen again, looking at her.

I thanked the woman and knelt by Becca. She nearly jerked, startled out of her reverie by me, who looked more like a patient than a visitor. On closer inspection, I saw she looked exhausted.

"Becca? My name is Jordan Poteet. I wondered if I could talk to you privately for a minute. It's about Jenny."

"You're not a doctor, are you?" she asked.

"No, I'm not. But I need to speak with you about Jenny. Please, it's important."

She watched me with those spectacular eyes. I guess I wasn't found wanting; she tossed the magazine to one side and got up, telling one of the other girls that she'd be back in a few minutes.

We went silently to the cafeteria, where I offered her a cup of coffee. She opted for a Diet Pepsi instead and we sat down at a glaringly orange plastic table. I don't know why hospitals, filled with the injured and the worried, buy furniture in colors designed to shock and nauseate. Becca sat across from me. Folding her hands rather primly, she left her soda untasted and watched me. There wasn't just beauty there; a keen intelligence gleamed from her. There would be no kidding around with this girl.

"I understand that you're Jenny's best friend," I said.

"Yeah. We've been close since the second grade."

"Good. Then I'm sure you're very concerned about her."

"Yeah. So what did you want to talk about, Mr. Poteet?"

I plunged ahead, telling her in detail my adventures at the Loudermilks. At no point did she interrupt or ask for clarification; but I could see that she was shocked. When I finished, she tapped a fingernail against the garish tabletop before answering.

"Wow, Mr. Loudermilk gave you the shiner? He's—he's got a temper."

"I believe Parker's got a violent temper."

"And you think Jenny was hiding something about him?" Becca watched her polished fingernails instead of my face.

"I don't think. I know. And I think you know, too."

Green ice looked into my face. "What do you mean?"

"I was there right after Greg Callahan's body was found at the Mirabeau B. Your phone number was written on the notepad by his phone. I've also heard tell that Greg might have been romancing both Jenny and her mother. That could have given Parker or Dee a potent motive to kill Greg." I wasn't about to suggest to Jenny's best pal that Jenny might be a murderer as well. "Now Jenny's turned to drinking and taking Valium. There are some connections here, Becca, and I want to know what they are."

She didn't look at me.

"Haven't the police already talked to you? They must've contacted your family."

She kept her eyes glued to the table. "I told them I didn't know any reason why Greg Callahan would have our number."

"There is a reason. Now, for Jenny's sake, can't you tell me?"

Becca Johnson slid back into the hard orange plastic

of the cafeteria chair. She popped the top on her warming can of soda and sipped, taking her time to answer me. Finally she said: "I don't want Jenny to get into trouble."

"Hon, Jenny's already in trouble. Big trouble. I think you know that. If you're a friend, you'll help her get out of this mess."

"Why should I tell you anything, Mr. Poteet?" Her right eyebrow arched.

"Because the truth has to come out now, Becca." I softened my voice. "Jenny said to her mother she couldn't keep protecting him—whoever him is, and I think it's her father. I'm going to wager the pressure of that secret is why she poured those Valiums into her palm and washed them down with a bottle of gin. If the secret's out, the pressure's gone. There's nothing to hide."

"Nothing to hide," Becca echoed. She ran a finger up and down the condensation of the can, in eerie imitation of Jenny and her glass of gin earlier in the day.

"Well?" I asked.

Her tongue covered her top lip for a moment, and she glanced around quickly to assure herself no one could hear us. The only other people in the cafeteria were two older black ladies, laughing quietly in conversation by the cash register.

The words came slowly, like paste squeezed out of a tube. "Greg was seeing Jenny. He had been since he got here. They met when he came out to talk to Mrs. Loudermilk. Jenny's impulsive about men. She has a bad thing for older men—she's dated a guy in his late twenties over in Bavary. No one else knows about that but me." She shot me a look that said: And you better damn well not tell either. Or get any ideas in your head about her.

"There's no reason to discuss her past relationships, Becca. I'm not going to judge Jenny."

"Anyhow, she ended up going to his room at the

Mirabeau B., and well—" She blanched. "They got intimate."

"And her parents didn't know?" I asked.

She shook her head. "She wouldn't let him call her at home. So he'd call me and leave messages for her. He used the name Don Miller. So I just told them Don was a friend from over in Bavary I met through school. Just a friend, not a boyfriend. So they didn't ask about him, except my mom teased me about how much this boy Don was calling me. He'd call and tell me where and when Jenny could meet him, and then I'd call her and give her the details." She stared into space above my shoulder. "I told her this was stupid, really stupid, falling for a much older guy who wasn't staying in town. But he kept telling Jenny he would be coming back to Mirabeau a lot, what with the condo resort getting built."

Don Miller. Not too far off from Doreen Miller. I leaned forward. "There is no condo resort, Becca," and I told her of Greg's fraudulent plan to resell the land to the Houston chemical waste company. Her face hardened.

"That son of a bitch. I was right about him."

"Then why did you help her?"

She smiled, ever so slightly. "Because it mattered to her, and she's my friend. And there was something terribly silly and romantic about them. I mean, you knew it wasn't going to work, but they had all this passion." She paused. "But her parents found out."

"How?"

"I don't know. Jenny's not a good liar, so they probably caught her in a contradiction. Or they got careless around town and someone ratted to Mr. and Mrs. Loudermilk."

"What about the possibility of Dee having an affair with Greg? How does that strike you?"

Her eyes met mine. "It strikes me as possible. Isn't that awful, Mr. Poteet? I guess I should think better of my best friend's mother, and Mrs. Loudermilk's always been good to me, but yeah, I could see her doing it. She does what she wants, I think. That whole family does. After all, they're Loudermilks. And she's a very"—Becca paused, searching for the right word—"*touching* person. I don't mean emotionally touching, but physically. I could see her having an affair just for the sheer pleasure. But if she did fool around, I think she'd make sure no one ever caught on. She's tough."

I thought of the look of ecstasy on Dee Loudermilk's face as the wet clay spun into texture and shape beneath her smeared fingers. I nodded.

"Jenny never mentioned anything about her mother and Greg, and if she had known, I'm sure she would have said something to me. We don't have many secrets from each other."

"So do you know anything more about the Loudermilks?"

"Yes," she said, staring down at her soda can. She finally looked up at me again. "When her folks found out, her father was furious. He's scary. I don't know how Mrs. Loudermilk took it—Jenny said she didn't seem upset at all. She was trying to defend Jenny against her dad. Mr. Loudermilk—" She broke off for a moment, then surged on, bolstered by some inner courage: "He's one of those men everyone says nice stuff about, but I don't think many people like him. And he's never made me feel entirely comfortable. There's something a little bent about him."

I thought again of the odd joy in Parker's eyes watching the Mirabeau B. burn and of Jenny's snide comment about her father getting excited by fire. Not to mention the hair-trigger temper and the violent streak. I had to agree with Becca that Parker's bathroom didn't appear to be fully tiled.

"This will sound really strange, Becca, but did Jenny every say anything about her father and the bomber?"

Becca blinked. "No, not that I remember. I mean, the

bomber's been all anyone's been talking about." She narrowed her eyes at me. "Why, you don't think that Mr. Loudermilk . . ."

"He could be. He owns a construction company. He's worked with explosives. And he really seems to enjoy watching fire. I noticed it when the Mirabeau B. burned and Jenny commented on it to me." I paused. "And the room of the man who was having an affair with his daughter gets blown up. Is that supposed to be coincidence?"

Becca took a long, studied breath. "God, I never thought of that. When Mr. Loudermilk found out, it was late Thursday night, after they'd had that meeting at the library about the land development."

"I was there," I said.

"Whoever ratted on Jenny did it after the Loudermilks got home, but I guess that they'd seen her arrive at the meeting with Greg and that just added fuel to the fire. No puns intended. Jenny and her dad had a big fight and then he stormed out. Jenny said her mom didn't fight with her—she was stone-cold icy to her. Jenny called me and I said I hoped that her dad had gone for a drive to cool off and not to go confront Greg. She was supposed to have met Greg around midnight, but she was arguing with her parents and there was no way they were letting her out of the house."

Lorna had heard a door slam down the hall around midnight—an irate Greg returning from a lonely rendezvous or angry that his young lover hadn't shown up?

"I mean," Becca continued, "Greg was guilty of statutory rape. Well, when I said statutory rape, Jenny just had a cow. She said she was going over to the Mirabeau B. and make sure her father hadn't hurt Greg. She hung up on me. I got worried that Jenny would go over there, find her father and Greg fighting, and there'd be a big scene." She stopped to rub her eyes. "God, this was only a couple of days ago and now it seems like years and years. I've hardly slept since."

"What happened?"

"I don't live far from the Mirabeau B., so I snuck out and walked over. I thought if there was trouble, I could at least be there for Jenny. If her parents knew how I helped her, I'd be in deep shit with them, but I wasn't really too worried about that. I thought Jen needed me. I got there and saw Mr. Loudermilk barreling out of the side door of the bed-and-breakfast—"

"Wait a second, Becca. What time was this?"

"Very late. Around two." Interesting. That was around the time Lorna had ventured into Greg's room, gotten tied up, and locked in a closet. She hadn't mentioned hearing an argument then, though. Did that mean that Parker Loudermilk had silently killed Greg Callahan, then left?

"Anyway, he was hurtling out of there just as I saw Mrs. Loudermilk's car pulling up. I don't think he saw them, he'd parked behind the house. He got into his own car and left. I nearly came out of the shadows then, but I wanted to see what was going to happen. Maybe if Mr. Loudermilk and Greg had already had it out, then I wouldn't have to get involved. I still didn't want the Loudermilks to know how I'd helped Jenny and Greg get together. They might not want Jenny and me to be friends anymore." She sighed, sounding older than she should.

"They sat in their car for a minute or two, then slowly drove off. I'm sure the Loudermilks would be very upset if all of this about Jenny and Greg came out."

Especially if Parker murdered him over it. I didn't voice that thought, however. "Did you approach Jenny?"

"No," she confessed. "I went home to bed. I still haven't even told Jenny that I was there."

I licked my dry lips. "Did you see if Parker was carrying anything? A pair of gloves, or a bag of some sort?"

She closed her eyes in concentration, her face as still

as a statue's, caught in a representation of eternal thought. "He didn't have a bag or anything. But he was shoving something into his pockets as he left. I couldn't see what it was."

Gloves, I thought. Maybe a pair of work gloves to protect his hands from the prick of the barbed wire. Parker would have had time to drive out to Dee's land, cut the barbed wire (or even take the barbed wire from Dee's studio), go to Greg's room, kill him, tie up Lorna, and leave. Parker Loudermilk was at the murder scene about the time that Lorna had gotten grabbed and locked up—and a time that fit for Greg to be murdered. And Jenny Loudermilk, reading the account of her lover's murder in the paper, must've felt crushed under that knowledge. What had Dee told her when Jenny found out Greg was dead? Keep your mouth shut about where your father was last night? What could Jenny have thought about her erratic father, except that he was a killer? Alcohol hadn't made her pain go away, so she'd supplemented it with something stronger. I felt a surge of pain for Jenny Loudermilk, and indignation toward Greg Callahan and the Loudermilks.

It didn't answer one question, though: why had Freddy Jacksill been blown to bits outside of Greg's room?

"Becca," I made myself ask, "how did you find out that Greg was dead, and what was Jenny's reaction to his death?"

"I saw it in the paper. And as soon as I heard, I called Jenny. She sounded like a dead girl on the phone—tired, like her mind had been shut off. I tried to give her comfort, but she didn't want to talk to me. She didn't want to talk about Greg." She stared down at the table, embarrassed by her emotion. "I tried to tell her that I was at the Mirabeau B. that night, but she hung up on me when I mentioned Greg and her father. I guess she just wanted pills and booze." Becca buried her hands in her face.

"And when Junebug came to talk to you—"

She looked at me through her fingers, tears streaming down her face. "I—I don't like Mr. Loudermilk very much, but I couldn't think he was a killer. My God, I've known him practically my whole life, and he's the mayor! He's Jenny's dad! I figured it had to be ... someone else."

I leaned back against the creaky plastic of the chair and closed my eyes for a minute. Dee must've known that Parker killed Greg when she heard about Greg's death. I tried to imagine her response: cover the precious Loudermilk ass. She'd sworn Jenny to secrecy. Then why had she shown me the barbed wire in her studio? Showing me the wire pointed more fingers at her family, not fewer.

I opened my eyes and made myself swallow past the heaviness in my throat. Unless she was sending us a signal. Maybe she was afraid of that vaunted temper as well, but wasn't willing to risk herself—or her daughter—by coming forward. If the police fingered Parker, she wouldn't have to—at least not until the trial, when he would safely be in jail.

I could understand Dee's fear, but I thought she'd taken the wrong tack. The tough, cool Dee might be able to keep a horrifying secret, but Jenny, pulled between loyalty to her father, terror over what she thought he'd done, and grief over her dead lover, hadn't coped with the pressure.

"Okay, Becca. I know this has been tough. Is there anything else that you can tell me? Did you see anyone else around?"

She shook her head. "No, I didn't. I was just glad there hadn't been a scene on the front lawn. I went straight home." She wiped sweat from her palms on her faded jeans. "You really think he did it, don't you?"

"It's possible, Becca. I won't kid you. I think Jenny must know. Did she ever have a problem with booze or pills before?"

Becca shook her head. "Not really. I mean, we drink beer every now and then at a party, but neither of us is much of a drinker. I don't like having to pee as much as you do when you drink beer and I don't think Jenny likes it. She just drinks to be cool." Suddenly tears filled her heartbreaker eyes. "God, I don't want to lose her."

I took her hand and she squeezed my fingers. "I think you just did a lot to help get her back. Let's go see how she's doing. Then maybe you and I can go see Junebug Moncrief together."

She wiped her eyes and nodded. We left the cafeteria; she walked with perfect posture. She wasn't going to show weakness, not in this case.

A doctor I didn't know was with Dee and the others in the waiting room. Dee's eyes went to Becca as we walked back in and then fastened on me. Her eyes, reddened by tears, stared into mine. Parker was nowhere to be seen.

"Mrs. Loudermilk, please, how's Jenny?" Becca attempted, but Dee cut her off.

"Jenny's not doing well. Hello, Jordan." Dee's voice had a forced calmness to it.

"Dee. Do you know where Parker is?"

She shook her head. "No, I don't."

"Why has he left town, Dee?" I forced myself to ask.

She took my arm and steered me away from everyone else, to the water fountain. I saw Becca and the gathered parents watch for a moment, then turn away to talk in quiet tones.

She sagged then, a little of the Loudermilk pride seeping out of her. "God, I'm a stupid bitch. Stupid, stupid, stupid."

I placed cautious hands on her shoulders. "Look. I know you saw him at the Mirabeau B. that night." She stiffened under my palms but didn't look at me.

"I guess you think I was protecting him," she said in

the most toneless of voices. Her shoulders shuddered and I steadied her.

"No, I think you were trying to protect yourself and your daughter. But for God's sake, why didn't you just tell the police you'd seen him there?"

"He's—my husband. And he's a dangerous man when he's crossed. I thought the police would figure out he'd killed Greg on their own, and that way—he'd never blame Jenny or me. We wouldn't be the ones to turn him in."

"Has he beat you, Dee? Or Jenny?"

She looked up at me with old, old eyes. "Oh, no. He's not the type to beat. He'd just kill us straight out if he wanted to."

I went downstairs to the main hospital lobby; Becca didn't want to leave while Jenny was still in bad shape and I was loath to try to convince her to do so. And after my talk with Dee, I felt sick and shaky. I could only imagine the guilt she felt over Jenny's suicide attempt. I found a pay phone and called Bob Don; but there was no answer. I called Junebug.

He sounded exhausted. "No one's seen Parker. He's vanished. I've got everyone looking for him to try and let him know about Jenny. You sure you don't want to press charges against him?"

"Yes, I do, and you might want to as well." After eliciting a promise that he wouldn't be mad at Becca for not immediately coming forward, I relayed her and Dee's stories. I heard Junebug's breath hiss out in a long sigh.

"What a goddamned mess. And him being mayor, too. This is just the sort of crap that those tabloid shows love to gobble up."

"Well, if you decide to run for mayor, I guess it would help if your opponent was serving time," I quipped. Humor seemed out of place, but I needed to avoid thinking about Jenny, even if just for a moment.

"Honestly, Junebug, who cares? We just need to find him."

"Let's say, Jordy, that you're right and Parker killed Greg. Still doesn't explain about what happened to Freddy."

I took a slow breath. "Look, I've wondered—and don't say that I'm crazy—if Parker might have something to do with these bombings."

"Yeah, I made that joke about him owning the construction company, but—"

"Listen, Junebug. I saw that man watching the Mirabeau B. burn. The look on his face was downright eerie, like he was getting nearly sexual pleasure from it. And his daughter told me he has a love of fire."

"Then he ought to be setting fires, not exploding bombs. And why kill Freddy?"

"I can't explain everything right now," I answered in a huff. "You've got to find Parker to get all the answers."

"God," Junebug muttered, and I could imagine him shaking his head in disbelief. "What the hell gets into folks? Why do they think murderin's gonna solve a single problem? I got to get a search warrant out for his house and his business. Lord have mercy, will this be a mess."

I leaned against the cool concrete wall of the hospital lobby. "I think I'm going home. Any luck on the Boston side?"

"Nope. Doreen Miller seems to be made of air." Junebug coughed, like he was coming down with a summer cold. "And you know, the whole setup with Intraglobal seems fishy. Their office space was leased in the name of Michael Beasley."

"Who's Michael Beasley?"

"He's listed as some officer of Intraglobal. I called Lorna a few minutes ago, and she claimed she never heard of him."

I thought of those files that Candace claimed Lorna

had obliterated. Was Lorna covering up for someone? Herself? This mysterious Michael Beasley? "Am I the only one who thinks this is getting goddamned complicated?" I asked.

"No, Jordy, you're not."

"What was Lorna doing when you called?"

"She said she and Mark were watching a movie. She was wondering when you were going to come home."

"She'll have to wait a bit longer. I'm going over to see Candace."

"I think that's a real good idea, Jordy." Junebug's voice sounded odd.

"What do you mean by that?"

"Just a good idea. I—well, hell, it ain't none of my business."

"Say whatever you're going to say, Hewett." I call him by his first name whenever I get impatient with him.

"Don't take her for granted, Jordan," he snapped back. "That's all I'm saying. Lorna's a nice girl and all, but Candace—well, Candace is special."

My jaw worked. I hadn't ever expected to hear such words regarding Candace from Junebug. I mean, they were friends and had known each other a long time, but I never thought that he thought she was *special.*

"Yeah, Junebug, she is special. I've always thought so."

"Good. I'm glad to hear that. Well, if we find Parker I'll give you a call."

"Thanks." I hung up and stared at the phone for a moment. Then I hurried out into the hot summer night.

CHAPTER FOURTEEN

THE LIGHTS WERE ON IN CANDACE'S HOUSE, and music drifted from the back porch. I paused at the side of the house, listening to Mary-Chapin Carpenter's sweet-edged voice sing a lament of forsakenness. Not a good sign. Candace always played Mary-Chapin's in-your-face songs when she was feeling mad. I tended toward Chris Isaak. And when we were feeling romantic, well, there was no one who could hold a candle to Patsy Cline. I thought I probably wouldn't be hearing Patsy's elegant voice tonight.

She sat on the back porch, sipping sangria she'd probably mixed herself, the music blaring without too much concern for the neighbors. I rapped on the porch's screen. She frowned at me and leaned over, turning the music down low.

"Have they carted her off yet to the hoosegow? Are you here to have a celebratory drink with me?" Candace asked dryly.

I sat down beside her on the porch swing, easing because of the soreness in my arm. "No, she's still there."

Ice barely rattled in Candace's glass as she sipped her wine. She set down her glass, went into the kitchen, brought out another glass, and poured me some sangria. She handed it to me and watched me take a sip. Sitting down again next to me, she said, "Jordy, we need to have a serious talk."

"I know. Would you like to go first or should I?" The rim of the glass was against my lip and I kept it there, afraid to drink, afraid to talk. I had a sudden fear: she's had enough of this mess, enough of me, and she's getting out. I sat frozen, not wanting to hear her, not wanting to say what was in my heart.

"I will." Candace swirled her sangria in her glass. "I take it you still haven't talked to Lorna about all her lies?"

"No."

"I see. Since Lorna's still roaming free, why are you here?"

I told her quickly, about Jenny's overdose and Clo's duplicity. She didn't say anything or look at me, watching the fireflies pirouette under the shadowy trees. Finally she spoke: "Clo is not the villainess here. She's a good person, and the best goddamned nurse you could have ever found for your mother."

This I was not expecting. "Listen, Candace, she lied to us! She was practically in cahoots with Greg Callahan to frame me."

"This is the way that it always is with you, Jordy," she said softly, her voice an arid whisper above the wind that moved through the trees like a dancer through a crowd. "The trust starts. You let yourself really get close to someone. And then you find fault with them, and you get the hell out. That way you don't have to deal with them anymore."

"I don't know what you're talking about. You make it sound like I was in love with Clo or something."

"Trust and love are different things, I think, although trust is a simple kind of love. That's something men just never seem to get." Candace shifted in her chair and sipped at her wine. She looked at me with her piercing blue eyes. "You haven't really trusted anyone since you found out that Bob Don was your daddy, Jordy."

I drank down some of the wine before answering her, collecting my thoughts. "That is absolutely ridiculous."

"Is it? I don't think so. Sure, you're upset with Clo, but having her gone means one less emotional connection in your life. Looking at her situation, it would not be hard to forgive her. You keep alternating between thinking Lorna is as innocent as the new-driven snow and thinking she's guilty as sin—maybe even Greg's killer. You're always bickering with Gretchen; God forbid you make peace with her and attempt to have a fully mature relationship with your father and your stepmother. And as far as you and I go, I'm really tired of only being your stout support."

She set her sangria down on the porch table and her gaze held mine. "You could have been killed when those mailboxes blew up. I came within inches of losing you and you didn't seem to notice how upset I was. Now you run off helter-skelter, sticking your nose in where it has no business being, and I wait for you to get hurt worse. Like that black eye. What if it hadn't been Parker Loudermilk beating you up but that crazy Tiny Parmalee? And now you've got your ex-girlfriend, who I know is a liar, shacked up in your house, trying to win you back. And I'm just supposed to sit here, not be bothered by this unholy mess, and watch."

"She's not trying to win me back," I answered automatically. I breathed in as soon as I said it, trying to suck the words back into my throat. Lorna had tried. I closed my eyes. I hadn't even thought what wear and tear these past few days had been on Candace.

"Yes, she is, Jordy. I'm not a fool. She's still in love with you. My only consolation is that she's even more messed up than you are, so I don't think she'll succeed. She loves you and she's more afraid of that than anything else."

A thickness sat in my throat, one I couldn't swallow past or cough up. Believe me, I tried. "She did try to get me back. She wanted me to go to bed with her. I told her no. I told her—I told her that I'm in love with you." I'd never said those words to Candace. I was afraid and there always seemed tomorrow. I wanted to reach out for Candace's hand, feel her warm fingers against my palm, feel her life. And, God, I didn't want her to turn away from me.

"Goddamn you, Jordan Poteet," she whispered. "If you were going to tell that to someone, don't you think it should have been me?"

"Yes, I should have. But I'm not good at this love crap, Candace. I don't know how to do it right; I mean, be a couple. Be in love." I felt like a dunce, the uncoolest person to ever draw breath.

"You're such a man. Hopeless." She shook her head. "You don't have to *do* love, Jordy. It's not like lunch or scoring well on a test. You just have to love. Don't you see the difference?"

I didn't answer and she reached over, touching my chin gently and turning my face back to hers. "You're scared to death of me, aren't you? Is that why Lorna still beckons—because you don't have to love her the way you love me? She makes life easier."

An odd tightness collected in my chest. The mysteries of women and love demanded bravery. "I never thought of it that way."

Candace studied me. "Then you go and think about it some." She stood up, collecting her pitcher of wine and her glasses. I watched her go inside, then come back to the door. "Good night, Jordy."

I stood. "Wait a minute! I told you that I loved you and you don't have anything to say to me?"

"You didn't tell me you loved me, Jordy. You told me you'd told your ex-girlfriend you loved me. Come back and sit a spell with me when you've learned the difference." And the door shut in my face, firmly, with a click that kicked at my heart.

It couldn't be true. I was not that messed up. I wasn't cutting myself off from folks; look how many of them I still had in my life. Candace was nuts or drunk. Then why did I feel like I'd been pierced with a cold steel sword and laid open like a surgeon's practice cadaver?

I leaned against my car, still parked out in Candace's driveway. The night air growled like a restless giant, and high above, heavy clouds dangled, ready to answer a prayer for rain. I wished the goddamned downpour would just come, come and drench me in the street, wash me clean of all my sins and failings. The clouded sky mocked me, rumbling flirtatiously, not offering even a meager drop.

Miss Twyla's house across the street was dark, except for one kitchen light. Poor Miss Twyla, I thought. Alone in this world. And I realized with a start that if I didn't have Candace, I'd feel a loneliness that Sister or Mark or Bob Don would not be able to fill. I'd never had a successful relationship before and now the one I considered good was crumbling like stale tobacco between my fingers. Because I was scared, and I was letting Lorna call the shots.

I glanced back at Candace's house. Was she watching me from a window? All the curtains were drawn. I hoped she was. I hoped she still had enough patience in her heart to want to watch me leave.

The light over at Miss Twyla's went out. She and Nina must be retiring to bed, exhausted from planning their battles against Lorna and adding coins to their war chest. I had my own battle to fight and those two would just have to stand in line. I got in my car and drove back to my house, letting my anger and resolve boil.

* * *

She was still up, watching the news when I got home. A bowl of popcorn sat in her lap and she was slowly nibbling. She was in a T-shirt and shorts and looked far, far too much at home in my house.

"Well, hello," she said as I walked in. "We gave up on dinner for you. Mark and I scarfed a frozen pizza and your mother had some tomato soup. Arlene called, she's not going to be back until around two in the morning. Do you want anything?"

I walked past her, snapping off the giddily grinning

meteorologist describing the storm alert we were under until three A.M. "Yes, I do. I want some answers."

"Uh, okay," she said, setting the bowl of popcorn aside. "What's wrong?"

"What's wrong, Lorna? Oh, that's rich. That's really rich. You waltz back into my life, try to get me back into your bed, your boss gets murdered, another guy gets blown up, a girl's tried to kill herself, the woman I love is ready to drop me, and you want to know what's wrong."

The words stung her. She stared up in defiance. "What is your problem? Are you laying all the blame for this on me?"

"Why not?" I shot back.

"Because Greg's the one that stirred up everything!" she retorted. "I wasn't the one who got someone pissed enough to kill me!"

"I'm pissed enough right now, Lorna." I took a deep breath. "You destroyed some of the files you accessed using Candace's computer. I know you did. You lied to me and you could have destroyed evidence in a murder case. Why those files, Lorna?"

Her dark eyes bored into mine. "I didn't destroy anything, Jordan."

"Quit your lying."

"What, did Candace manufacture this little story? Obviously she wants to turn you against me. She's pretended to be my friend, but she really loathes me. I can tell. She thinks she's better than me." Her tone turned ugly.

"If you're the liar I think you are, she *is* better."

Lorna looked away from me, her eyes traveling across the wall of photos of Sister and me in our youth. "You're so goddamned smug. So superior in your small-town rightness. You do belong here, Jordan, not in the real world. You live in some Ozzie and Harriet fantasy of what life should be like—"

"No, I don't. I live in the real world. I live in the

world of busting my ass and taking care of my family and having my friends and just trying to get by. And I don't lie to people."

"I told you, I didn't destroy any files."

"You know, there should be backup tapes of any of Intraglobal's files, Lorna. Most companies do that." I laughed hollowly. "But then, Intraglobal isn't most companies, is it? Most companies aren't committing fraud. Most companies don't have folks who do work for them getting blown up like poor Freddy. Most companies don't have silent partners who conveniently disappear." Her eyes widened. I leaned down into her face. "Like this Doreen Miller that they can't seem to find. Where is she, Lorna? How can you work with Greg and not know her?" I leaned back on my heels. "Unless you're Doreen Miller."

"You're nuts!" Her tone was outraged. "Even if I was in on Greg's fraud—which I wasn't—it wouldn't be much of an out for me, would it? Since the cops are looking for her."

"They're looking for her in Boston. Not here. And you never did answer my question about the backup computer tapes. Or did you destroy the evidence on those backups before you came down here?"

"I'm not Doreen Miller. I've never even met her, never talked to her."

"Candace and I are going to go to the cops. Here and in Boston. Candace will tell them that she saw you destroy those files." I took a step toward her. "Look, Lorna, whatever mess you've gotten yourself into, I'll try to help you. I'll help you as much as I can, but I've got to know the truth. Otherwise, what can I think?" I lowered my voice. "I don't want what I'm saying to you to be true, but it could be. You could've killed Greg. Did you know what he was up to? Did he threaten you if you told on him? Lorna, for God's sake—"

She was shaking her head at me, her lovely gray eyes

wide in the dim light from the lamp Mama used to read her books by. "My God. You *do* think I killed him."

"As long as you don't tell me the truth, I have to assume the worst."

"No matter what I once meant to you?" I could barely hear her question.

"No matter."

She held her breath for a moment, then let it out in a long hiss. "I am many things, Jordan, but I am not a killer. I didn't kill Greg, and I sure didn't kill Freddy." Indecision framed her face, and she pressed the back of her hand against her mouth. The last time I'd seen her do that was when she'd gotten the phone call that her father had died.

"I'm afraid you won't believe me. I don't want you to hate me, Jordan."

I sank to the couch. "Lorna, for God's sake. I don't hate you. I don't understand you anymore, but I don't hate you."

She leaned against the back of Mama's chair. Her fingers left long red lines across her cheek as she dragged her hand down her face. "I found files in the computer back in Boston. Copies of letters. Letters from me to Gary Zadich, the guy that owns the chemical company in Houston, the one you said Greg was going to sell the land to."

"So you had known! You had been in touch with him!"

"No! Someone faked those files, Jordan, I never saw them before. I never heard of Gary Zadich, or of any plan to resell the land. But those letters in the computer were going to make it look like I had. Someone's trying to set me up."

I stood in the gentle quiet of my living room, listening to her, trying to weigh her words. "How do I know that you're not making this up, Lorna, that you're just trying to cover your tracks? Why didn't you just leave the files alone and tell the cops that they're faked?"

"I was afraid. I checked the files; they were created long ago. But they were in Greg's directories, ones I'd never seen before until I started trying to track down what he was up to. I made a mistake, I panicked. I got rid of them." She paused. "Don't you believe me? For God's sake, Jordan, this is *me*! You know me better than anyone else, how could you think I would lie about this?"

"I don't know what to think anymore," I said, sitting down. My stomach felt tied in knots. I stood back up. "We better call the cops again and tell them this." Let Junebug decide if she was lying or not. I didn't want the responsibility anymore. The phone rang just as I was reaching for it.

"Hello?"

The voice was breathless with fright. "My God, Jordy, this is Twyla Oudelle. I need help and I can't get ahold of Junebug. Tiny is—" And the phone went dead.

I held the receiver in my hand, feeling coldness creep over me. "Miss Twyla? Miss Twyla?" There was not even the normal hum of the dial tone. I hung up and tried to dial Miss Twyla's number. There was only mocking silence. I tried to call Candace—she was only across the street. No answer. Either she wasn't at home or didn't want to chat.

My heart pulsed in my throat. "Mark!" I bawled. He came running down the stairs, disheveled with sleep.

"Look, there's something wrong at Miss Twyla's. See if you can get hold of Junebug. He's probably still out looking for Parker Loudermilk. I'm going over to Miss Twyla's."

"I'm coming with you," Lorna said. I didn't bother to argue with her. All the fight was out of me.

Horrible thoughts played in my mind on the short drive over to Miss Twyla's, like a bad B-movie festival. Tiny strangling Miss Twyla with the phone cord he might have yanked from the wall, Tiny snapping Nina's thin neck with a flick of his wrist. I thought of that far-away day on the playground, his weight against my throat, him trying to shift the life out of me with slow resolve.

"You better stay in the car when we get there," I said to Lorna, my anger with her temporarily eclipsed by my concern for Miss Twyla and Nina. "Tiny can be trouble."

"You sure you trust me to stay in the car? I might try to hot-wire it and steal it." Her voice was back to the peculiarly Northern brand of sarcasm that she could excel in. "For God's sake, Jordan, don't be both judge and jury of me. If we could get out of Mirabeau for a while, talk about us—"

"There's no us, Lorna." I pulled up in front of Miss Twyla's darkened house. I couldn't help but glance across the street to Candace's; it was darkened, too, and her car was gone.

Lorna stayed silent; we got quietly out of the car, me taking along a flashlight I always kept in the glove compartment. She wasn't going to wait in the car, and I didn't argue. I wasn't used to sneaking up on houses, but I had toilet-papered many a one in my roguish youth, so I made a beeline for where I thought the bedroom window was.

I kept an ear up to the glass but heard nothing. I considered shining my light into the room but decided that might be a bad idea, especially if Tiny was waiting inside. I gestured to Lorna and we carefully cut around to the backyard. It was dark back there, the outline of the fixtures of Miss Twyla's backyard hardly visible: the scattering of pink plastic flamingos that Miss Twyla goofily referred to as her pets, the low shadow of her tornado shelter, its doors a slight bulge out of the grass, the silhouette of a vase-shaped birdbath, the dark hulk of her house. I began to move toward the back door, not yet turning on the flashlight, not wanting to advertise our presence yet. I didn't want to think about Miss Twyla lying inside, maybe dead.

I had taken about four steps toward the house when Lorna whispered: "Jordan! Here!"

I turned back to her and in the darkness she grabbed my arm, her hands fumbling for mine, seeking the flashlight. I turned it on and she pointed the beam toward her own feet.

She'd been wearing open-toed sandals—not always a good idea in yards round here because of the threat of fire ants; but you couldn't expect Lorna to know that. And I saw with horror that blood smeared her toes.

A wet blotch of red stained the lawn. Lorna's hand tightened over mine. "Oh, God, Jordan, let's get out of here," she pleaded.

"Not without Miss Twyla. You go on back to the car. Or go over to Candace's and see if you can get Junebug." I shoved my key ring at her, holding out Candace's key.

"Uh-uh. I don't want to go off alone. . . ."

I slipped the keys back into my pocket and played the light along the freshly mowed grass. There was a thin trail of blood leading to the doors of the tornado shelter.

I'd sat through enough horror movies at the old drive-in over in Bavary to know what not to do; namely, go down into that shelter where something from another planet was eagerly awaiting an opportunity to eat my face off. How many times had I sat watching those movies, seeing the hero or heroine act like an idiot, my lips pleasantly bruised from making out with my date during the dull parts? Here was my conclusion: *If they're stupid enough to go into that attic that's dripping blood, then they deserve to die.* And those foolishly bold characters almost did always find a terrible demise. My hand tightened on the flashlight and I thought of Miss Twyla, her unconditional kindness, her erratic and always amusing demeanor, her bold assertions about the vitality of the elderly, her outlandish lectures in her laboratory classes during my student days, her special reputation in town as the last of those crazy Oudelles. Of all the folks in town, she'd called me when she needed help. I moved to the shelter doors.

The light showed they were unlatched. As I reached to open the door and pull it back, Lorna grabbed my arm again. "This is nuts. Let's get out of here, please."

"I said you could go. I'm finding Miss Twyla."

"God, you're stubborn." Lorna breathed in my ear, but she didn't leave.

The door fell back against the ground with a thud. Darkness as black as the devil's soul beckoned. I shone the light down the ten or so steps that led to the concrete floor. Blood speckled the two bottom steps. I played the light along the wall of the stairwell; I couldn't see a lightbulb or a switch by the doors. I took a tentative step in, Lorna right behind me. Behind her, thunder rumbled, as though the storm had finally and inopportunely decided to make its debut.

After several other tentative steps, I was at the bottom of the shelter. The Oudelles, in their eccentricity, had spared no expense on their tornado shelter. I remembered the shelter out at my grandparents' farm; the floor and walls had been dirt, more a burrowing hole in the ground than something fit for people to occupy for a long time. It had always reminded me of a grave waiting to be filled. The walls of Miss Twyla's shelter were concrete block, with cots and shelves lined with food in case the main house was destroyed in a twister. I played the light and found a door in the wall, slightly ajar.

I had taken two steps toward the door when I smelled it, the sickeningly sweet odor of bubble gum. I whirled as from a darkened corner of the room a fist lashed out, catching me squarely in the chest. I coughed and stumbled, my light dancing around the room but catching Tiny Parmalee's brutal face in its beam. He struck me again, backhanding me hard, shoving me through the ajar door that led into the inner room. I landed on my back, skidding in the darkness into a piece of furniture. My arm throbbed and my chin felt numb. Hearing Lorna scream, I yanked my arm from the sling, trying to get enough breath to get to my feet. I'd made it half-way when a light snapped on and Nina Hernandez stood with a gun pointed at my head from the opposite side of the narrow room. A shrieking Lorna was thrown down on top of me. I pulled free of her and stood in a crouch, trying to absorb what I was seeing.

This inner room was larger than the outer room, and it held far more interesting secrets. Nina with a handgun, not looking like she cared a great deal about the Mira-beau ecosystem at this moment. Tiny smiling down at me, hate in his eyes. Miss Twyla sitting in a chair next to where Nina stood, her mouth, chin, and nose blood-ied, her hair hanging in her face, her eyes angry. And along the wall, shelving that held boxes of wires, pliers, a canister marked KClO₃ (POTASSIUM CHLORATE), sacks of sugar, batteries, watches and egg-timers, a dusting of finely powdered aluminum, and a stack of metal pipes.

Oh, my God.

I steadied Lorna, who had stopped screaming and was fearfully watching Nina's gun. Nina held that gun rock-steady and the small dark bore locked on my head.

"Miss Twyla, are you all right?" I managed to cough out.

"Yes, Jordy, thank you for asking. At least one of my former students is behaving like a gentleman." She shot a daggered look at Tiny, who seemed inordinately pleased with himself, smiling like a badly carved jack-o'-lantern.

"Obviously, you don't want to make any sudden moves," Nina said to me. "I'll shoot you before you get across the room. And even if I miss you, I shoot Miss Twyla. You don't want that, do you, Jordy?"

"You wouldn't really, really hurt Miss Twyla, would you, sugar pie?" Tiny rubbed his lip with the back of his hand. "I mean, you didn't really want to slap her like you did."

Nina favored Tiny with a look the painted angels on the Sistine Chapel might give to devout worshipers. "Of course not, Tiny dear. But let's not forget that we're dealing with dangerous criminals."

"What?" I asked stupidly. Lorna leaned hard against my back, hiding behind me.

"Don't try to fool Tiny, Jordy, he's far too smart for you. He understands how Miss Twyla's gone crazy, bombing places around town, and how Lorna's the same kind of con artist that Greg was."

It took a couple of seconds to register. How could she know? Oh, God. "You—you're Doreen Miller?" I heard myself say.

She didn't give me a direct answer. Instead she smiled at Tiny, who stood near the doorway. She fired twice, in rapid succession. One bullet exploded into Tiny's left shoulder, founting blood, and the second hit him in the right side, vanishing into his big frame. The double roar was deafening in the enclosed space. Lorna didn't scream, but she seized my shoulders in a death grip. Tiny collapsed against the wall, a look of bewilderment on his face, and tumbled to the floor. I couldn't tell if he was still breathing.

Miss Twyla stood, her fists clenched, and Nina motioned for her to resume her seat, the smoking end of the gun waving gently. Miss Twyla sat, but her anger was a physical presence in the room. "Why, Nina? Why?"

"He's the most dangerous person here, Miss Twyla. I mean, after you." She laughed mirthlessly. "And Tiny's done his part for me."

Lorna had gone and knelt beside Tiny's slowly stirring form. "He's still alive," she moaned.

"He'll die soon enough, bitch," Nina snapped. "You'll be past worrying about him."

I took a long breath. "Let me guess. As Doreen

Miller, you planted those files that made Lorna look as if she knew about Greg's land fraud. She's your fall guy."

"Unfortunately now, she has to be a dead fall guy."

"You betrayed me." Miss Twyla's voice was low, the voice that only outraged old Southern ladies can muster. It could frighten a tyrant. "I brought you into my home to fight for a cause I believed in, and you lied to me. You stole from me and then used me to kill another human being."

"Miss Twyla," I said, watching the gun that still aimed in my direction. "I think I know the story now. Nina's real name is Doreen Miller—or at least, that's the name that Greg knew her as. The land resale to the chemical waste company is just a fraud, a cover. Greg and Nina are scam artists. They come to a town, they create a crisis. Greg threatens development that could ruin the river; Nina heads up the opposition, rallying folks and their finances against what Greg proposes. They specifically target towns where both development is needed and environmental concerns could run high; that's what Greg had Lorna looking for when he hired her. After they've squeezed money out of both sides, they vanish, taking the money with them. Then they set up office somewhere else and start again. Maybe they set up a fall guy to take the blame; that's what happened here."

I pointed at Nina. "You faked the files on Greg's laptop that said he was going to resell the land to the chemical waste company, and you faked the same files on the computers up in Boston to let Lorna take the blame. No matter how much that waste company denied that they'd ever heard of Intraglobal, folks wouldn't believe them. So you sail free with all the money Miss Twyla and Eula Mae raised, vanishing off into the night, and Lorna looks like the fool and the criminal."

"She is a criminal." Nina smiled. "There are more files up there she doesn't even know about that will make her guilty of land fraud. Posthumously, of course."

"Why did you kill Greg?" Lorna demanded. Her fright had evaporated, at least on the surface, and in her face, I saw the anger of a cornered animal that is tired of being toyed with and wants the fight.

"Profit margin, sweetie. Greg was getting greedy and I just didn't want to share the pots anymore. Don't feel bad about him—he was all for you being the patsy when we blew town. I took that nice little length of barbed wire I got from Dee Loudermilk's property and ended my partnership with him."

"And left Lorna alive so you could have your blame fall squarely on her shoulders." I said. "But what about Freddy?"

"Freddy got nosy, and Freddy got greedy. Since he was already stupid, he got dead." Nina said icily. "He made the mistake of overhearing a phone conversation between Greg and me and trying to get money out of me. He was too idiotic to see that if I'd killed Greg 'cause I was tired of sharing, I wasn't about to split the pot with him." She shrugged. "I conned him. I told him he needed to plant more evidence in Lorna's room, in a suitcase, that would make Lorna look like the solely guilty party and make it easier for him and me to take the money. All it took was a timer, and Freddy was history. I just borrowed one of Miss Twyla's contraptions."

I shook my head, remembering Linda Hillard's talk about Freddy getting rich. "Too many people now, Nina. You act like you intend on killing us all. This many people, there'll be an awful lot of questions."

"I can handle that, Jordy. I'm used to vanishing. And for all the money I'm getting out of the Intraglobal accounts and that dingbat Eula Mae, trust me, your lives are worth it." She straightened her shoulders as Tiny stirred and groaned. "We'll have to make this look good for when the fire investigators get here. Obviously Tiny and Miss Twyla were unhinged; her little pranks just got more destructive, and you and Lorna bravely tried to stop them. Everyone knows what a nosy snot you are, so no one will be very surprised. I think maybe one bullet in you, Jordy, will be enough—" She wasn't prepared, taunting me, for Miss Twyla to throw herself at her gun arm. One bullet smashed into the concrete flooring as the old woman tried to grab the pistol away from Nina.

Lorna and I, from different corners of the room, launched ourselves at Nina. I saw Miss Twyla fly off, shoved hard against the shelving by the spitting con artist, and then the gun whirled toward me. There was a flash and I felt agony in my leg, far worse than any I felt before—like a sharp, hot stab with a needle that'd been sitting in fire, turning molten. I screamed and fell to the floor, holding my thigh. Blood seeped over my fingers.

I heard shrieks and I managed to get my head up to look, half making my peace with God in case a bullet slammed into my head or detonated one of Miss Twyla's playthings. Lorna and Nina fought for the gun, Lorna with an obvious height and size advantage. The gun spurted fire once, striking the ceiling. Lorna shoved hard and the gun broke from Nina's grip, skidding toward Miss Twyla. I pulled myself painfully toward it.

I heard Lorna scream "Goddamn you!" and glanced back. My former ladylove belted Nina with a strong right hook, wincing as she did so. "I'll kill you for what you've done to us! You shot Jordan, you bitch!" Nina fell to her knees.

"Lorna! Lorna!" Miss Twyla barked out. I glanced over my shoulder. Miss Twyla had the gun in her hand, aimed steadily at Nina. I nearly collapsed with relief.

"Move away from Nina now, dear," Miss Twyla ordered. Lorna took a reluctant step back. I could see that her face was scratched and her hands flexed into fists. Nina stared at Miss Twyla, hate in her eyes. "Don't move, Nina. I will shoot you."

I breathed a huge sigh, wincing at the burning pain in my leg. This whole nightmare was over.

"Y'all go on. Go ahead and get out." Miss Twyla's voice was preternaturally calm, after the echoing hell of gunshots in the enclosed space.

"Lorna." I found my voice. "Go call the cops. Get an ambulance for me and Tiny." I tried to stand but fell into a crouch. Lorna was at my side instantly.

"Both of you go," Miss Twyla ordered again. "Don't wait for an ambulance. And take poor Tiny with you." Through my haze of pain, even that request sounded odd.

"I don't think we should try to move Tiny, Miss Twyla." And as I said it I looked up at her. She still had the gun leveled at Nina with one hand, but in the other she pulled two wires from a box, keeping the ends of the wires separated with two fingers.

"You'll have to, dear. Neither Nina nor I will be leaving." Miss Twyla's voice was firm, the same one she'd used on us in that long-ago chemistry class when we got too boisterous.

I didn't comprehend at first, the pain blocking my thoughts, but Lorna did. She stood. "Oh, Miss Twyla, no. Let the police and the judges do their job. You don't have to do this—"

"But I do, dear," Miss Twyla insisted. She nodded toward Nina, who had begun crying and shaking. "She killed Freddy using one of my projects. That's my fault. Don't you see that I must pay for that? And I'm not going to take a chance on a jury letting her go. It's so much better this way, don't you see?"

"Go, Lorna," I said. "See if you can get Tiny up the stairs and go."

"No! I won't!"

"You crazy bitch," Nina managed to whisper. She sat huddled on the concrete, her eyes wide and staring at Miss Twyla.

"Hurry, dear." Miss Twyla sounded almost sad. "My

hand is getting tired, and when these wires touch, that's it."

"Lorna, go. Trust me." My voice didn't sound like my own, but it was. "Please. I'll be okay."

She stumbled over to Tiny, talking to him, trying to pull him to his feet. Suddenly she sobbed and let go of his arm. "He's dead. He's dead."

"Oh, how awful," Miss Twyla murmured. "Poor misguided thing. Then go, dear. You help Jordy—"

"No." I shook my head and spoke through clenched teeth. "I'm not leaving without you, Miss Twyla. You just get that into your head." I turned to Lorna. "Just go and call Junebug."

Indecision played on her face. I motioned toward the door. She turned and ran.

I turned back to Miss Twyla, her gun still steady on Nina. "Miss Twyla, now you just listen to me. The police will be here in a minute. Nina's not going anywhere, not with you holding that gun on her, so you just put those wires away."

"Oh, no, Jordy. Don't you see how much better it is this way, now that I've been found out?" Her tone indicated I'd made a perfectly stupid suggestion. "I just couldn't abide all the talk I'd have to hear about how crazy I was. I never wanted anyone to get hurt and I was so careful. But then you were injured. . . . I just started my little projects as a game, because I did get so bored and to show little old ladies could do so much more than attend quilting bees and bake sales. We're all so underestimated, don't you think, Nina?"

Nina pulled her tear-streaked face from her hands, staring at the gun and then turning to me. "Talk her out of it, for God's sake! She's crazy!"

"Miss Twyla, Please, please, just put the wires down and come with me. You're not well, you don't want to do this. You're not thinking straight because Nina hit you." I attempted to hobble toward her.

"Jordy, you're always so optimistic, never seeing the

ugly side of life." Miss Twyla smiled gently at me. "But this is going to happen. I'm not going to some crazy farm, and Nina has to pay for what she did. So you get going. You have a whole life to live. Now go."

"I'm not leaving until you promise you won't put those wires together. Promise me!" A sob escaped me and I leaned down, clutching my leg. My jeans were blood-soaked and I felt dizzy.

"You don't want to bleed to death like poor Tiny," Miss Twyla advised. She sighed. "Very well, if that's how it must be. I promise. So get going."

She made her promise. And God, I wanted to live. As if of their own accord, my feet turned and began a slow hobble toward the door. My breathing shuffled along with my feet.

"Don't leave me!" Nina screamed. "Don't leave me here with this fucking crazy woman!" Her screams turned into a sobbing wail of hysteria. I didn't stop.

I glanced back at Miss Twyla when I reached the door. Both her hands were still steady and she smiled kindly at me.

"If something should happen ... think of me often, Jordy, and be nice to my memory. I do like daisies, so maybe if you'd remember to put them on my grave, I'd be most appreciative." I saw with mounting horror that reason had left those eyes. I mouthed the words *you promised* at her, and she nodded silently. I stumbled past the doorway, pulling myself up the stairs in agony.

A shriek of sirens sounded above, in the real world where men and women loved and fought and ate and lived. I felt like Orpheus crawling from some dank hell, except I had no Eurydice to bring home with me. Behind me, I could hear Nina's inchoate scream, words that could haunt a man for a lifetime:

"Jordy! Jordy! Please, please don't leave me here—"

Rain kissed my face as I pulled myself out of the shelter. It was pouring, and hard. Behind the shimmer of water I could see the flash of Junebug's police sedan.

CHAPTER FIFTEEN

YOU'D THINK THEY'D PUT INTERESTING PIC-
tures on hospital ceilings. Or at least mount the televi-
sions so a soul can lie on his back and watch the
baseball games unfold between the tiles. Not that it
would have made much difference. I didn't want to look
at pictures or watch the Austin news play by, talking
about all the goings-on in the formerly tranquil town of
Mirabeau. I had enough pictures in my mind to make a
film, one I could spend my life watching again and
again and again; no sequel needed.

On the back of my eyelids, I could still see Junebug
and Lorna hurrying me away from the backyard shelter,
which exploded in an unholy blast, quickly followed by
a second, more violent detonation, as though demons
were breaking through the mantel to wreak havoc on
Mirabeau. The force'd thrown the three of us to the
shuddering earth, and I'd seen the tornado-shelter doors
cartwheel free from the opening, disintegrating into
flaming splinters. Lorna's arm had closed around me,
pulling me ahead, my leg in fresh agony, and then I'd
fainted. Not to ruin my manly image, but see how you
hold up after a night like that.

I'd become dimly aware of Candace and Lorna both
in the ambulance with me, one of my hands in each one
of theirs. They were arguing about me, I could tell from
their tone of voice. That didn't really make me happy.
I passed out again.

The next day blurred image after image. I was in a

bed, I was aware of my sister's crying (I'd know her sobs anywhere, having made her cry a fair amount as a child), and there was a voice telling her that my surgery was successful and I *was* going to be okay. She was told that she needn't carry on so; as soon as the shock wore off, I'd be just pert near perfect again. I slept some more.

Once I was sure Miss Twyla was in the room with me. If she was, I was probably dead, which was confusing, since I was still in the hospital. I suppose there's not a great demand for hospitals in heaven. I called for her, reached out for her, begging her not to do this foolish thing, but she vanished before my eyes, a gentle, forgiving smile on her face. I called for her again and Candace's kisses were on my cheek, the fragrance of her perfume in my nose, the gentle spill of her hair across my eyes. So I kept my eyes shut. I didn't want to see Nina if I opened them, begging me for her life.

I never did see her. But one night, a dream of Tiny fought through the painkillers, a shocked and disappointed look on his face as the woman he'd loved emptied his life for him. I woke, a sob in my throat. I had never liked him—hell, part of me had abominated him—but I could have wept for him then. He didn't deserve the cruelty he'd been given.

The days passed. I didn't talk much, not to Candace, not to Lorna, not to Sister, not to Bob Don, not to Eula Mae. They all tried to smother me with love, which I pushed away like an irritating blanket. Clo visited at least once, double-checking me everywhere, not trusting the nurses on duty to do their job right. Apparently she ran off a sheepish Billy Ray Bummel when he made an attempt to see me. I gave my statement to Junebug and signed it. His friend from the Austin Bomb Squad, Teresa Garza, was there, and I remember her squeezing my hand when I had to describe my final words with Miss Twyla. I could only imagine what Miss Twyla had thought when the bomb at the Mirabeau B. had gone off, and she'd sat, numb, with Nina and Tiny in his pickup truck, watching the town deal with the disaster. Did she try to delude herself at first that perhaps it was a gas explosion? Or did she know from the beginning that someone had taken one of her little projects and used it to murder someone? Why hadn't she come forward? Pride? Shame? Or, considering recent events, a need to extract her own revenge? I asked Junebug those same questions and went back to sleep. Only later did Sister tell me that after I'd slumbered, my old friend sat by my bed, quietly watching me for the longest damn time.

The doctors came and went as well, saying my leg was healing well from the surgery, and it was too bad I'd broken it when I'd tumbled to the ground, coming down on it at a bad angle. I'm not sure they believed me when I told them my black eye and gashed arm didn't result from the explosion at Miss Twyla's. Maybe that's when they sent the psychiatrist in.

I'd just as soon not talk about that part. It was painful to me, and like most men I don't believe in sharing every thought and feeling that I have. The psychiatrist was a pleasant young fellow with a mightily suppressed drawl who was bound and determined to make sure I didn't feel guilty about leaving Miss Twyla and Nina. I met with him a few times and let him think he was making progress. I heard hospital gossip that he was also treating Parker Loudermilk for his tendencies to resort to violence when angry. I thought Parker would make a prize project for him, far more interesting than me.

Sister told me Jenny had recovered from her suicide attempt. I closed my eyes; that girl must have been in hell. Sister said everyone said Jenny was doing so much better now that she knew her daddy wasn't a killer. I tried to take some pleasure in that, but it was fleeting; she still had Parker for a dad, which I felt was not an optimal situation. Dee visited me once, bringing flowers in a pot she'd made herself. I was glad to see this pot had no barbed wire. Candace told me that Parker had admitted to finding Greg dead; apparently Nina must have killed Greg shortly before the Loudermilks arrived. According to Junebug, Parker said he'd gone over there with a gun; that's what Becca had seen him stuffing back in his pocket when he fled the scene. I didn't want to think about him anymore; I suspected the voters of Mirabeau would soon give me a new boss.

So I sat in this introspective stupor for the days that I was in the hospital, not talking much, nodding, smiling, closing my eyes, letting myself be fussed over by the women in my life. I was glad when I got to go home and finally get some rest.

Everything else of interest happened one Saturday afternoon when I'd gotten back. Weary of my own bed, I'd used my crutches to get down to the couch, where I'd built my empire of tattered paperbacks and bowls of popcorn, watching old movies on cable. Out of harmless-style spite, I picked up a little silver bell that sat on the coffee table and rang it.

It was no lovely French chambermaid who answered my call, but rather a frowning Clo, heavy arms crossed over her barrel chest. "What do you want now? Your damned old pillows been fluffed enough."

"I didn't want anything from you. I just wanted to talk for a second." I gestured toward the chair. "Would you sit down?"

She sat warily.

"I'm glad that Bob Don hired you to look after me, and still help with Mama," I ventured. "I know we exchanged some harsh words. I think I had a lot of reasons to be angry with you. And you with me."

She stared down at the floor.

"But, that's past. You made a mistake in judgment. I've made several myself lately, so I'm not inclined to be critical. So, if you're still willing to be around here after I'm back on my feet, will you take care of my mother?"

She nodded and stood. "That all you wanted to tell me?"

"Yeah." I eased back onto the pillow and fumbled for the remote control. I'd muted Gary Cooper in *Sergeant York* on American Movie Classics while I'd made amends with Clo. I wasn't expecting it when she leaned down, kissed my cheek, and hugged me. It was so unlike her I forgot to hug back.

"Now, you keep that TV down," she snapped once my head was back on my pillow. "I'm on my break in the kitchen and I can't read the *National Enquirer* with all that jabbering."

"I didn't know you could read," I quipped gruffly, more relieved than I'd ever admit that my relationship with her was back to normal.

I hadn't had long to enjoy the movie when Gretchen came calling. She came into the living room, carrying a huge bouquet of flowers that could hide a beehive. She set them down so the giant blossoms blocked my view of the TV and made herself at home in Mama's chair, curling up like a cat before the mouse hole.

"I'm sure you'll forgive me for not coming to see you in the hospital, Jordy, but the doctors said you needed your rest."

"Oh, I did. Don't worry about it; Bob Don was there practically around the clock."

Her smile, pasted on for the visit, winced. "Well, dear, we're all just so relieved that you're okay. I must admit that I'm a bit surprised to see Clo still working here. I'd heard you weren't very happy with her."

"Oh, I wasn't for a while. But I'm less happy with you, Gretchen."

Her smile stayed pasted on. "Whatever do you mean?"

"I mean that I've given this some thought. When I found out that Greg had offered Clo all that money to frame me, I thought there must be some reason he really wanted to get me in trouble. I wasn't suspicious that he was committing fraud until after he was dead, so the land deal wasn't why he wanted me out. And when I found out he and Lorna had been lovers briefly, I thought he considered me a potential rival. But now I know that he was setting up Lorna to take the blame for his scam, so he wouldn't have cared about winning her. And I don't think that a con artist would have easily parted with as much money as he gave Clo, just to get me out of the picture. It just started me wondering who else might have paid cold cash to get me in such an embarrassing amount of trouble."

I wasn't sure that she was still breathing. "I don't know what any of this has to do with me, Jordy." She tried to laugh, and leaned over to rearrange the flowers.

"You're the only person that came to mind, Gretchen. The only one who would have had the money and the desire to see me humiliated with that sort of accusation. Of course, being accused of being the bomber wouldn't have held up; I'm sure truth would have won out in the end. You got upset when Billy Ray mentioned in front of me that you'd been seen having lunch with Greg. What did you tell him? That for his land deal to work, he'd have to get me out of the picture? That's not true, but you must've made him think so. Anyway, he was a crook to the bone. I'm sure once he knew what your goal was, he probably suggested the plan of action. Maybe he even suggested planting the bomb makings; I'm not sure I'd credit you with that much imagination."

She stood, her frozen smile now thawed into a grimace. "Obviously, you suffered some sort of impairment to your reason after that blast. How unfortunate."

"So why'd you tell me about Clo talking to Greg when the plan didn't pan out? Because you figured at that point that she intended to keep the money and you wanted to cause more pain to me by exposing her? Of course, with you blowing the whistle, no one would expect that you were the troublemaker behind it all. And with Greg dead, no one could rat on you."

"This is ridiculous. I don't have to come over and hear this abuse when I came to visit you on an errand of mercy." She fumbled in her purse for her keys. "Of course, you have no proof of this."

"No, I don't, Gretchen," I said softly. "But don't think you can ever hurt me again. You can't. So just give up this stupid war against me. You ever, *ever* try anything like this again and I will nail your ass to the wall. You try to hurt me, or anyone in my family, or anyone I care about, I will ruin you in this town, utterly, completely, totally. As long as we understand each other, I think we'll be fine."

She toyed with one of the pillows on the couch, and I thought she'd like nothing better than to shove it over my face and watch me squirm for air for a while. Instead, she patted my cast, a little harder than necessary. "You take care, Jordy. I'm sure you'll be feeling much better about all this unpleasantness real soon."

Her departure left me feeling more energized than I had in days. I sat back and watched Gary Cooper keep the world safe for democracy.

I dozed for a bit, then there was the clatter of footsteps and mild cursing on the stairs. Lorna, coming down, carrying a suitcase. I hate goodbyes.

She tossed her bag on Mama's chair and sat down next to me, gently pushing my leg out of the way. She examined my cast gingerly. "I didn't write enough. I should've written more."

"No, I think you've written more than enough." I couldn't see her scribbling from here, but I knew what it said: *To Jordan—Be on your feet soon so you can chase me around. All love, Lorna.* Candace had seen it but not commented. I figured the firestorm would erupt as soon as Lorna's plane left.

"Oh, I'd planned on writing lots more. Like in letters

and cards. But I'm starting to think that's not a good idea." She took my fingers, interlacing them with hers.

"Why not?"

"Because they have such a distance to them. Up-close communication is far preferable, don't you think?" She was leaning her face close into mine, her gray eyes as intoxicating as always.

I shook my head. "I think cards and letters and phone calls have a lot to recommend them. It's a good way for old friends to keep in touch."

She tugged at the bottom of my T-shirt. "But we're more than old friends, aren't we? Won't we be, still?"

"No, Lorna, we won't." I hated having to say it to her, but it was true. I'd made my choices, to stay in Mirabeau and have a relationship with Candace. I couldn't choose otherwise.

She leaned back. "I knew you were going to say that." She let go of my shirt. "Just don't give me that line that a part of you will always love me."

"It's true, though. But I won't say it if you don't want me to."

"No, I don't." She smoothed her pants legs with her palms, not looking at me.

"I'm sorry if I've hurt you—"

"What do you know about hurt? You got enough painkillers here to numb King Kong. You ain't feeling any hurt, country boy." Her voice was teasing, light. I wondered if she was hiding behind mild flirting, shielding herself from disappointment. I reminded myself that was her problem, not mine.

"Whatever you say, Lorna."

She looked at me then, tears welling in her eyes. I didn't have a handkerchief to offer her, but she leaned down and kissed my forehead, with sudden speed as though she were afraid I'd refuse. I wouldn't have, not for the world.

"I better call Junebug. He's giving me a ride to the

airport in Austin. I think he's got a hot date with that bomb sergeant he's warm for."

"Have a safe trip." So much hung unsaid between us, but that was the nature of broken relationships; they weren't concluded as neatly as business meetings. "Now, don't talk off Junebug's ear the whole way there. He's not used to that annoying Boston accent of yours."

"He might find it cute, Jordan. The same way you did. I'll weave a spell on him with my wicked New England charm, and before you know it, I'll be a Mirabeau housewife. Mrs. Junebug Moncrief. I don't think the Wiercinskis would be quite prepared for that." She stood by her suitcase and picked it up.

"Goodbye, Lorna." There was a range of emotions in my voice as it said those two words. Some I didn't care to identify. I just kept thinking: This is right for you both. You know it.

"This is me riding off into the sunset." Her voice sounded a little ragged.

"I know. Ride careful, now."

She picked up her suitcase and, without a backward look, walked outside. A minute or so later I heard a car pull up, doors slam, Junebug's drawl answering some tease of Lorna's, and then the distant whine as the sedan pulled away.

I sat with my eyes closed. I had cared for her. I still cared for her, in that I wanted her to be happy. But I didn't want her for myself. I knew what I wanted—all the craziness, all the aggravation, all the passion.

"Clo? Would you bring the cordless in here, please? I need to make a call."

She brought it in, fussing at me that I'd skipped the nap I needed every afternoon and surely wasn't going to get it by prattling on the phone all day. She was still complaining as she went upstairs to check on Mama.

I dialed the seven numbers slowly. She and I hadn't talked much since I'd returned from the hospital; apparently words had been exchanged in the ambulance between her and Lorna that made each other's company unbearable. But we hadn't had a chance to fix what had gone wrong between us. That didn't matter, though. What mattered was the loving pressure of her hand on mine as I'd faded in and out at the hospital, the homemade peanut-butter fudge she'd snuck into my room for me, the gentle kiss of her lips on mine when she thought I was numbed entirely by the medications.

She agreed, hesitatingly, to come over. When she arrived, Clo suddenly remembered she'd promised to take Mama over to Eula Mae's for a visit. We watched her bustle out. Candace sat down on the side of the couch, brushing her heavy brown hair over her shoulder. We made small talk about my broken leg, my messy coffee table, the merits of Gary Cooper as an actor as he mutely eliminated half the Kaiser's army on the screen. If Gary could perform heroic deeds, maybe I could, too.

Deep breath. "Candace?"

"Yes?" Her hand was buried in the bowl of popcorn, but her eyes came back to me. They looked like bits of blue heaven. I took her other hand in mine, interlocking my fingers with hers.

"I love you."

Kisses are better than painkillers for easing what ails you.

JEFF ABBOTT

Do Unto Others

After a few good years of city life, Jordan Poteet returns to his small hometown of Mirabeau, Texas, to work as a librarian. Yet his quiet domesticity is shattered when he locks horns with Miss Beta Harcher, the town's prize religious fanatic, in a knock-down, drag-out battle over censorship. When Jordan finds her murdered body in the library, he learns that Beta dead is much more dangerous than she ever was alive—not only for poor Jordy, whom the police are itching to throw the book at, but for countless others. In fact, thanks to a cryptic list the police find stashed next to her fanatical heart, Beta Harcher has the whole town in a death grip....

Published by Ballantine Books.
Available in your local bookstore.